the Whole World was Watching

the Whole World was Watching

LIVING IN THE LIGHT OF MATTHEW SHEPARD

Romaine Patterson
with Patrick Hinds

Advocate BOOKS

NEW YORK

Manufactured in the United States of America.

This hardcover original is published by Advocate Books, an imprint of Alyson Books.
P.O. Box 1253, Old Chelsea Station, New York, New York 10113-1251.
Distribution in the United Kingdom by Turnaround Publisher Services Ltd.,
Unit 3, Olympia Trading Estate, Coburg Road, Wood Green,
London N22 6TZ England.

ISBN 1-55583-901-0

Credits
Jacket photography by David LaChapelle.
Jacket design by Matt Sams.

for Michael and all of the angels in my life

Author's Note

In October 1998 my good friend Matthew Shepard was brutally murdered by two young men who tied him to a fence in Laramie, Wyo., beat him senseless, and left him there to die. He was 21 years old. The incident touched off a media frenzy and brought national attention to the problem of antigay hate crimes in America. A year and a half later *The Laramie Project,* a play based entirely on interviews with the people of the town where Matthew was murdered, hit the stage and met with phenomenal success. In 2002 it was adapted by Moisés Kaufman into an HBO film with an all-star cast. I was one of its central characters.

In October 2004, as the five-year anniversary of my friend's murder approached, I was confronted by my younger self and all of her idealism and excitability as I rehearsed to play her in a staged reading of *The Laramie Project,* to be performed in New York City to commemorate the event. It was sort of amazing to meet that young woman again, knowing that, like everyone in *The Laramie Project,* the 20-year-old Romaine Patterson is no more than character, frozen in time, a piece of a piece of art inexorably linked to Matthew Shepard and his murder. And it was surprisingly satisfying to realize not only how much I had grown, but how much I still had in common with that feisty young Romaine who was once so widely referred to as "that girl in the leather jacket who was Matthew Shepard's friend."

A big piece of that growth has been the transition from my work as a professional activist to my job as the witty cohost of the satellite radio talk show *Derek & Romaine*. I've discovered a whole new me in that studio, a sort of lesbian Howard Stern, who once encouraged a porn star to slap his "monster" against the microphone and who often dives without hesitating into such raunchy topics as licking celebrity snatch or the thrill of substituting a sea sponge for a tampon. When I first invented—or unleashed—her, I wanted this new Romaine to be totally inappropriate, to turn on truckers in Middle America by talking about her big tits and nights of hot lesbian sex. She'd have fun at work *and* in life. And she'd also get to say "fuck" a lot. Her style was seductive, and I fell in love with her because she stood in stark contrast to my "angel" identity, so different from the serious activist role I'd taken on since Matthew died. She was, and continues to be, a perfect means of escape.

My radio persona is the fallen angel: filthy, uncensored, and kinky. However, the evolution of Romaine from one end of the spectrum to the other helped me to see that the greater journey was finding my way to the middle, to the place where I could be both—the friend who helps carry on Matthew's legacy and the sexy girl radio host who likes to talk dirty.

There's a clear distinction between my friend Matt and the Matthew Shepard who became a piece of history. I miss Matt, the kid who couldn't dance, the kid who smoked too many bowls, the kid who'd sit and chat for hours while I served up espressos in Denver. And I mourned him for a long time, the same way I mourned my brother Michael and my father. But that day in

October, five years to the day after I last spoke with him, when I would play the role of 20-year-old Romaine Patterson for the first time ever, was not about mourning. No, it was about throwing a kick-ass party for my friend, a guy who gave so much to the world, and even more to me.

This book is for you, Matt.

Your light has changed the world.

Foreword

On the evening of March 31, 1997, in the small college town of Caspar, Wyoming, I heard a determined knock on the door of my apartment. When I opened it I was dazzled by a pair of sparkling eyes and a radiant smile. I had no idea who this beautiful young woman was. She wore a black leather jacket, which made me wonder if she'd come on a motorcycle. I don't think she was expecting to see me because she looked a little confused. Still, she very politely asked for my son, Matt, and I pointed her in the direction of his apartment down the hall. Well, it turned out this polite girl was none other than Romaine Patterson, Matt's feisty new college friend with—as he put it—the "most unusual but infectious laugh." Matt was throwing her a party for her 19th birthday.

Since that evening, over the years, Romaine has been my angel, my friend, my honorary daughter, and my teammate—with all the intense emotional fluctuations and complexities these roles imply. I have come to admire her ability to say what she thinks. (We should all be so forthright.) She is very loyal to her family, not an easy thing in today's society. (Time and space are hard to overcome.) And, perhaps most amazing is her ability to be true to herself in the face of outside influences. (Romaine is not the sort to buckle under pressure.)

Perhaps the best example of this quality, this rare ability to not only know what is in one's heart but to act upon what is in one's heart, is her creation and pulling together of the angels. I first heard about the angels the evening of April 5, 1999. It was the night before Russell Henderson's trial was to begin. We all knew Fred Phelps and his family were planning to be there and that the press would be all over them. It was extremely upsetting that the reason for the trial would be lost amidst the flurry of media coverage of Phelps's hateful demonstrations. When I heard of Romaine's plan and the participation of so many of her friends and their friends, I thought it was a perfect way to counteract an expression of hate and intolerance. It would be a display of God's most important message: Love thy neighbor as thyself.

Since the initial appearance of the angels and their immortalization in the play and film *The Laramie Project*, their message of love and understanding has been a very powerful answer to the hateful rhetoric surrounding the issues facing the GLBT community at large. I am so grateful to Romaine for the concept of the angels. I know that many other people have used her idea and have felt empowered by its simple message of love.

Reading this book was somewhat painful for me. Though I definitely feel like I know more about Romaine's life, I was struck by how different memories can be for everyone. We all remember things as they relate to us and where we were in our lives when they occurred. Some of Romaine's recollections about Matt differ from mine. That doesn't make either of us right or wrong. It only proves the relevance of what each person—his mother, his friend—brings to a situation in how memories are formed. Regardless of perspective, these fragile, dynamic memories form the fabric of our lives.

This memoir doesn't just tell the story of my friend Romaine Patterson. It depicts how a person's life can be changed, formed even, by pure circumstance. Of course, we shouldn't be surprised when this happens. It's how all our lives are formed. Some circumstances seem bigger or more life changing, but the result is the same. We are forced to look at what is important to us and how we can make things better. No one has answered that call as swiftly as, or more resolutely than, Romaine.

—Judy Shepard

Part One

1 | *The Frog Lady*

When I was 9, the kids on my block called me "the frog lady." And with the denim legs of my overalls soaked and rolled up to my knees as I waded into the irrigation ditch down the street from my family's house in Ranchester, Wyo., I took tremendous pride in embodying their would-be insult. Located at the end of my street, the ditch skirted along like a jagged old battle scar through a mucky patch of land overgrown with sun-bleached weeds and prairie grass droopy from malnourishment. It was built to keep the neighborhood lawns fortified, but for me it served a much higher purpose: This was where my friends lived—the turtles, the snakes, and most important, *the frogs*. Wet and slimy, with tiny sparkling eyes that shimmered with anticipation, they came in all shapes and sizes: big and green with bumpy backs, little and brown with floppy long legs. A girl's got to be fast to catch a frog—and patient. She's got to have sharp eyes and the ability to hold still long enough to calculate making that one swift, almost imperceptible, grab. I had it all down to a science.

Every time I caught one it was a thrill. Through the thin skin of its belly the little frog heart fluttered against the palm of my hand. I'd slip the little critter into a pocket or let it balance on my shoulder or my head, anyplace it could rest comfortably. And when

I had a whole bunch of them I strutted—I never walked in my life; I *always* strutted—down the middle of the street back home, with mud drying and cracking on my face, my hair in a matted ponytail, dirty water dripping off me like from a rain cloud, and my frogs clinging like parasites to a host.

Once home I'd de-frog myself on the back porch, where, one at a time, I introduced the little creatures to their swank new digs—a habitat my dad helped me build out of a plastic swimming pool, which provided my pets with mud, water for swimming and drinking, and dry land for roaming. Frogs, I learned, are a patient breed. I loved to watch them as they sat immobile, feeling the place out with their eyes. Eventually they'd begin to hop clumsily, careening against the side of the pool as if swept there by a gust of wind.

Once my dad took me down to a pond where we collected frogs' eggs to watch them grow up from tadpoles. It seemed to happen so quickly and so slowly at the same time, the way they developed out of nothingness into full-grown entities. Letting the frogs go the following spring—both the ones from the ditch and the ones Dad and I had caught as tadpoles—was the hardest part. I remember the stubborn fit I threw as Dad tried to explain why we couldn't keep them. I gave him the silent treatment as we drove back to the original pond to release them. He looked over at me where I sat next to him in the cab of the truck. I was his devastated little tadpole. He took a deep breath, then spoke the words I'd remind him of years later when it was time for me to spread my wings. "Romaine," he said, "no creature can thrive in captivity. All things have to be set free."

Frog collecting aside, I was always seen as a rather strange child. My quirks were tacitly accepted by my parents until my fourth-grade teacher, upset because I refused to get involved in classroom "girl drama," pegged me as the class tomboy and called my mother in for a conference. My poor mother, who by then had given up on the idea of normalizing the seven eldest children but would be damned if she dropped the ball on the last one, immediately started buying me Barbie dolls. Oh, those fucking Barbies! I have such distinct memories of sitting in front of the TV after school watching *The Teenage Mutant Ninja Turtles,* quietly stroking my doll's matted hair. With a quick, deft motion I'd tear off an arm or the head, imitate a muffled Barbie scream, then do my very best turtle impersonation by throwing the freshly amputated appendage into the front lawn and screaming the Mutant battle cry: "Cowabunga, dude!"

It's funny how much the Teenage Mutant Ninja Turtles influenced my way of being in the world. (Because of the Turtles I discovered martial arts—tae kwon do, specifically—studying throughout my early teenage years, up to the black-belt level. But more important, my predilection toward the more macho aspects of the cartoon, and rowdiness in general, endeared me to the neighborhood boys in grade school, who let me into their secret club with minimal fuss.

These same boys would desert me years later when I came out—in fact, they would be some of the main proponents of the abuse that made my high school years so difficult. But back then it was all about the after-school football, baseball, and soccer games. I was damn good at them all, but football was my gift. I insisted on being the quarterback, but I couldn't really be tied to any one position. I was all over the field. Nothing gave me more pleasure than, ball in hand, colliding with some cocky boy to send him flying.

Every time Mom insisted on buying me a Barbie, I insisted she balance it out with a toy gun. My guns were the newest, the shiniest, the loudest, and absolutely the biggest envy of the neighbor-

hood. This was a major bonding point between my dad and me. I'd
be his sidekick when he went hunting, and one day when I was 12
he handed me his .22 pistol and coached me through the proper
way to hold, aim, and shoot. I will never forget the invigorating
weight of that gun, the precision of the crack it made when it
fired, and the intensity of Dad's attention on me throughout.
Shooting became a regular thing we did together.

"What are you thinking, girl? That's not how you're going to kill
that damn rabbit," he'd say in his husky, fatherly way. But the best
times were when he didn't say anything at all. Sometimes I'd surprise him by hitting a target dead-on, then quickly look over to see
his reaction. Strong and vital, he'd be leaning against a tree, arms
crossed in front of himself, wearing a pair of jeans, a plaid farmer's
shirt, and a baseball hat. He'd nod his head with a slight smile—a
smile I wouldn't even have noticed if it weren't for his eyes, big and
blue and wide-open, proudly taking in his little girl with the gun.

Yes, I was a tomboy, and I was the best tomboy there was. My
father loved it and my mother hated it. In his later years my father
must've looked back over the times he took me fly-fishing and
taught me the tricks for tying flies, or the hot dusty summer afternoons when he brought me into his garage workshop to show me
how to use power tools, and wonder how much he'd contributed
to my being a lesbian. But he didn't think about such things back
then. Back then I was still just his little buddy.

My mother never understood why he didn't encourage me to do
more girlie things, one of the few parental decisions they didn't see
eye to eye on, but she let it go. My relationship with my father was
truly as important to her as it was to him. He was diagnosed with
lymphoma when I was 11 years old, so there was always a sense of
urgency in our spending time together—as if every second were
something precious and way beyond the ordinary.

2 | Bad News

From where I sat at the other end of the ugly avocado-green couch, which had overstayed its welcome in our house by over 10 years), I was jealous at how comfortable my father looked. (By now he'd been told by the doctor, "Stay in remission another seven years and you'll have it licked.") With only the weight of my mother's head on the bulky part of his thigh to distract him from the *M*A*S*H* rerun we were watching that night, he had it good. I, on the other hand, when she had decided to lie between us—covering herself in an afghan before absently thumbing a Louis L'Amour Western—got her icy unsocked heel in the center of my thigh. My quadriceps twinged and threatened to charley-horse, so I shifted big, like I was stretching—even faking an exaggerated huffing yawn—and slid out from under her. She hardly noticed. And so, bored, I went back to twirling the front of my hair—my rebellious attempt to keep the mother-enforced shoulder-length nappy until the next school year, when I'd be a tenth-grader and, "if I still wanted to," would be allowed to cut it all off.

Disinterested in *M*A*S*H*, as usual, I looked around the room for what must have been the millionth time. From the brown shag carpet to the enormous wooden-box television—complete with rabbit-ear antennae—our living room was so '70s it was painful. The only thing missing was the tacky orange wallpaper.

The ringing phone was like an answered prayer to get me the hell out of there. I jumped up and ran into the kitchen to answer it, and was psyched to hear my brother John's voice. He was my favorite of all my seven grown siblings because he spoiled me the most. With the care packages he sent me every birthday and holiday, complete with wall decorations, candy bars, cash, and whatever else he thought I was into at the time, it was basically impossible for the others to compete.

Usually when he called and I got to the phone first he'd ask me how I was and we'd chat for a few minutes before I handed him over to Mom or Dad. But that night he just said flatly, "Romaine, I need to talk to Mom."

When I handed her the phone she took it with that sort of head-cocked-to-the-side, furrowed-brow expression people make when they're confused. I stood there and listened for a minute, hoping to catch a piece of whatever it was that was so important. But my mother just wrapped a piece of the loose phone cord around her hand, turned her back on me, and dragged the phone halfway down the basement stairs—something we all did when we wanted to have a private conversation.

I went back into the living room and sat on the couch next to my dad. He'd changed the channel and was fully engrossed in the last half hour of *The Magnificent Seven,* blissfully unaware. About 20 minutes later Mom walked back into the living room. Her face was pasty-white and she was crying. I got up to make room for her next to my father, and as I watched her robotically sit, then collapse into him, it was clear something really fucked-up had happened.

I knew my brother Michael had moved in with my brothers John and Sabin because of something to do with his health. I can't

say for sure if I knew the call was about him, but the idea must
have hit me somewhere. I suddenly felt like I had to get away. I
went to the closet, grabbed my jacket and baseball cap, then
turned to my parents. "I'm going outside to play basketball." They
didn't respond. I looked at them sitting there, holding each other,
and, for the first and last time in my life, saw tears stream down
my father's face.

I had to get out of the house, away from the sight of my parents falling apart. So I turned on the floodlights over the driveway,
went out into the cold night, and shot hoops until I was exhausted. When I came back inside an hour or so later, it was like the
phone call had never happened. My mother was cleaning the
counters in the kitchen and my father was in the living room
watching another Western. Nothing like good old Irish denial.
"Time to get cleaned up for bed," sang out Mom. Things were back
to normal.

"OK," I said, and went upstairs.

After that we started making the eight-and-a-half-hour drive to
Denver every other month to see my brothers over the weekend at
their townhouse on Downing Street. Sabin—the youngest of the
three, a college student looked after by the older two like a
scrawny puppy rescued from the pound—lived in the basement.
Michael and John each had a big bedroom on the second floor,
where there was also a third bedroom that had been converted into
a TV room. The ground level boasted a beautifully decorated living room and a dining room, used (John told me) "for formal
events only"...a little odd for a houseful of guys, but whatever—I
wasn't really one to question things back then. There was also a
spacious kitchen that looked out onto a fenced-in patio and a
patch of grass.

Though John had done quite well for himself in Denver's real estate industry, it was clear his true passion lay solely in the domestic realm. Roly-poly but in an attractive way, he was Mother Hen, the self-appointed plant waterer, keeper of the garden, and cleaner of all things house. And to watch him work was to see how much meaning and joy he derived from creating order out of chaos. I don't think I ever saw him do it without a smile.

Michael, by contrast, was a jeans-and-collar-up-polo-shirt kind of guy. He was slender and handsome and had a meticulously maintained black mustache. He was the oldest of the three and had worked in the banking industry in Denver for as long as I could remember, so he had money and had been the one to put up most of the capital for the house. This fact, he felt, entitled him to bark at the other two with cleaning or grocery shopping orders in his hilarious trademark bitchy voice.

Cute, skinny Sabin was the youngest by seven years. He adored John and Michael and—whenever he took a break from studying—absorbed their advice like a sponge.

Those weekends in Denver were incredibly exciting for a wet-behind-the-ears kid like me, who had never even been stuck in a noisy traffic jam—never mind speaking to, let alone seeing, an actual black person. With Michael in the kitchen baking most of the day and John coming and going from work—or one of his many social engagements—all the while engaged in the bitchy banter that was the backbone of his and Michael's socializing—

"Mad cow," Michael, unprovoked, would shout at John.

"Bitter old queen," John would shoot back.

—and Sabin constantly arranging and rearranging things in preparation for his future as an interior designer, those weekends were like a miniature version of the family holidays I loved so much.

Because my seven siblings were so much older than me, I was

raised pretty much as an only child except for those holidays when every member of the Patterson clan made their way back to Wyoming to be together. Michael cooked, my sisters drank, and my father, brothers, and I hiked into the woods, picked out the perfect Christmas tree, and dragged it back to the house, where it would be resurrected in the archway by the stairs my architect father had designed with Christmas trees in mind.

For my parents and me, the hardest part about those weekend trips to Denver was leaving at the end of the weekend.

To make it easier, we established a routine: Everybody went around and hugged each other goodbye, then my brothers helped us out to the car with our stuff. Mom, Dad, and I piled into our silver Mazda, and Dad let it idle for just a minute before we pulled away. Michael stood in the window, waving at us. Dad and I smiled. Mom waved back a little frantically then would start to cry. She cried every single time we left, until we'd get to the highway.

Only once did I ask why we were making so many trips to Denver.

I was sitting in the backseat, adjusting the seat-belt strap so it wasn't so tight across my enormous new boobs. My dad had flipped on the radio and started humming along with this Loretta Lynn song that we had caught halfway through. I was exhausted and annoyed—it was way too early for humming—and wondering how I was ever going to make it through another eight-and-a-half hours in the car with my parents listening to the horrible country music that they loved. I sort of blurted out, "Why do we make these trips all the time?"

Dad stopped humming and looked quickly over at Mom. He bit his lower lip. His expression said, *Uh…why don't you take this one, honey?*

Mom didn't turn around. No, she just wiped her nose with a

tissue and said, "We just want to be with your brothers as much as we can." By the tone of her voice, I could tell: This was going to have to be good enough for now.

3 | Sabina and My Three Gay Brothers

With her milky complexion and thick, rippling hair—so dark it shone in the middle like a moonlit lake—my sister Sabina was the picture of Snow White's badass twin. For eight long years she was the baby of the family and, having quickly learned of the getting-away-with-murder rights bestowed upon this position, she absolutely adored being the family's little hellion. Then I was born. To her credit, she could have hated me, but instead, she conceded her position graciously and did her best to teach me the ropes. Sometimes she'd even get maternal.

When I was 14 she took me to Wal-Mart and insisted that I pick out the blush, eyeliner, eye shadow, and mascara I thought would complement my face. She took me home and ushered me into the bathroom, where she stood between me and the door as she layered it all on. I humored her, even forced a smile, when she turned me toward the mirror to have me confront myself as a Tammy Faye Bakker–style drag queen. "Thanks," I said, then got out of there before she could tease my bangs and force me into a pair of hoop earrings.

The Halloween after John's phone call about Michael, I had

agreed to babysit her two daughters, Haley and Chelsie, so that she could go to a party. They were living in a tiny house about 15 miles from my parents, in a town called Sheridan. It had two bedrooms, a little kitchen, and a living room. The place was cute enough except for the horrible blue shag carpet splattered with food stains and cigarette burns. The house was particularly trashed that week thanks to a real "rager" of a party she'd never gotten around to cleaning up after. After batting a couple of juice boxes and some empty bags of potato chips onto the floor, I tried to eat my dinner—fish sticks and microwave pizza—on the sofa. Of course, hunching over a coffee table cluttered with day-old ashtrays and beer cans is not the most appetizing dinner arrangement, so I grabbed her rocking chair and slid it up to the empty beer keg in the middle of the room, where I plopped my plate down, grabbed the clicker, and surfed cable channels until I found an episode of *Rosanne*.

Around 11 P.M. I heard my sister staggering up the driveway. She pulled the front door open with a little too much force and was only able to maintain her balance by grabbing the door frame with both hands and hanging on for dear life. Then she stood there, taking deep, snorelike breaths and trying to get her bearings. *Wow,* I thought. *She's pretty fucking drunk—even for her!*

Her costume was in shambles. Where there had once been an oversexed fairy-angel princess—complete with fake wings, glittered halo, low-cut halter top, miniskirt, and purple spiked heels—there was now the sister I knew and loved: an overworked single parent who'd partied too hard and had clearly been mauled by her date. Her halo had fallen and was tangled in her hair. Her wings were torn and lopsided. The bags she had painted so beautifully under her eyes had run down her face and dried on her cheeks, as if she'd cried then tried to wipe away black tears. She was one hell of a glorious mess.

My sister said nothing, just stumbled right past me en route to the bathroom. As I sat there listening to her stumble from wall to wall while she tried to pry herself out of her clothes (and laughed at herself the whole time), I had to laugh too. If nothing else could ever be said about her, Sabina—the girl who learned everything the hard way—sure could take a licking and keep on ticking.

When she came out of the bathroom about a half hour later, she'd changed into a baggy sweatshirt and a pair of pajama bottoms. Her halo was still tangled in her hair. She tottered over to the couch and sat next to me, eyeing me for a second the way she often did before saying something she felt would be of monumental importance. "I want to have a talk about the birds and the bees," she slurred. I could smell the cheap beer on her breath.

Oh, my God, here it comes, I thought, the conversation I had successfully avoided with my mother over and over again. And now I was sure to get the XXX version from Sabina.

"OK," I said reluctantly.

Then she launched into it. No holds barred—from "the only thing guys want" through "you can have the best orgasm of your life if you…"

Sabina flailed her arms in front of her like a sloppy orchestra conductor as she spoke. As for me, one hand was clenched and sweating in my lap, while the fingernails of the other were thrust into my mouth where—though I knew it was a habit I needed to break—they were being chewed like crazy. I tried not to flinch every time she said the dreaded words "penis" and "vagina" *—but I couldn't help it. (*Footnote: All the crasser variations were just fine to my seasoned ears.) They just weren't words I ever thought I'd get used to hearing out loud.

Then, lowering one of her hands to my chin and turning my face to look directly into her eyes, she dropped the bomb. "You always have to practice safe sex, Romaine. Or else the same thing will happen to you that happened to…Michael."

"What are you talking about?" I said.

"Oh." Sabina looked down at her trashed shag carpet. She fooled with the halo still stuck in her hair. "Mom and Dad haven't told you yet?"

"No…tell me *what*?"

"I can't tell you if they haven't told you yet."

"Yes, you can, Sabina," I said, grabbing her elbow. "And now you have to."

She looked at me, thought about it for a second, then said, "Oh, all right, I'll tell you. It's stupid that you don't already know. Haven't you noticed that you guys take a lot of trips to Denver?"

"Yes," I said. "What's that all about?"

"Mom and Dad just really want to spend a lot of time with Michael."

"Why?" I said.

"Well, because Michael is really sick."

"He doesn't look sick," I said.

"Well, he is sick. He's very sick. It's very, *very* serious."

"OK…" I would have been satisfied if the conversation had ended there.

"Romaine," Sabina said. "Michael has AIDS and he's gonna die. Do you know what AIDS is?"

I thought back to a video I had seen in school about a little boy named Ryan White who was a hemophiliac and had gotten AIDS through a blood transfusion. All I knew was that it was a disease, a deadly disease that didn't have a cure. "Yeah," I said. "I know what it is."

"Oh, and he's gay too," she said. "So's John and Sabin."

"What!" Now it was all getting too out of control. It didn't seem possible that all of this could be happening in my own family, and without my even knowing about it. Life was so fucked-up right then. *How can they be gay?* I wondered. *They didn't look gay. And Michael didn't look sick,* I thought, *so how could he have AIDS?*

Sabina was on a serious roll. "Yep," she went on as if talking to herself, "all three of our brothers that live in that house are gay. Oh, and you know that guy, Brad, who's always with John for the family holidays and stuff? *He's* gay too. He's Johnnie's boyfriend."

At this point I started to pace the living room, totally freaking out. It was almost like having three gay brothers was harder to understand than the fact that one of them was dying of AIDS. "So, by 'gay,' you mean—"

"That they sleep with guys, Romaine." She finally extracted the halo from her hair. "It's not that big a deal."

"You're drunk," I said. "You don't even know what you're saying."

"No, no, honey, it's true," she told me. "Three of our brothers are gay. Michael has AIDS and he's dying. The doctors have given him six months."

I let the information process for a few minutes while I paced. It all made sense—even if I didn't want it to…the phone call from John…the weekend trips to Denver…a formal kitchen and dining room, used only for special occasions…how Mom cried every time we left…

Finally, I said, "So, our brother is going to be dead in, what, six months?"

"Yes." Sabina stared at me hard.

It seemed so strange that I wasn't instantly devastated. It felt more like how I imagined it would be if it was happening to my next-door neighbor, Mr. Laya, who I'd only chatted with briefly at the supermarket a few times.

"Are you OK?" Sabina asked.

"I guess so," I said. "I guess I just don't really know much about Michael."

"Yeah," she said. "He was pretty much gone by the time you were born."

I folded my arms in front of me and stared into the corner, where a day-old pizza box was being scouted out as a living space by a family of ants. "Well, this is going to freak me out every time I see him."

"You know what?" she said, and her tone was so different, so much more hopeful, that I instinctively jerked my head around to look at her. Her face was bright and childlike, as it always is when she decides she's just come up with the most brilliant idea ever. "I think you should take the time to get to know him."

"How?" I asked. "He's going to be dead in six months."

"You know what I would do? I'd write him a letter. Why not? Write him a letter and tell him you feel like you don't really know him very well. Tell him how you feel about him dying. It'd be good for you. It'd be *great* for him."

That ended up being the best advice Sabina—or anyone, for that matter—ever gave me.

4 | The Pill Dispenser

Three weeks later my parents and I went back to Denver, this time to spend Thanksgiving with my brothers. It was my first holiday outside of Wyoming and the first Thanksgiving I could remember that my entire family would not be together. Sabina, Trish, and my other brothers, Charles and Patrick, stayed away that year so it would be more restful for Michael.

I'd decided not to tell my parents what I knew about Michael. I wanted to get a sense of how I felt about things on my own, without being tethered by the leash of overprotectiveness inevitable in the wake of any conversation about AIDS. For now, playing dumb was definitely the way to go.

With Michael in the kitchen cooking all day, John and Sabin worked overtime trying to fill a house having only six Pattersons with 20 Pattersons' worth of fun. His belly a little more prominent than usual, John handed out mugs of Irish coffee—overly spiked for the adults—and Michael's signature sugar cookies, humming "I Feel Pretty" from *West Side Story* in his forced musical theater vibrato. It was endlessly entertaining. Sabin stuck close to our parents, who seemed as happy as they always were, sitting on the couch while their dutiful youngest son told stories about college and made quips about life with his "crazy older brothers."

I spent the day wandering between the kitchen, where I tried to be of help to Michael, and the living room, where I sat on the leather footrest of Michael's recliner and watched. It looked like a family holiday, but it somehow didn't feel like one. Who was this tiny Stepford-like family? And what had happened to my wonderfully large, strange, and flawed one?

At dinner I just sat there, not saying a word—just poked at my food and took everything in. We ate in the formal dining room on a cream-colored linen tablecloth. John had dimmed the lights and there were candles on the table. Michael had prepared more food than the entire family—including my missing siblings—could've eaten in a week. I kept looking at John; then at his boyfriend, Brad, who sat to his right; then at Sabin; then Michael, as I was just totally freaking out inside. *These guys are gay!* It was such a strange and fascinating thing. I had never heard my parents talk about my brothers as gay; I wondered if they even knew. So I watched the boys for the slightest implications—whether John's hand would rest on Brad's shoulder or a smile exchanged while Mom and Dad weren't looking.

I studied Michael closely while he cooked that afternoon and while he ate his dinner that night. Though I wasn't sure what I was looking for, I did notice that his skin was pale, and that he looked a little thinner than usual. He didn't seem very hungry either. Other than that I couldn't see any sure signs of death. No trembling hands while he carved the turkey. No running to the bathroom in between bites to vomit. Could he really be as bad as Sabina said? Mom and Dad didn't seem to pay any extra attention to him. Only one detail was different: the conversation. I kept waiting for our favorite topic—how we'd make the next holiday even bigger and better—to be brought up. Usually it was Michael who'd say something like, "All I know is that next year I'm getting *two* turkeys because you all are a bunch of pigs." Then we'd all riff on which sibling would be divorced by then, which ones would be married with twins, and who wasn't going to be invited back because they never helped clean up. That conversation, which would take place after everyone was wasted, was an unofficial family tradition, and I wondered if I was the only one who noticed that this was the first year it didn't happen. It wasn't until the drive home the next day that I realized why we had avoided, and would continue to avoid, discussing the future with Michael in the room. There was no guarantee he'd be there to enjoy it with us.

It was the next morning, as my brothers were saying goodbye to my parents, that I snuck up to Michael's room with the letter. Scrawled onto a piece of notebook paper, the handwriting barely legible, it said:

> Dear Michael,
> I don't really know anything about you because you were out of the house by the time I grew up. All you've ever been is the three piece suit that walks into the house at Christmas time and makes really yummy cookies. I feel like I don't know anything about you and now you're going to die. And I'm really sorry that you're dying. I kind of wish I knew you better. Love, Romaine

As I went to put the letter on his night table, I discovered something I'd never seen before: a long blue plastic box divided into seven compartments, each labeled by day of the week. The box was crammed with pills—pills of various colors, shapes, and sizes, and I knew immediately what they must be: Michael's AIDS medications. Pushing my other hand deep into my pocket, I replaced the pill dispenser on top of my letter on the table.

Once my father had let the car idle for a minute, we waved to Michael as we drove past the house. My mother cried while I sat wondering in the backseat about how long it would take my brother to find the letter, and what his reaction would be once he did. I was sure he'd think it was silly or else be mad that Sabina had told me. But I was still relieved to have done it. At least everything could be all out in the open now.

A few weeks later, on a freezing Wyoming afternoon, I decided to have a talk with Mom. Christmas was coming soon, I still hadn't heard from Michael, and I didn't think I could handle another Twilight Zone holiday. I came home from school and found my mother in the kitchen, wearing the big-house-with-the-white-picket-fence apron she somehow always managed to keep spotless. She was in the early stages of fixing my father's favorite meal—strip steak and baked potatoes.

Before she even had a chance to ask me how my day went, I said, "Thanksgiving was sort of an interesting holiday, don't you think?"

Mom was stabbing a raw potato with a fork. She put down the fork and just looked at me.

I pulled a chair away from the table, finished unwrapping my scarf, and sat down. "Look, I had a talk with Sabina."

Right away she knew. She picked her fork back up, said "Oh?" then went back to the potato, stabbing it hard and fast, probably imagining it was Sabina's head.

"She told me what's going on with Michael."

Mom nodded and continued her assault. Once the poor spud had suffered enough, she stopped, wiped both hands on the back of her jeans, looked up—but not at me—and asked, "Are you OK?" Her tone was forceful and leading, like a school nurse dealing with a third-grader known to be a faker. It said *The jig is up—there is only one right answer.*

"I'm fine," I said.

"Good," she said.

And that was that.

A few weeks later Michael called and, after speaking briefly to my mother, asked to speak to me. I still remember her suspicious-sounding voice: "Sure, Michael, but why do you want to talk to Romaine?"

As Mom handed me the phone, my heart pounded in anticipation.

"Hey, Romaine," said Michael.

"He-e-ey." I sounded shy, shyer than I'd wanted to.

"Thank you for my letter," he said.

"OK. I mean, you're welcome," I answered him.

"Listen, I haven't talked to Mom about this yet, but you're right. We don't really know each other very well. It's not very fair, is it?"

"No, not really." I wondered where this was going.

"How do you feel about coming and spending the summer with me, or part of the summer with me, here in Denver?"

"OK."

Damn, I wished I could come up with a better way of expressing how happy he'd made me. The idea of spending my first summer away from home, living in a big city with my three brothers, who would surely spoil the hell out of me...I mean, what more could a teenage tomboy want? My only trepidation came from knowing they were all gay. Gays were supposed to be perverts, right? But these guys were my brothers. That couldn't include them, could it?

"OK, great," he said. "Don't say anything to Mom now. Just let me talk to her and see if I can convince her, all right?"

I don't know when that conversation took place, but Michael did let me know it took a good amount of convincing, which ended with him, ever the drama queen, asking, "How can you deny a sick man his dying wish?"

5 | *Wowed by Vanessa*

The ugly brown suitcase lay open on my unmade bed. I always hated that thing. I never would have used it for, say, a class trip or a church-sponsored weekend retreat. But I packed for a summer with my brothers, vowing that once I returned the generation-old hand-me-down to them it would never again see the light of day in Wyoming—even if I had to bring my shit home in trash bags at the end of the summer. Then I began to see why the broken-latched relic had had such staying power in my family—because you could fit everything you owned in there, and that was basically what I was trying to do.

Of course, I'd packed for weekend trips to Denver before, but that was nothing like this—my parents had always been with me for those mini vacations, and as annoying as that could sometimes be, nothing could ever really go wrong with them around. But on the eve of my being left alone with my brothers for the first time ever, as I tossed my dirty white Keds on top of the erupted volcano of my unfolded clothes, my mind began to reel. The superficial worries of getting cold in the middle of the night and having nothing to wear, or of being given chores I wouldn't be able to handle, were just a cover for the real panic that had been festering in my mind since I decided to go: *What if my brothers were crazy?*

What if they'd managed to put their sane faces on for our quick little weekends together, but as soon as we left they morphed right back into stark raving lunatics. Would I be able to leave if that happened? Should Mom and I come up with some sort of get-me-the-hell-out-of-here code words like "pink flamingo" that I could say into the phone when she called to see how things were going? Or would I have to escape into the night, dressed in black with shoe polish smeared on my face, climb out the second-story window, and make a break for the highway, where I'd thumb a ride home? Did I know where the highway was? Did Mom and Dad even have shoe polish I could steal? Would they notice if it were gone?

"Romaine?" my mother said, pushing my bedroom door open without knocking.

I swear, I jumped 10 feet into the air—before I said, with my back to her, in my coolest voice, "Yeah, Mom?"

"I just wanted to let you know that your father and I have decided to spend the weekend in Denver with you after we drop you off. You know, to help get you settled."

With my back still to her, I closed my eyes and thanked the heavens. "OK," I said. "Whatever."

I felt a lot better when I saw what would be my bedroom during my stay, a spare room on the third floor that had previously been used as storage space. Michael was an organized person who couldn't stand clutter, but he had outdone even himself. There was a twin bed, a little oak bedside table, new curtains, and most important, closet space. They even supplied the hangers. I know it seems funny to be so moved just because my brothers had made room for my clothes—but it was such a nice gesture. And it made me feel welcome. I was completely reassured.

On Sunday we took a family trip to Denver's Mile High Flea

Market, which is essentially an elaborate yard sale five city blocks long. That day was about dumping the ugly Keds and reshoeing the tomboy—I was really jonesing for a pair of Doc Martens. After wearing a dress to school in the fourth grade and having all the girls in my class laugh at me, I had put my foot down against all outfits that implied even the slightest hint of femininity. Much to my Catholic mother's chagrin, my progression was to take it one step further: I wanted clothes that were not only void of femininity but were antifeminine. So I had to find some boots. They had to be Doc Martens, they had to have at least 10 eyeholes, and they had to be purple. We found this street vendor—a chubby little Mexican guy with a thick accent and a giant handlebar mustache. When I told him what I was looking for, he grabbed his belly and laughed good-naturedly—he thought that, because I was a girl, I must have been joking. When he saw that I was serious, he quickly looked to my father, who gave an *I don't get it either* shrug.

Looking back at me, the vendor smiled a big yellow-toothed smile that said "Only in America" before digging through his boxes. When he pulled them out, I snatched the box eagerly while he and Dad negotiated a price. I ran them over to Mom, who was looking at purses. "Look what I found!"

Mom staggered back, her feet narrowly avoiding a box that would have sent her flying onto a table full of fake Kate Spade bags.

"Oh, honey..." she said. "Those are...your favorite color. Isn't that nice?"

Once we got home I went up to my room to put them on immediately—eager to break them in and get the whole excruciating process over with—only to find out the salesman had sold me two left feet. Nothing comes easy, I guess. My family thought it was hilarious—but I was devastated.

After breakfast the next morning we all walked my parents out to the car. It felt strange to not be leaving with them. My mother hugged John first, then me—whispering in my ear, "You behave yourself, young lady"—then, as always, she hugged Michael last and longest. As Dad started the car, Michael took my arm. "Come on, we'll wave to them from the front window." We ran up the front steps and got to the front room just as the car was going by. Michael and I waved, Dad smiled, and Mom, locking her teary eyes with mine for just a second before shifting their focus to Michael, waved frantically.

Later that afternoon Michael had to leave for a doctor's appointment. John announced that he and I were going to jump in the Jeep, pick up one of his friends, and do some errands, which would include stopping by the flea market and exchanging my boots. As we drove down oak-lined streets, past church playgrounds and hilly front lawns, John took the opportunity to fill me in on some things. "Listen, I need to tell you a little bit about this girl we're going to see. First of all, she's a lesbian." He paused for effect. "Are you OK with that?"

"Yeah." I still wasn't completely sure what exactly a lesbian was anyway.

"The second thing you need to know is that she's kind of crazy."

"OK."

John pulled into the driveway of a rickety yellow house. "And the third thing you need to know is that she's got a big dog."

We got out of the Jeep and I eyed the house warily, half expecting a giant dog to come bounding out from around the side. The structure seemed to have settled comfortably on its foundation while leaning to its right, making it more oblong than square. It was a spooky place, with cracked yellow shingles and crooked shutters, the kind of place that children dare each other to get nearer and nearer to at dusk.

I followed John around to the back of the house, then, seeing where I was being led, stopped with such certainty that I almost tripped. There in front of me, clinging to the side of the house but drooping to its heavy, unsupported right side, was a crudely constructed and weather-beaten staircase. John jumped over the first two steps and landed hard on the third.

I closed my eyes in anticipation of the entire contraption collapsing in a cloud of smoke under his weight, but instead, it just gave a little—then sighed like the bray of an old donkey.

I let John get about halfway up before I followed, figuring that an even distribution of weight would lessen our chances of our plummeting to our deaths. By the time I reached him he'd knocked twice on the door then let himself in. I followed him into the kitchen and had only glanced around when I felt this massive force behind my shoulders that sent me tumbling onto my stomach. Next I felt a warm tongue licking my neck followed by a gentle growl, then the weight of four paws as they jumped onto and off of my back.

"Oh, my God, Saphie! Saphie! *Saphie!* Get off of her, you bad girl, you," came a voice from the back of the apartment. Then the monster was gone. As I was brushing the dog's slobbery black hair out of my eyes, I felt a little hand slip inside mine and help pull me up.

"Well, you must be Romaine," she said. "I'm Vanessa. It's very nice to meet you."

"Yes," I said as I opened my eyes and took in this woman for the very first time.

All powers of speech left me. I was overcome with lust and awe as I stood there and just stared. In a white tank top and army-green cargo pants, she was petite and sprightly. Her dark hair was short, spiky, and looked like it would crunch if you tried to run your fingers through it. She had four hoop earrings in one ear and two in the other—but those were details I memorized later. In that moment it was her eyes I locked onto: a shade of blue I'd seen only in the stained-glass windows of a church. And they sparkled like little stars.

Vanessa's lips continued moving, but I had no idea what she was saying. I just stood there, paralyzed, sinking fast into this quicksand of feelings I had never, *ever* felt before. *Oh, my God. Who is this tiny goddess?*

A half hour later we were all in the Jeep—John and Vanessa in front, me in back. "So, what's up, girl?" John said, and Vanessa started in on the most insane story I had ever heard. "You know I'm crazy about Cathy, right? I totally *love* her and *miss* her and can't get *enough* of her!" With my eyes glued to the back of her beautiful head, I watched her shake it as she mockingly stressed the words "love," "miss," and "enough." (I guessed this "Cathy" was her girlfriend back in Laramie or wherever, and I immediately hated her.) Then, in a brighter, more devious tone, Vanessa went on: "But now that I'm in Denver, I have all these other girlfriends. I mean, do you have any idea how many women in this town want my box? They try to pick me up in bars, the park, supermarkets...I mean, these women are seriously crazy and I'm not kidding when I tell you that I have to sometimes physically fight them off. Like, there was this one girl I turned down at Elle the other night who literally tried to climb through the window of my car and make out with me as I was driving away."

I was mesmerized. Nothing in the world could have pulled me away from this conversation. I finally got what a lesbian was, and it was fantastic! Suddenly, Vanessa stopped herself mid-sentence. She turned around in her seat and said, "So, where are we going anyway?" It took me a second to process the divine miracle that she was talking *to me*, but finally I grabbed the box with my boots in it and said, "We're going to exchange these." I pulled one out and showed her, and she said, "Oh, wow, cool."

I celebrated internally—*she thinks my boots are cool! Victory! Victory!*—as she turned back around and continued giving John the details of her latest sexual exploit.

And so it went for the rest of the afternoon—Vanessa telling stories about who did what to get into her box, John telling her what a whore she was, and me trailing behind them, wishing I could take notes.

At the end of the day when we dropped her off, John asked if she'd be coming to our Pridefest party the following weekend on the morning of the parade. "Oh," she said, "you *know* I'll be there. And in addition to Cathy, I'm going to bring along another girl-friend. Her name's Lindsey."

"Girl," John said. "Is there any woman in the state of Colorado you're *not* doing it with?"

Vanessa punched him in the arm. "You're just jealous 'cause I get more play than you, Michael, and Sabin put together." She then vaulted out of the Jeep without opening the door.

"Slut!" John shouted.

"Bitch!" Vanessa yelled back, grabbing her tits for effect.

"Whore."

"Hey, a girl's got to make her money somehow." Vanessa walked around to her rickety old staircase, draped one leg over the side and hump-jumped her way up, moaning in mock ecstasy the whole time.

Vanessa's show so excited my brother that he threw his head back and laughed, then began clapping like a little girl. "You bet-ter WORK! Shake that boo-tee!"

Doing my best to conceal my shock—displays like that would

never have taken place in Wyoming—I smiled to myself as I moved to the front seat, content because I knew I'd see her again.

When we got home, I used wanting to try on my new boots as an excuse to go up to my room and be by myself. When I got up there, I sat on my bed and pulled a piece of notebook paper out of the little drawer in my nightstand. I needed to draw Vanessa right then, before I forgot a single detail. My pencil moved intently for over an hour, making her perfect; and all the while I was becoming just a little surer of what it meant.

6 | *You're Too Young to See This*

Every year at the end of June, Main Streets all over the country are transformed. The oft-used parade routes for homecomings and Fourth of July extravaganzas are lined with gay dads decked out in seersucker, unabashedly holding hands and pushing a stroller. Behind them is a butch dyke wearing a spiked dog collar. Directly behind her is her nervous-looking girlfriend—a tall blond who's in public as a lesbian for the first time in her life. Up and down the street the scene repeats over and over and is added to by groups of young men in tight T-shirts and long shorts, and by drag queens in three-foot wigs and couldn't-look-less-real breasts. Everyone is waiting for that sound—the wonderfully horrible roar of a herd of motorcycle engines signifying the arrival of the Dykes on Bikes and the beginning of the Pridefest parade.

Michael's Pridefest party, which he held every year on the morning of the parade, was his baby. He'd been working on it for weeks, and once I showed up he made me his bitch for the remaining three days that were left before the party. He made me clean the backyard, weed the garden so all of his roses and sunflowers could be seen, drag a bunch of old card tables out of the basement, and polish his special party dishes. "And while you're down in the basement, could you find a ladder so I can hang my decorations?" He was an evil slave driver—busting my balls all over the place—but I swear, we laughed the whole time.

Two days before the party he took me grocery shopping, which was kind of irritating. He was just so goddamn picky! We had to get exactly the right brand of everything. *And* the colors of the crackers had to match the colors of all the various cheeses. *And* we had to meet the full spectrum of the rainbow with the fruit salad—even if we had to use food coloring. Yes, you read me right: *food coloring.* To top it off, each item had to somehow fit into his chosen party theme: "Under the Sea in '93."

The day before the party we spent the entire evening in the kitchen. Michael drizzled icing over his specially made coffee cakes and added dashes of cinnamon and nutmeg to his home-made granola, while I mixed pitchers of mimosas and took directions from him as to how to make the perfect Jell-O shot—which basically meant adding as much vodka possible because "We can't have those bitches leaving here sober—or they won't be back next year."

After that we hit the backyard and worked well past midnight setting up the decorations he'd not only bought but had spent hours crafting especially for the occasion. We hung paper fish cutouts from the trees with fishing line to create, as Michael put it, "a free-floating effect," then surrounded them with blue and white streamers that rustled in the gentle Denver breeze as if caressed by an underwater current.

I watched him that night under the lights of the backyard. He'd hang a fish, then stand back from it, cupping his chin in his hand. Then he'd move it an inch this way or that, an imperceptible difference to anyone but him. While doing all this he was careful with himself: He didn't move too quickly or lift anything too heavy. He stayed off ladders and held onto the railing of the stairs as he walked in and out of the house. Though he wasn't fragile, it was unsettling for me to realize that he wasn't sturdy either. I don't even think he noticed that I noticed, because by then he had been sick long enough to have grown accustomed to doing the things he could and avoiding the things he couldn't. That moment reminded me of why I was there.

At 5 the next morning Michael knocked on my bedroom door. "Romaine! Wake up, honey. I need you to go out and buy me nine bags of ice." Oh, God—that fucking ice! He was crazy about that ice and had been talking about it for days. His worst fear was that we would run out before all the guests had had their fill of Bloody Marys.

I had to make three trips to King Soopers—or Queen Soopers, as the market was nicknamed in my brothers' gay neighborhood—then was asked to run down there again to pick up some last-minute odds and ends. I finally finished my errands around 9 A.M., just as the guests were starting to arrive. Some had gotten there even earlier—ostensibly to help set up, but really they wanted to get in as many free drinks as possible before the parade started at noon. As I worked at setting up the liquor table—my appointed responsibility—people continued to trickle in down the narrow path that ran against the side of the house and led to the back patio. I'd been told to walk around and introduce myself to the guests, then lead them over to the liquor table and get them what they wanted. The only problem was that, since every guest had the original idea to pressure me into having "the first drink of your life," within a half hour I was pretty well plastered.

I was standing with my back to the patio gate when I felt a finger flick my earlobe. "Hey, Romaine," said Vanessa. "You gonna let us in?"

I jumped out of the way, and Vanessa—with two ladies, one on each arm—walked into the yard. "Romaine," she said, "I'd like you to meet Cathy and Lindsey. Cathy and Lindsey, this is John and Michael's little sister, Romaine."

I didn't want to stare, but I'd been waiting for this moment all week, and now here they were—three real live lesbians standing right in front of me. The two new specimens couldn't have been more different from each other. Cathy was tall, with long, matted brown hair that—in a couple of places—tangled into these gnarly-ass dreadlocks. She had more body hair than my father or any of my brothers, but there was still something alluring about her. Lindsey, on the other hand, was slim and well-shaven—at least her legs and armpits were. Then there was Vanessa.

Wearing that same white tank top and a pair of baggy cargo shorts, beaming like the sun had risen that morning with the sole purpose of shining directly upon her, and standing in the middle of a pair of hot babes, Vanessa grinned like the cat that ate the canary. She was clearly loving life. "Let's get our drink on," she said as she tousled my hair. "Lead the way, Romaine. Time for you to do a Jell-O shot with us."

Sabin stood with a couple of his college buddies near the liquor table and saw us approach. With crossed arms and a big old smile, he shook his head and blocked my path. "Ah, ah, ah—I don't think so."

"Out of the way, Mary," Vanessa said, shoving him hard with one hand, and with the other sticking three fingers deep into as many Jell-O shots before turning and offering them to us. I don't remember how many we did, but I do remember seeing it as a coolness test. Hence, I was determined to not only go shot for shot with them but to do it with a smile and without passing out. To puke would also have been way out of the question.

Before we all left for the parade, Michael called me inside. "Come into the kitchen. I've got a little present for you." When I got there he reached into the pocket of his Levi's and pulled out a silver dog-tag chain with six little colored rings, each one a color of the rainbow. "OK...these are called freedom rings. You wear them around your neck to show your support of freedom and equal rights. I'd like you to wear these today—if you want. They'll help you fit in a little bit at the parade. And besides, they'll look pretty on you." The compliment made me blush, and I put the rings on immediately. "OK," he said. "Now let's go!"

The parade route was only five blocks away. Drunk as I was, I stumbled and swayed and almost fell into traffic before Vanessa released one of her women and wrapped a protective arm around me. It was a lovely gesture, but once she spotted a liquor store that had just opened, I was flung from her embrace in favor of a 40-ounce Bud.

At first I thought it was all a drunken hallucination—the bare-breasted, leather-clad Dykes on Bikes, who revved their engines and waved their fists in the air as they roared by; the flatbed trucks converted into floats where boys in thongs gyrated to pounding house music; the garish drag queens in their lacy dresses and spiked heels (I was so damn green then that if Michael hadn't told me, I never would've known they were dudes); and the bare-assed leathermen with their chains, collars, and whips. There was such excitement and passion all around. Everybody was ranting, chanting, or screaming about Amendment 2, which would change the state's constitution to legalize certain forms of discrimination against gay people.

"HEY, HEY, HO, HO! AMENDMENT 2 HAS GOT TO GO!"
"HEY, HEY, HO, HO! AMENDMENT 2 HAS GOT TO GO!"
Michael got really tired about an hour into things. When we

couldn't find John, he agreed to leave me with Vanessa and the girls. "All right, ladies, now don't you go corrupting my little sister."

"Girl, please." Vanessa slipped her arms around her women and pulled them tightly to her. "We're the most wholesome playmates she's going to meet all summer."

I swear, my mouth actually watered when she grabbed my wrist and pulled me away from my brother. She wrapped one arm around my neck and held up two fingers. "Scout's honor, no harm will befall this child."

"All right, all right," Michael said smiling. "I'm out of here."

As soon as he was out of sight the girls slipped a beer into my hands, and when the last float passed we all jumped into the street and followed it down to the Capitol building, where the pride festival was in full swing. T...After a raucous chat with a very tall transvestite—a friend of Vanessa's—we all collapsed under a tree, wiping massive lipstick kisses from our cheeks.

It was turning out to be a hot day. We rested for a little while, then walked over to a big concrete fountain in the middle of the pavilion. Clusters of people in various stages of undress were cooling off in the water. I sat down on the edge of the fountain and took off my purple combat boots, dipping my feet to cool off my new blisters. As I watched the paradegoers wading, swimming, and splashing around, I couldn't get over the celebratory atmosphere. There was such a feeling of camaraderie. In fact, the only sound that overpowered the party's booming music was the collective laughter from in and around the fountain. It seemed like everyone had something to be happy about.

I waded in too, anxious to be a part of it.

About 20 feet away two women, completely soaked, held hands and faced each other. They had this look, an intensity about them

that made me think, *Wow, there they are, knee-deep*
of a fountain, surrounded by hundreds of other people
all that exists for the other. Then they leaned in and kissed.

In a few seconds, my understanding of everything I had ever
thought about myself changed. There was such a sense of certainty in their kiss, a certainty and a security I had never imagined
existed. Now that I knew it existed, I wanted it. And more than
that, I wanted it with a woman.

Like most kids my age, I'd been subjected to the myths,
rumors, and taboos of what being gay was all about—perverts
fucking perverts, then burning in hell for it—but that moment,
that kiss, changed everything. I realized it could be about so much
more than having sex—like about love and companionship and
happiness. It was like something clicked in my head—the proverbial lightbulb came on—and I knew that I was like them, and that
being like them was that unnameable thing that had always made
me different.

After a while Vanessa found me again. "Time to head home,
Romaine. Hey, where's John?" We couldn't find him, so I went
back to her place with her and her two girls. When we got there,
they asked me how I felt about ordering Chinese food. I hate
Chinese food but said it would be great. Vanessa decided that we
should all watch a movie and relax for a while because she and the
girls had a big night of drinking ahead of them. She put in the lesbian classic *Desert Hearts*—a movie about an English professor
who leaves her husband and takes a vacation on a ranch out West
where she's seduced by a younger woman—a younger, incredibly
hot woman, I might add. I was sitting on the floor with my back
against the foot of the bed and one arm draped over Vanessa's dog,
Saphie. Vanessa and the girls were on the bed—and becoming
more and more entangled, I noticed with every peek I was able to

sneak. Then the inevitable bedroom scene began. For six long seconds the entire room went quiet while the screen was aflutter with bare breasts, soft lips, and yes, a close-up of a saliva strand. Vanessa screamed and spilled a carton of fried rice. "Close your eyes, close your eyes, Romaine, you're way too young to see this!"

"Leave her alone," Cathy said.

Lindsey agreed. "Yeah, this is frickin' hot stuff."

Saphie, who had been asleep, broke away from me and started wolfing the fried rice.

"Oh, my God, Romaine, don't you *dare* tell your brother I let you watch this. He'll kill me!"

I didn't respond. I couldn't. My mind was far too overloaded. I started to laugh. What else could I do?

Just then, John called to see if I was there. Vanessa rolled her eyes at the phone. "Well, duh, of course she is." She listened to him for a moment then told me, "Hey, Romaine, your big brother wants you back home, but I told him you were moving in with me now, OK?"

"OK," I said, enjoying the joke.

On the short walk back I tried out the words "I...am...a lesbian." This was the first time I'd ever said it out loud. The experience was scary and liberating at the same time.

When I got home John and Michael weren't speaking to each other.

7 | Car Fish, Bed Fish

A few days later Michael and I were back at King Soopers, walking though the meat-and-poultry department and talking about his most recent tiff with John. John had been in the doghouse with Michael anyway, ever since he drank too much at Pridefest, passed out under a tree for four hours, then showed up at home without me. But the very *same* night John had come stumbling home at 2 A.M. stinking drunk and waking up the entire household. Michael held up a package of whole dead fish and flashed from under his mustache an evil, knowing smile. "It's time we exact our revenge," he said. "What do you think of these?"

(When Michael and John were in high school, Michael had done something to piss John off, and in retaliation John had gone on a fishing trip, brought home a trout, and put it in Michael's bed.)

Shooting a hand to my mouth to muffle a gasp, I said, "Oh, my God, they're perfect, he'll never see it coming."

When we got home John's Jeep was parked in front of the house. We slipped out one of the fish and stuck it under the windshield wiper like a sick-ass parking ticket. Giggling like girls, we hurried inside to unpack the groceries. The rest of the fish was stashed at the back of the freezer—under a bag of frozen mixed vegetables Johnnie would never touch.

An hour or so later we said goodbye to our unsuspecting victim as he left the house to meet his boyfriend for dinner, then practically peed ourselves laughing as we heard him start the Jeep and drive off.

Like most nights in the kitchen with Michael, this one would involve a cooking lesson. We were going to make what he called "beat-the-meat chicken." In preparation, he handed me a wooden mallet, a stack of chicken breasts, and said, "OK, Romaine, beat it."

"What?" I said, holding a breast in my hand.

"Beat the meat."

"What? How?"

In full drama queen fashion, he snatched the breast right out of my hand, threw it down on the cutting board, took the mallet, and gave it one good whack. "Beat it," he said, and handed the mallet back.

I raised my hand, brought the mallet down with a weak little thud, then looked to him for approval. When I got no reaction, I raised my hand again.

THUD!

"Beat the meat, Romaine!"

This time I brought that mallet down with some serious force. To my surprise, the breast seemed to give a little bit. I did it again, harder, and it gave even more.

"BEAT-THE-MEAT! BEAT-THE-MEAT!" Michael chanted as I whacked the chicken harder and faster. THUD! THUD! THUD! THUD! Little pieces of fat started to fly in all directions, and Michael tucked a little dish towel in the front of my shirt. When I finished, whatever was left was so thin, it was almost impossible to peel up without tearing it in half.

Michael cracked a small smile. "Well-done, kid."

Over a delicious three-course dinner that included pounded-thin chicken breasts wrapped with bacon around a variety of special cheeses, Michael and I sat alone together at the small kitchen table, talking about nothing much in particular. Suddenly he blurted out, "You know I don't have HIV, right? I want to make sure you know I have AIDS—and that it's full-blown."

I didn't really know the difference between HIV and AIDS back then. But during the night recently I had been hearing him get sick. Usually it was vomiting, but sometimes it was severe diarrhea in the middle of the night. Or else, first thing in the morning, I would see him take his bedding downstairs to be washed because his night sweats had drenched them while he slept.

I stared at him across the table for just a second. I was conscious not to stare too long, but I wanted to take him in. "Yeah, I know," I said. And I did. I did know.

"Well," he said, grinning through a mouthful of food, "I only bring it up because I'm wondering what you want me to leave you when I die."

Playful or not, I know that's a question that should have made me sad, but at the time it didn't because it was just so *him*. This is the same guy who, less than five months after being diagnosed, had planned his memorial service down to the letter, including everything from what hors d'oeuvres would be served at the reception to exactly which rendition of "Amazing Grace" would be played while the family spread his ashes. Looking back now, I realize that all this planning gave him a little bit of power in the face of so much uncertainty.

"I guess I haven't really thought about it," I said.

"Well, think about it. If you could have anything of mine when I'm gone, what would it be?"

I thought about it for a second. "You know what I'd really love?"

"What's that?"

"Your leather jacket." Leather jackets had become my thing ever since I saw Madonna wear one in *Who's That Girl?* Michael's was a sleek black one with zippers and silver snaps, made of tough leather that made the jacket heavy and caused it to squeak when you moved in it.

"Well," he said, "I've already promised that to Sabin, but you know what, I think it would suit you better. Let me see what I can do."

And with that, the AIDS conversation was over for the evening.

As we were cleaning up, Michael and I heard John's Jeep pull up and park in front of the house. We exchanged smiles.

"You guys are never going to believe this," John said as he lumbered in through the front door, "but when I went out to the car earlier, there was a dead fish under the windshield wiper."

I thought for sure Michael would say something like "Well, isn't that fishy?" and give us away immediately. But he didn't; in fact, he said "What? That's crazy!" with so believable a sense of bewilderment that for a second I thought he'd forgotten we were the culprits.

"Yeah," John said, "and of course I didn't want to touch it, so I got in the Jeep and turned on the wipers, which just smeared the thing all over the place. It must have been cooking in the sun out there all day."

"What?" Michael said. "That's so gross!"

"No, the grossest part is that its eyeball came out and rolled onto the hood of the Jeep, and I had to pick it up to get it off."

At that point I had to laugh. But Michael shot me a look that said *Don't blow this!* and I shut up.

A little while later John went out again and, before Michael and I went out for the night, we took the second fish, wrapped it in Saran Wrap, and threw it into his bed.

When we got home John's Jeep was parked out front. The first dead fish was lying on the ground next to it—so of course we picked it up and put it back under the windshield wiper. Then we went inside and were walking upstairs when Michael, a few steps ahead of me, slammed his right hand over his mouth, gasped, and pointed directly in front of him with his left hand. Then I gasped too, for in the doorway of the TV room, hanging by its neck from a coat hanger that had been twisted into a noose, was Michael's favorite toy—a little wooden duck he'd had since childhood. "This is war," he grumbled under his breath as he freed his little duck.

The next night John went out again, and Michael and I got to work. We dug out the third and final dead fish and wrapped the same coat hanger John had used to hang the duck around the mid-section of the fish. Knowing that when John stumbled in at the end of a night out he didn't turn any lights on until he got into his bedroom, we then hung the fish—sans Saran Wrap—exactly at face level in the door frame of John's bedroom.

Sure enough, around 3 A.M. John came stumbling in, tripping over himself as he walked up the stairs. The anticipation—as he lingered in the bathroom, brushing his teeth and washing his face—was killing me. Then it happened: He walked face-first right into that fish. There was a small scream of shock, a second of silence, then the yell heard round the world: "GODDAMN YOU MOTHERFUCK-ERS!" His bedroom door slammed and that was that.

A few months later, once I'd gone back to Ranchester, I got a card in the mail with a picture of two trout on the cover. Michael had written underneath them: THE CAR FISH, THE BED FISH.

8 | *Freedom Rings*

The sunglasses had been Michael's idea. They were wonderfully ugly, cheap, and plastic in a sort of *Back to the Future* lightning bolt–shaped way, and he and I had decorated enough for the entire family. We'd superglued pink, gold, and blue sequins to the rims, black-and-white feathers to the rest of the frames, then finished them off with glitter. They were to be a surprise tribute to Sabina, our wild-child sister who would relinquish her rebellious existence upon my return from Denver that August of '93—she got married two weeks later.

As a special treat for the occasion, I'd been stuffed into a horrendous peach bridesmaid's dress with puffy shoulders and a bow tied in back. It was made of the kind of material that always itches and never fits right. As my sister walked down the aisle in her beautiful flowing white dress, I stood on the altar, shifting uncomfortably, clutching the small bouquet I wished was big enough to hide behind altogether.

What struck me, throughout the ceremony, was how traditional it all was—and how untraditional I was in contrast. As I watched my sister's new husband, a stocky little guy named Pat Nowak who was cute in that runt-of-the-football-team kind of way, slip his ring onto her finger, I envied her and felt sorry for her at the same time. For myself, I felt relief, because I finally knew what made me different. I finally knew what it was that had always nagged at my brain and my heart every time I tried to conform. I was gay.

After the vows were exchanged and the groom kissed his deceptively virginal-looking bride, a slight amount of shuffling was heard on the bride's side as my siblings, parents, and cousins reached into their purses, pockets, and handbags. We bridesmaids delved into our flowers just as Sabina and Pat turned to face their family and friends as man and wife. Then, just as we'd hoped, there was a small scream then a fit of amused laughter from Sabina. The entire Patterson family looked like we had all chosen variations on the same awful costume for a masquerade ball. And poor Pat—who shot a quick look to the confused-looking groom's side of the chapel—knew us all well enough by then to have expected something like that. The man just rolled his eyes.

Michael pulled his glasses down on his nose, caught my eye, and winked at me. *Our plan has worked,* his grin said. And I thought, *Screw tradition.*

A few days before I left Denver, Michael took me on a shopping spree. "By the end of the day you'll have a whole new wardrobe," he said as he pulled into the Foley's parking lot. "It's time the clothes matched the lady—sexy, sophisticated, and sweet." While the idea of sophistication wasn't exactly what I was into, his approach soared above anything I had ever experienced with my parents. I mean, he actually asked my opinion. "Now, Romaine," he told me, "I don't want to know what you think *I'd* like to see you in. I want to know what *you* think is pretty and what *you* think you'd feel comfortable in."

On our way back home we stopped by the honorary gay pride

shop in Denver, a place called Tom's Floral. It was there that he bought me my own pair of freedom rings.

Every year at the end of summer the town of Sheridan holds a rodeo carnival. It's a tradition I had always loved, but I was especially excited that year to see friends I'd missed in my month away from home.

The first friend I ran into that afternoon was Laudan Rajhimi, a pretty girl with olive skin and long thick dark hair. Laudan had moved to Ranchester during our grade school years, and though we'd never been especially close, we always chatted when we ran into each other socially.

"So," she said. "How was your summer?" It was a question I was dying to have asked.

I started to answer excitedly, "Oh, it was great, I've been in Denver with my brother and you'll never guess what I discovered—"

But before I could finish, she grabbed the rainbow freedom rings that dangled from around my neck and said, "Oh, my God, Romaine, what kind of necklace is this? This is the most beautiful thing I've ever seen."

"These are my freedom rings," I said, fingering them with a proud smile.

"Freedom rings, what are those?"

"They're what gay people wear to show off their pride."

A dead silence followed while Laudan considered what I told her. "Are you...*gay*?"

"Yeah. Yes, I am," I said. "That's what I discovered about myself. I'm a lesbian."

"Oh. OK..." She sounded as though she were about to laugh. "Ah...I gotta go. Bye." She turned around so quickly that her long black braid almost slapped me in the face.

It almost makes me laugh now to think of how naive I was, but in the moment I was completely confused by Laudan's reaction. Granted, she and I weren't close, but it seemed odd that she didn't express any sort of excitement for me. I wasn't necessarily expecting a hug or even congratulations, but since she was technically the first person I ever came out to, a slow, interested nod or a "Wow, good for you" would have been nice, to say the least.

I attribute my naïveté in part to the summer with my brothers. The accepting environment they had fostered helped smooth my transition from awkward tomboy to raging lesbian, but three weeks of watching women make out in fountains and monitoring Vanessa as she jumped from girlfriend to girlfriend in no way prepared me for the reactions of people like Laudan, who wasted no time spreading the news among my peers.

It wasn't until a few weeks later, during "Ranchester Days," that I began to realize just how extensively the word had gotten out. Ranchester Days was—and still is—a sort of celebration of the small town–ness of the town. There's a small parade down Main Street, complete with mounted horses, a hay wagon, a float or two, and a contingent of old men dressed as cowboys from the Old West, wearing spurs, chaps, bolo ties—the whole nine yards. It turns into something of a street dance where onlookers can jump in and follow the parade down to the park.

There's food and music and everyone in town goes to socialize. I went down by myself that year and was making my way to the park when I saw David, my next-door neighbor, walking toward me. I can't remember a time in my life when I didn't know him; our parents had been neighbors since long before either of us came along. We'd been born within months of each other and as kids had played together practically every day. Back in those days—while David and I ran around shooting BBs at baseball cards and playing soccer in the middle of our street—I think our parents wondered whether someday we would marry.

But as we got older the social hierarchy of adolescence began to take shape. He became popular with the kids who played sports and went to parties on the weekends. I became obsessed with the world of band and chorus. By the end of middle school we had completely stopped speaking to each other. Still, we'd acknowledge each other with a nod when we saw each other at the bus stop.

Tall and thin, with light-blond hair, David had grown into a good-looking kid. It had been years since we'd talked, and as he stood in front of me, not yet speaking, I couldn't imagine what would be important enough that he'd seek me out mid-festival.

"I hear you're gay." He phrased this more like a concerned question than an accusation. But still, it caught me off guard. I couldn't imagine how he'd found out, and why, after all this time, he'd want to talk to me about *that*.

"Yeah," I said. "I spent the summer with my brothers in Denver and it just kind of dawned on me. Isn't that great?" (I didn't mean for it to come out so sarcastically.)

"Well, no, actually. It's kind of fucked-up. Gay people are sick and wrong."

I stood there, speechless, feeling the weight of the rings at my throat.

"Gay people are sinners." His nostrils flared and his eyes were as wide as I'd ever seen them. "And sinners go to hell." With that, he turned and walked back into the crowd.

I stood there alone for a few minutes, feeling myself begin to shake. I was scared—less of the idea of going to hell than of how personally threatening David, one of the most popular kids at school, had sounded. But within seconds I was smiling and I realized that I felt invigorated too. In my naïveté I'd told one person the truth about myself, and now everybody was going to know. The burden of having to hide had been lifted—and it felt too good to let fear fuck it up. I made the decision then and there that I would not take it back no matter how hard things got once school started.

9 | *Fireworks*

The whispering started the first day of my sophomore year. At first it seemed less mean than bewildered: a hallway full of people I'd known since childhood staring at me. Did they want me to explain myself? To stand on a soapbox? *"Gather round, everybody. I can assure you, what you've heard about your friend Romaine Patterson is not true."*

But the thought of appeasing them never occurred to me. Ever since my run-in with David, I'd made up my mind to tell anyone who asked: "Me? A lesbian? Why, yes." But, of course, nobody had the balls...so they just whispered: indiscernible bursts of words, ending in a snicker here, a cruel fit of laughter there. Feigning a confidence I hoped would become real, I strutted from class to class, past the giggling girls, the snorting boys, and the teachers who saw what was happening and either thought I deserved it or were too weak to do anything.

I became incredibly lonely. It surprised even me how sad and hurt I was by the way my classmates treated me. People seemed to fall for my whole tough facade, but I didn't know how long it could hold up. I really felt like I would crack if something didn't change soon. I desperately needed a friend who could see me for who I was; who loved me not in spite of, but because of, all the things that made me different. Then one day, in the middle of November, she materialized.

The first time I saw her, she was standing in the doorway to the band room. She had short brown hair with blond highlights, milky-white skin, and a set of twinkling blue eyes that, beautiful as they were, were immediately upstaged by her smile, then her huge tits. She was new to the school and looked lost, though that didn't seem to bother her. She just stood there grinning, her round cheeks blushing a little as a result of all of the attention she was getting from everyone who passed.

I watched her, transfixed by how beautiful and confident she was. I felt a warm intensity in my stomach that reminded me of the first time I met my brother's lesbian friend, Vanessa. Holy shit! This girl was someone I simply had to know. I pushed my way through the crowded hallway right in her direction. I didn't know what I was going to say or how she would react, but three months of being an outcast made me a girl with nothing to lose.

"Hi, I'm Romaine," I said when I finally reached her.

"Romaine. That's an interesting name," she said. "I'm Suzanne." With both hands behind her back she'd been rocking back and forth from heels to toes. She stopped as soon as we started talking, cocked her head to the side, and squinted a little as she looked at me, like she was appraising a piece of antique furniture. She had a cluster of tiny, oddly shaped freckles on the right side of her nose. I smiled when I noticed them, and she smiled back.

"You look a little lost," I said. "Can I help you find something?"

"Oh, how sweet of you." Suzanne held up her flute case and shook it a little, like she was ringing a bell. "Actually, I'm joining the band—I'm here for rehearsal."

"I'm in the band too—I play the saxophone," I said. "If you

want, I'll take you into the practice room and show you where you can store your stuff."

"That'd be great."

Because every other room in the school was dominated by the evil cool kids and therefore made me feel like shit, I thanked my lucky stars we'd met in the band room—the one place I could assert any authority. It had become a second home, a sanctuary where I could just be "Romaine" instead of "Romaine the Dyke," as the boys in my science class called me, or "Romaine, that freaky girl who thinks she's a lesbian," as I was referred to in the girls locker room. Suzanne and I talked for the few minutes it took to put our instruments together, then took our seats for rehearsal. The saxophones sat a few rows behind the flutes, and as I sat there tapping my foot in time to the music, staring at the back of her head without blinking, I realized that something terrifying was happening to me.

A panicky feeling took over my body—desperation began to bubble in my stomach, causing actual physical pain. I blew harder on my saxophone, bit harder on the reed, and played through it. All I knew was that this girl was the first person who had been nice to me in months and I wanted to know her. I needed to be close to her. And there was a very good chance that once rehearsal had ended, Suzanne would get up and leave without so much as a backward glance.

When the bell finally did ring I stayed in my seat, pretending to make notations on my sheet music. I allowed myself to look up only once, and when I did I caught Suzanne's eye. She winked playfully, then got up, flute in hand, and walked out of the band room.

My plan had been to make Suzanne more mine than anybody

else's, and by March the next year it had worked. Her being the new girl in a small school inhabited by kids who'd known each other practically since birth had worked to my advantage: None of the cliques seemed particularly interested in opening up and making room for her. If she hadn't been so pretty and downright charming, nobody would have bothered with her at all, and I would have had her completely to myself. But as it was, a few of the boys were crazy about her; she even went on a date and fucked one of those bastards. Afterward, unsure about the boy she'd done it with, she called me at home to ask my advice. Sitting halfway down the basement stairs, where the jealous tapping of my foot loudly echoed the enraged pounding of my heart, I wrapped the loose phone cord around my hand and pulled it tight—like a noose around the neck of the boy Suzanne was telling me about. She was chewing gum and, frustratingly, telling the story almost absent-mindedly—like it wasn't the most important thing in the world.

"We did it in the back of his car," she said as the circulation slowly dripped out of my hand.

"Uh-huh," I mumbled.

"And I'm no virgin or anything, but I didn't think it was supposed to be like *that*. I mean it was over in, like, five minutes then he drove me home and practically shoved me out of his car." She was quiet for a second then said, "I don't know, he's just a stupid football player...what do *you think I should do?*"

Tell me where he lives so I can find him and cut his dick off is what I wanted to say. Instead, I growled, "I think you should break up with him immediately."

My point was moot, though. They never spoke to each other again.

Suzanne and I were fascinated with each other's lives. She loved hearing stories about my summer in Denver, which provided me an outlet to talk about Michael. My brothers being gay and my being a lesbian didn't bother her at all. I think it had to do with her East Coast upbringing—she'd simply been exposed to more of the world. It seemed her mind was open to anything—and in the back of *my* mind, I couldn't help wondering just how open she was.

We snuck off during every break and study hall we could—forging hallway passes when we had to. The band room was our home base. There was a big hole in the wall in the back of one of the practice rooms where the tubas were stored, and every day during lunch we'd pull the tubas out, cram ourselves into the hole, and talk. Sometimes we'd hold hands or rest our legs on top of each other's—gestures so casual she seemed almost unaware of them. As for me, I couldn't move a single muscle for fear she'd pull away.

During one of those afternoon talks we decided to spend our enrichment week—when classes are suspended so students can focus intensively on a particular interest—together in a band clinic.

By the time enrichment week started that March, my crush on Suzanne was taking over my life. By the second day she knew something was up, and when she asked me about it, I was vague, saying, "I've got a crush on this straight girl, but I can't tell you who it is." It was so hard not to tell her, because I couldn't help but wonder if there were a chance she might feel the same way about me. Though I knew she was straight, I just couldn't believe it possible that I could have all these romantic feelings for her while she did not feel anything in return.

By the last day of enrichment I had gathered my courage and was planning to tell her that I was in love with her—when she upped the ante. I was pushing open the door to the practice room where we were going to put our instruments away when she said, "I just wanted you to know that I have a crush on somebody too."

The room's stale warm air rushed out at us as we entered. My eyes dried up immediately, and I got caught in a fit of frantic blinking before I even had a chance to play it cool.

"Who is it?" I said, and my voice cracked. My desperation was showing, but I couldn't help it. I felt like I'd die if it wasn't me.

"Well," she said wickedly, "I'm not going to tell you mine if you're not going to tell me yours." She began to disassemble her flute, polishing it with the silk cleaning rag she kept in her case. The absentminded look on her face, meant to imply indifference, was so exasperating I almost laughed. I paced the room, watching her, and finally took my freedom rings off, walked over to her, and put them around her neck.

"What's this?" she asked with genuine surprise.

"I just want you to wear something of mine that means a lot to me. I'll feel good knowing you have them on."

"Oh, Romaine, that's awfully sweet." She played with the little rings for a second before slipping them inside her shirt.

We stood there for a second, silent under the hum of the fluorescent lights, looking at each other. I was completely incapacitated. Have you ever just not been able to say something? I desperately wanted to take a chance, to trust my gut—but what if my gut was wrong? What if I made a move then lost the only friendship that meant anything to me? A dozen times I felt myself about to speak then stopped myself. I tapped my foot in anticipation. I was about to do it. Then the bell rang.

"Ah, I guess I'm going to take off," Suzanne said.

"Uh...OK." *Goddamn it!* I cursed silently.

Just as she got to the door I shouted, "Suzanne, wait!"

"Yeah?" she said, slowly turning to face me.

"Before you go, I just want to say that, you know, the crush I have..."

"Yeah?" she coaxed again. And her mouth widened into that smile that said, *Come on, sweetie, you can tell me anything...*

Though it would have been to myself, I think I said "fuck" out loud. Terrified of her, realizing how powerful she was, and knowing there was no turning back, I took a deep breath, looked her in the eye, and said as quickly as I could, "It's you." Then I hung my head.

I closed my eyes and waited for her to say something. My heart was echoing in my ears, but it had felt so good to tell her.

A silence hovered between us and, with my eyes still closed, I felt the words I had just spoken still hovering within it. I didn't want to take them back, but I did want them to disappear so we could get rolling with whatever was going to happen next. I heard the click of her shoes on the tiled floor as she walked toward me. And I felt her stop when she was close enough to whisper, "Yeah? Well, who said I just wanted to be your friend?"

Then she turned on her heel and walked out.

When I opened my eyes I was dizzy and stood there gathering myself for a minute before following her out of the band room. I was shaking. *Does that mean she likes me too?* I ran through the gym—a shortcut to Suzanne's locker, where I knew she was headed—then down the long L-shaped hallway to where she stood trying to fit her flute case into her cute purple backpack.

"Are you fucking kidding me?" I asked.

"About what?"

"About wanting to be more than just my friend?"

"Oh, about *that*. Nope, I'm very serious. I have a crush on you too, honey."

When she said that, I had to take a few steps back. It was all happening too fast. "Suzanne, I'm kind of freaking out here. But I think I want to kiss you."

"OK," she said. Then, like a schoolgirl in some black-and-white silent movie, she laced her fingers behind her back, rolled forward onto her tiptoes, closed her eyes, and puckered her lips.

Oh, my God, I thought, *this is really going to happen*. I started to pace again, thinking, *I don't have the energy, I don't have the courage*. Then the second bell rang.

Having waited long enough, Suzanne opened her eyes and said, "Romaine, either you're going to stick your ass out in the wind and come over here and kiss me or you aren't, but either way, I have to go. If I miss the bus, my mom will kill me."

And so I did it. I clenched my fists, walked over to her, and kissed her. In an instant, everything was relaxed. My muscles unclenched, my stomach stopped hurting. Suzanne slipped her hand into mine and we wound our pinkies together. And, just like in the movies, there were fireworks.

10 | *Gay Visibility*

At the end of March the local paper ran a small piece requesting volunteers to help the Names Project display pieces of the AIDS Memorial Quilt to the public on the evening of April 6. I invited Suzanne to volunteer with me—and this became our official first date.

The event took place at the Golden Dome, a big ugly golden goose egg that houses a basketball court. With all the bleachers pushed back and the walls cleared, the space was barely large enough to accommodate the massive traveling quilt. We got there early to help set up, then found ourselves free to wander around.

I had only a vague understanding of the quilt back then. I knew that the panels, created either by those living with AIDS or by their loved ones, were sewn into the larger quilt when the person died. But that was about it that I knew. There was no way I'd expected how tangibly the quilt reflected life itself. Suzanne and I were mesmerized by it. Some of the panels were stitched so intricately and with such detail that we could almost feel the sense of determination that had gone into creating them. Others were painted with primary colors, depicting stick-figure children with balloons, yellow suns, flowers, and open skies, conveying our carefree and childlike sides. There was sadness in much of the poetry, and joy in the splashes of glitter.

A special section was on display that night, made by people around the country who'd been moved by the story of Ryan White. By then I had learned more about him. When he was 13 he and his family discovered he'd contracted AIDS through a blood transfusion. The fear and ignorance he encountered in his community resulted in his family being forced out of their town. By the time Ryan died at 19, Elton John—among other celebrities—was his friend, and Ryan was one of the world's most renowned voices in the fight for AIDS research and education. Seeing the many Ryan White panels was especially moving because his story helped me understand what was going on with Michael when I first learned of his illness.

Suzanne and I signed the special panel from the people of Sheridan, then went up to the mezzanine where the wraparound balcony had a view of the interior. We were all alone up there, and that felt so safe. As we stood against the railing, gazing down at the quilt in its enormity, the reality of its message swept over me like a panic. Michael was going to die. Of course, I already knew, and had been working on accepting it, but my day-to-day routine had enabled me to not really deal. For the first time, while face-to-face with this beautiful tribute, the inevitability of Michael's end—the permanence of his death—looked like something.

I was on the ground at Suzanne's feet before I even realized I had let go of the railing. I was crying and hyperventilating. My throat was closing. Suzanne knelt down on the ground behind me and hooked her arms under mine as she struggled to get me into a seated position.

"I know," she said, and I knew that she did. "I love you and I've got you," she said, and she held me until I was better.

Suzanne and I had become visible at school. We couldn't help it; we were in love.

Tongue River High School had very strict policies about everything. If you forgot your pencil, you got detention. If you got below a C, you didn't get credit for a class. As far as public displays of affection were concerned, students were allowed to hold hands—that was it. Hugging, kissing, or any other show of affection on school property was strictly prohibited.

In the weeks since we had officially hooked up, Suzanne and I could barely keep our hands off each other as we snuck kisses between classes or on our way to the band room when we thought no one was looking. And, for a little while, we felt like we were getting away with it.

By mid May of that school year, just as Suzanne and I were settling into a comfortable place with our young romance, some of my classmates became more aggressive toward me. There were three boys in particular who had almost seemed to have gotten over their initial shock about my being out, yet upon discovering that I had a girlfriend (forget about her being a totally hot one!), they made it their mission to make my life a living hell.

These guys were like the Three Stooges—only their version would've been called the Three Religious Knuckleheads. David was my old childhood friend, the one who'd informed me I was a hell-destined sinner in the park during Ranchester Days. Tim, whose father ministered to many of the local community churches, had been instilled with such staunch Christian values that he refused to attend the evolutionary portion of any and all science classes. And finally, there was Steven. Steven Serna was born the day after I was. His father, celebrating in the waiting room with mine, asked if a marriage could be arranged between the two of us babies at that very moment in time. And no, he wasn't joking.

The boys and I all had a science class together—a class taught by a young student teacher who exerted no authority and therefore had no control.

I liked science; I even liked participating in class. But every time I raised my hand to answer or ask a question, from the back of the room one of the three boys would yell, "Excuse me, teacher-woman, that dyke down there has a question." If it wasn't that, it was some sort of gay sexual innuendo. And no matter how many times it happened, it never got easier to take. Sometimes I'd look to the back of the room where the "real" teacher, Chuck Bailey, sat observing his petite young protégée. Usually he wouldn't look at me, but on the rare occasions when our eyes did meet he'd just raise then drop his shoulders, as if to say *What can ya do?*

Finally, one day at the end of May, I stormed into Principal Edwards's office. Bob Edwards was a hunting buddy of my father's; a big man with broad shoulders, he's good-looking in a clean-cut, sharply defined, former-military way, and he believes strongly in etiquette and manners.

"What's on your mind, Romaine," he said, leaning forward to rest his folded hands on top of his desk.

"What's on my mind is that we have a problem, Bob." I used his first name to let him know I was serious.

"Do we now?" Bob motioned to a wooden chair in front of his desk. "Why don't you take a seat and tell me what's going on?"

Ignoring his invitation, I started to pace the room. "I don't think I have to tell you about my situation or about my relationship with Suzanne."

"No," he said. "I think I have a pretty good understanding."

"Well, good," I said, "because I'm having some problems."

"With students or teachers?"

"With both," I said, "but mostly with this one group of guys right now—and I'm coming to you because I need you to do the right thing."

"Tell me who they are and what they're doing and we'll take it from there," he said.

I told him everything, from David's impromptu you're-going-to-hell speech up through their harassment in science class.

"Romaine, I had no idea this was going on," Bob told me, which I knew was 100% total bullshit.

Now I was pissed. "Yes you did, Bob. You know everything that's going on around here."

He thought about that for a few seconds, then nodded. "To be really honest with you, we didn't talk about stuff like this when I was in school. I really don't know how to deal with it...but I just now have an idea," he said, pressing his palms on his desk. "You wait here for a few minutes and I'll be right back."

Bob came back a few minutes later, and trailing behind him were David, Tim, and Steven. The look of confusion on all three boys' faces almost immediately turned to comprehension when they saw me. As they exchanged knowing glances—interspersed with glares at me—Bob shut the door to his office. Then he slowly walked past the boys, eyeing each one individually before finally taking his seat. "Romaine, why don't you pull up a chair over here and sit next to me. You boys can stay standing."

I moved the chair next to his and sat down.

"So I've just had an interesting little chat with Romaine. She told me some of the things you guys have been doing and saying to her in science class."

Each boy's face dropped its mouth open and completely lost its color as Bob spelled out word for word exactly what I had told him. At different times I saw David or Steven or Tim struggle with the urge to interject, to deny the charges, but as Bob continued to talk,

I watched them each slowly surrender to the truth of his own behavior. They were immobile, and I loved it. The only thing they moved was their eyes, as they darted around in an effort to avoid Bob's own—especially when Bob said a word like "dyke" or "lesbian," mocking their tones of voice. I found it difficult to not laugh, but I also felt like crying—finally someone was acknowledging this.

When Bob was through, he asked the boys if they had anything to say for themselves. It was a trick, and they knew it; any attempt to defend their actions would only implicate them further. And so, in unison, they whimpered ashamedly, "No, sir."

Bob then turned to me and said, "All right, Romaine, you punish them." There was a collective gasp—from the boys and from myself. That was the last thing any of us expected. "That's right, Romaine," he continued. "You know better than I do what sort of punishment would fit this crime, so I'm leaving it up to you. In-school suspension, a month's detention, whatever you want."

That was a tough one. Of course I wanted these guys to know how shitty they'd made me feel, but I had no idea how to make them care. Then it came to me.

"I've got your punishment," I said as I turned to look at them. And they were terrified.

I knew none of the things Bob mentioned would have had any lasting effect. In a few weeks, after the terms of the punishment were up, things would go back to the way they'd been and nothing would have changed. "I want you to go home and think about how hurtful your words are," I said. "I'll give you guys the benefit of the doubt and assume that up until now you didn't know how much your making fun of me hurts my feelings. But now you know. It makes me feel like shit, and it won't be acceptable in the future."

David actually seemed to be affected by this. He hung his head and even grumbled, "I'm sorry, Romaine." This was, after all, the same kid who played Tinkertoys with me every day of our preschool years. Steven nodded with David's apology. But Tim—ever the pastor's son—remained stone-faced, completely unmoved.

The prom was held in June that year at a sprawling ranch in the nearby town of Dayton. Suzanne and I had told our parents we'd be going stag but hanging out together for support—and that seemed fine with everyone. (Mom, who was no fool, had begun by then to wonder about my relationship with Suzanne. And though she never would have directly asked me if I was gay, once that May—in the car on the way to band practice, gripping the steering wheel like she was trying to choke the life out of it—she asked me, in a tone so cool it was almost gossipy, if Suzanne was my girlfriend. I lied of course, saying "No," trying—and failing—to insert the required note of disgust into my response.) I wore a black pantsuit and my purple Doc Martens. Suzanne wore a black tuxedo dress she'd chosen because, as she put it laughingly, "it shows off my ample bosom." She wore no jewelry, and her highlighted brown hair was barretted and pinned to spiky perfection.

We arrived separately, then lined up together for the couples march. Like all the other sophomore couples, we marched arm in arm, step by step to the area where camera-toting parents had been assembled to snap photos for the family album. Years later my mother told me about some of the remarks she was subjected to as Suzanne and I came marching into view. One mother, speaking to nobody in particular, elevated her voice. "Can you believe the nerve of those lesbians, ruining such a beautiful event as this? What a mockery."

My poor mother—who just wanted her kids to live the kind of normal existence she had—took it in stride. But it couldn't have been easy for her. She is the same woman who'll tell anyone who will listen the story of a young virginal maiden in Trinidad, Colo., who at the age of 20 was outdoors one day feeling sad and lonely about the fact that she still hadn't found a husband. Suddenly she heard a plane flying overhead and spontaneously looked up into the heavens and said out loud, "Dear Lord, please send me a man who will love me, and let him be on that plane." And sure enough, God delivered to her, from that very plane, my father, who was at the time flying in the Air Force.

My parents held hands at the dinner table, and my father—who with his children used the words on the most special of occasions only—could be overheard telling my mother that he loved her just about every hour of the day. They were the strongest people I knew because they had each other. They prided themselves on the family they had created together, and so I can only imagine how hard it was for them to have to stand around listening while people they'd known for as long as they could remember gossiped angrily about their daughter. It must have been awful. They could have let it ruin the night for Suzanne and me, but of course, they didn't. As always, they were troopers—willful soldiers in the battle of denial. They just took a few pictures of their daughter and her friend, told us how beautiful we looked, and went home.

Toward the end of the evening I went over to the DJ—a short and skinny little guy with two pierced ears and a nose ring—and handed him a CD by the Flirtations.

"The last track on this album is called 'Everything Possible,'" I said.

The DJ flipped the case over to check it out then nodded his head. "Yeah?" he said.

"It's, ah...sort of me and my date's song," I said. "Do you think you could play it for us before the night's over?"

He thought about it for a second. "Never heard of these guys," he said, now looking at the CD cover. He looked up at me and must have seen the pleading in my eyes. "Yeah," he said, "I'll hook you up, sister."

"Thanks," I said, then went back to our table and asked Suzanne if she'd take a walk with me. We walked over toward the pool area, which was all but deserted because everyone was trying to get in some last-minute dancing before the prom ended; the popular dance hit "The Sign" by Ace of Base was playing. We talked about how funny people's reactions to us had been during the couples march and about how difficult it would be to be apart for the summer.* (*Footnote: She'd be going to Ohio to see her family. I'd be going back to Denver.)

"I really do love you, you know?" Suzanne said as she hiked up her dress and sat down on the wall between two tiki torches.

"I love you too," I told her, "and, actually, I got you something just to remind you of that." I knelt down and pulled a little ring out of my purse. It was sterling silver and had a little pink triangle etched into it. I slipped it onto her finger. "This is a little token of how much I care about you."

Suzanne didn't say anything. She stood up, took my hand, and kissed me.

As we strolled back to the tent, holding hands, still feeling a little awkward in our heels, Suzanne heard the opening notes to "Everything Possible."

"Oh, my God, Romaine, is that DJ really playing our song?" Her stunned question was answered when all our classmates froze in place, then came wandering off the floor, annoyed that a slow song they'd never heard before now blasted from the speakers.

"How did you..." she started, then changed her mind. "You know, we still haven't slow-danced tonight," she said.

"Do we dare?" I asked, looking at the completely empty dance floor.

"Hell yeah, we do."

And so we did. We strutted out on to the vacant dance floor. She put her arms around my neck, I put mine around her waist, we both closed our eyes, and we danced.

A few minutes later a few of the other class "freaks"—straight girls who knew about my relationship with Suzanne and were in total support of it—partnered up and slow-danced alongside us.

"*And the only measure of your words and your deeds,*" sang the voice from the speakers, "*is the love you leave behind when you're gone. Anything and everything is possible.*"

11 | Summer of '94

It was a little harder to convince Mom to let me go back to Denver for that second summer. She was nervous about the influence my brothers were having on me.

"I'm not sure I like some of the changes I've seen in you since last summer," she said to me one afternoon in early June. We were outside de-rocking the front yard so my dad could mow it. Of course we both knew she was talking about my having become a lesbian, but we also both knew that her inability to talk about it made arguing her case impossible. And so, angling my foot to kick a pinecone out of the yard and through an imaginary goalpost, I played the trump card.

"What changes, Mom?"

She thought about it for a second before letting her rake drop. Then, reaching with more force than I think she intended to, she grabbed my shoulder hard and held it tight for a second before, a little bewildered by her own frustration, she relaxed her grasp but didn't take her hand away. She looked at me then. It was an intense sort of stare where eye contact was established and remained unbroken for a solid couple of seconds. And though it was sort of uncomfortable, I stood my ground, fighting the urge to break away from her because I knew it was a moment we had to share. I remember thinking as I watched her take me in that it was a big moment for her—the moment in which she began to resign herself to the idea that, like it or not, I was not going to become the person she had always hoped I would become. And it was a nice moment for me because that afternoon, in the front yard of her house on the corner of Betty and Carl streets—streets on the other side of the picket fence that had been named after her and my father—I really believe my mother's perspective began to change and, though it was hard for her, for the first time in both of our lives she was beginning to be able to really *see* me.

"Oh, I don't know," she said as she subtly shook her head before bending over and picking her rake back up.

Of course, she folded when Michael hauled out and dusted off the old "last dying wish" speech again. But there was one surprise condition: "All right, young lady, you can go back to Denver if you get a job while you're there."

Her words instantly scared the shit out of me. "What? Me, work?" I said half joking.

"That's right, Romaine. You need to start saving for college."

My job hunt began my first weekend in Denver. On my second day I noticed Diedrich Coffee down the street had a HELP WANTED sign in the window. The manager, a big bear of a man named Carl Nixon, later claimed to have been "taken with" me from the moment I asked for an application. "Do you have any work experience?" he asked me.

"Um, no," I told him, and he chuckled good-naturedly.

Then—either because he felt sorry for me or because he needed a lesbian to balance out a staff composed entirely of gay guys and fag hags—he offered me a job.

Right from the start I knew I was going to love it there.

Diedrich's was designed to be a comfortable place that made you want to linger for hours. There were overstuffed couches and armchairs, all the daily papers, and an ever-changing array of local artwork on the walls. The back door opened onto a patio, and in good weather it was kept open to keep the air and the aroma of freshly ground coffee circulating. And since Diedrich's was smack-dab in the heart of Capitol Hill, the gayest part of Denver, all sorts of interesting people hung out there.

So many characters came in and out of that establishment over the years, but a few stand out in my memory. There was Latte Jim, who always got a large and liked it extra sweet with vanilla syrup; and Sheri, the old lady who rode horses; and Sheri's husband, who insisted on bringing in his cup of 7-Eleven coffee because he thought it tasted better; and crazy-man Elias, who waited patiently outside the door every morning just to be the first one in at 6 A.M. It was with these regulars, the people I had known longest in Denver (next to my brothers), that I would share a sense of loss and anger three-and-a-half years later when my good friend Matthew, the tiny little man who occasionally shared a table with one of them, was so brutally murdered. And it would be among them that the national dialogue over Matthew's death would be born.

My brothers rarely visited me at the coffee shop that summer. Michael, when he was feeling well enough, came down and saw me occasionally. He'd have a cup of chamomile tea and read *The Denver Post*, then sit tiredly for a little while before heading back to the house to watch *The Young and the Restless* and *Guiding Light*. He was considerably sicker this summer, and for the first time I was able to *see* the disease on him. He had never been a pudgy guy, so he didn't have a lot of weight to lose when the thinning effect of the AIDS virus began in him. I noticed it first in his ass, an area of his body that had always been flat but by that summer was completely gone. His jeans hung off him in back as if there were nothing there at all. Then it was his legs...he was so self-conscious about them that he covered them up at all times, with a blanket if he was lying around the house or with baggy pants if he was going out. His cheeks hollowed out so much, they looked perpetually sucked in.

But he never lost his humor. He got up with me every morning and sang his own special version of "Supermodel" by RuPaul from the kitchen, where he fixed our breakfast as I would be getting ready for work. The words were changed to celebrate my employment: *"You better work, cover girl, work it bitch, do your thing at the café."* Our afternoons were spent in the TV room, where we'd scarf day-old Diedrich's pastries, watch soap operas, and bitch about John.

Though Michael had many good days that summer, even managing to volunteer a few hours a week with the Colorado AIDS Project, I left Denver unsure whether there would be a next one with him.

12 | *An Illness in the Family*

I was 11 when my father was first diagnosed with lymphoma. I remember driving with my parents up to Billings, Mont., for his treatments. In the small lounge where I sat and waited while my parents were in with the doctors, there was a comfortable couch and a big brown coffee table that always had a half-finished puzzle spread out across it. After each bout of chemo Dad was totally incapacitated, so Mom always drove home. She and I would help him up the stairs to the bedroom, where he'd spend the next few days vomiting and screaming in pain.

My triumphant working-girl return to Ranchester that fall was marked by more bad news. My mother broke it to me over lunch one afternoon at the Ranch House—the restaurant she used to take me to when I was a little kid for her weekly lunch with the library ladies. Back then, if I behaved myself, she'd end the meal by handing me a pack of Life Savers.

"Over the summer," she said, "we found out that your dad's...condition has come back."

It annoyed me that she couldn't say the word "cancer." "Why didn't you guys call and tell us any of this?"

"You had enough to worry about, honey," she said, "What with your new job, and Michael not doing so…" Welled-up tears began dripping down her cheeks. She cut herself off. "And anyway, your dad's fine for now. We're going to start with radiation treatments this time and put the chemo off for as long as we can. And who knows, maybe he won't need chemo at all this time." Then she said with mock cheer, "I think we should all just try to look forward to Thanksgiving."

Over the course of the weeks between that lunch with Mom and the Thanksgiving trip to Denver, Dad and I didn't talk much about his health. And thankfully, except for some sunburnlike skin irritation, he didn't really seem that sick.

Michael's health, on the other hand, hadn't improved much since the summer. His energy levels was so depleted that he could only be up for a few hours before needing a nap, and he was cold all the time, always wrapped in an afghan or his favorite parachute blanket.

That parachute blanket was Michael's safety object—so much so, in fact, that had he been a 5-year-old he would have called it his "blankie." Like a doily—the fancy kind they use to line coffee saucers at expensive restaurants—the thing was white, frilly, and round. And when his health was on the downswing, the blanket almost never left him. If he was on the couch, he was buried underneath it; if he was cooking in the kitchen, he had it wrapped, folded, and tucked around himself like a toga or, if he was feeling extra queeny, an intricate wedding dress. Despite the number of times a week John or I wrenched it away from him in order to wash it, the blanket never lost Michael's deep, musky scent. I swear, the blanket—fresh from the dryer and alone on the couch—could fill the TV room with the smell of my brother.

Suzanne, after weeks of trying to convince her mother, was

finally permitted to spend Thanksgiving with us. Between Michael and me, it was hard to tell who was more excited that she was coming. Ever since I dropped the bomb that I'd gotten myself a girlfriend, he'd become sort of obsessed with knowing everything about her. When we showed up and she was wearing the simple silver ring I'd presented her at the end of the summer (making clear my intention to marry her someday), Michael loved her immediately. And—as with everyone he liked—gave her a nickname he knew she'd hate. Because of her voluptuousness, he called her Hildegard, and she cringed every time she heard it.

He put forth a grand effort but couldn't hide his exhaustion. And for the first time he let us all help with more than just the cranberry sauce. But we all knew where the line was: If the actions of any of us were in any way construed as catering to Michael's illness, there would be hell to pay. So we stood around the kitchen while he cooked and, like assisting doctors to the chief surgeon, fetched him whatever he needed. He drank a lot of water and sat at the small kitchen table when he needed a break. From there he would shout directions until he had the strength to get back up. And he *always* got back up.

Michael was more active that week than it seemed he had been the entire summer. He took me, amid near hysterical protests from my mother, to see his friend Randy, a hairstylist, who gave me my first official short-short lesbian 'do. And he got tickets for the entire family to see *The Phantom of the Opera*—complete with long-stemmed roses for Mom, Suzanne, and me, and we even went out for our favorite brownie-bottom sundae after the show. Michael outdid himself. But the extravagance of it all clearly drained him.

Even as I lived through it that night at the theater, I knew this would become one of my most treasured memories, because of the opportunity it presented to share Michael with my girlfriend and my girlfriend with Michael. A deep sadness took hold of me as I tried, nuance by nuance, to commit the evening's every detail to my memory.

There was illness all around me that winter. I dealt with it all by trying to disappear, to avoid taking away attention from the needs of my father and brother. Then I became sick myself. I had all but stopped eating and was dealing, secretly, with stomachaches that had grown from minor annoyances to a sudden pain so tremendous I sometimes couldn't stand or walk.

Whether anyone in my family knew I needed help I'm still not sure, but in pictures of myself from that time I certainly look like someone in serious trouble. In one I'm standing in front of the window in the living room of our new house. I'm wearing a baseball hat and a T-shirt that, tucked into a pair of jeans, clearly shows the emaciation of a girl who went from 140 pounds to 106 in three months. I'm so gaunt in that picture and my face is so small. Dark-blue circles shone like bruises under my eyes. Though the changes in my physical appearance were dramatic, I was in total denial that I was starving myself. And my parents, who were usually very conscious of any fluctuation in my weight, never said anything about the fact that I was visibly fading away. I wonder now if it's possible that they were so preoccupied with their other worries that they just didn't notice, or if they did notice but were too exhausted by the thought of taking on more illness to try to help me. Suzanne, of course, was worried—she was always trying to get me to eat—but, other than that, hadn't the slightest idea of what to do.

Besides Suzanne (who still proudly wore my ring), my salvation that year came in the form of the speech team. I joined as a result of prodding both from a teacher and from Michael, who'd been on the team when he was in high school. Michael and I decided that Original Oratory, in which you write a 7- to 10-minute speech about any subject, would be the best category for me. Suzanne joined the team as well so we could travel together, and she and I decided to also do a duet from Lily Tomlin's *The Search for Signs of Intelligent Life in the Universe.* For my oratory piece Michael and I chose AIDS as the subject then, with my love of the multicolored freedom rings as our inspiration, we broke it down by the colors of the rainbow—each color representing a different group of people who were affected by the disease, with the exception of blue, the color that represented hope.

Because I was new and nervous—and hadn't bothered to memorize my speech before I even got on the bus—I was entered into the novice competition for the first meet. It was the equivalent of being put on junior varsity, and it stung my ego, but in a way I was psyched. There was less pressure on me—and I knew my speech kicked ass. My round was held in a classroom and was attended by four people, including Suzanne and the judge. Suzanne sat in the front row, using the rainbow charm bracelet I bought her to subtly guide me through my speech.

I shocked the small Wyoming speech community by taking first place that day. As soon as I got home I called Michael. His reaction—a scream followed by a demand to "tell me everything"—was all I'd hoped it would be.

Out of sheer determination, a sort of compulsion to always make Michael that proud, I went on to place in the top three in all of the next six speech competitions. Having been yanked from the novice group by the team's coach, I quickly earned a reputation as the young interloper from Tongue River High who was going to be a force to be reckoned with.

My participation in the speech team that year helped me find my voice as an aspiring activist. But it was Michael's support, encouragement, and help—especially with that first speech—that spurred me on to hone that voice. And though we'd worked tirelessly on it together, he never saw me perform with it. He had the opportunity in March when I competed in the district meet. Tongue River was required to send a judge/coach to accompany me; Michael qualified because of his years of experience as a competitor, so I took him. He judged a number of rounds but never came to see any of mine.

I think it just would have been too emotional for him to hear me talk about how it felt to have a brother dying of AIDS, to hear me say those things in my own words. I understood that, so I didn't push him on it.

Of the 100 or so students who participated in rounds that day, 10 of us had made it to the finals. Of the 10 finalists, the top three won spots to participate in the national meet that coming June in Fort Lauderdale, Fla. I remember Michael sneaking in and out of the judging meetings all day long, trying to see how I was doing. The other judges adored his enthusiasm, so they tolerated it. But when it came down to the finals, they kicked him out.

When Michael accompanied me to the awards ceremony that windy March afternoon it was difficult to tell which one of us was more nervous. My fingernails were chewed ragged. Michael squirmed in his seat like a kid. When one of the judges got up to make the announcement, I closed my eyes, feeling like I'd never wanted anything so badly in my life. The judge, after saying that the names would be read in no particular order, called out a first name then a second. Neither one was mine. A wave of disappointment hit me as I became sure that the third and final name would be somebody else's. I opened my eyes and focused on Michael as the judge read the last name. I don't even think I heard my name being read—I just remember Michael's face exploding into an open-mouthed smile. My heart pounded, and light-headedness swooped in and clouded my senses as I walked to the front of the room, shook the judge's hand, and took my place next to the other winners.

"It gives me great pleasure," the judge said, indicating the three of us, "to present 1995's speech champions of the state of Wyoming."

I had kept my eyes focused on Michael, who'd kept his on the judge up until that moment. He looked at me then, still beaming with that proud smile, and gave me a double thumbs-up. The image instantaneously burned itself into my mind: My brother, proud and happy, waving his thumbs, having momentarily forgotten about all of life's other circumstances—wanting, as much as I did, to live in the moment forever.

13 | Busted in the Girls Room

One afternoon in May of '95 I found Suzanne crying in the girls bathroom after yet another fight she'd had with her mother over her stepfather's asshole-like behavior. I was hugging her, trying to calm her down, when the home economics teacher, Ms. Swanson—an uppity woman who wore flowered dresses and believed every girl should know how to sew—walked in. Clearly pleased at having caught the school lesbians in the act of breaking Tongue River's "no hugging" rule, she told us she was going to take the issue up with Bob Edwards.

A few hours later, in the band room just before rehearsal, Bob stormed in and demanded to speak to Suzanne and me. The band teacher, Mrs. Knutson—our biggest supporter—asked to be part of the meeting, and we all went into her office.

Bob was furious. He told me he had already "told everything" to my father, who—coincidentally and despite his health problems—was substituting at the school that day.

"That's called outing somebody, Bob," I said. "You have no right to do that."

He didn't respond. Instead, he announced he was about to call

Suzanne's parents and have the same talk with them.

Suzanne, who'd been crying since we sat down, became hysterical—which brought out the crazy in me.

"You can't call her parents, Bob. They're nuts!" I shouted.

"Yeah, my parents are n-n-uts," Suzanne said between sobs.

"I have to," Bob said unapologetically. "It's what we do."

"It's one thing for you to out me to my father, Bob. Even though he'll probably have my ass in a sling when I get home this afternoon, at least we know he won't throw me out on the street," I said. Then, shoving Mrs. K's heavy wooden chair into her metal desk, creating a loud, hollow boom like rolling thunder, I went on. "Because some parents do that, Bob, and Suzanne's parents are those parents, so if you are going to call them, you better be ready to take her in when they throw her out."

In the end, though Bob didn't believe Suzanne's parents would go that far, we were able to convince him not to call them, in return for a slew of detentions.

Back at home, though I was never sure if it was more because I was gay or because of the embarrassment he suffered from his old hunting buddy being the one to tell him, Dad was slamming cabinets around in the kitchen. When he heard me come in and make a beeline for my bedroom, he shouted—and these are words I'll never forget—"Goddamn faggot bitch!"

You'd have to know my father to understand why those words didn't make me turn on my heel and run into the kitchen screaming "How dare you!" He was a man who had wanted eight sons, settled for five, was dealing with three of them being gay, one of them dying of AIDS—this on top of the fact that he was probably dying himself—and now his baby had just been outed as a lesbian by one of his oldest friends. Our big kitchen was the place where he went to work out issues like these. And if the kitchen had been

his gym, well, then its sturdy "buy once, buy right" wooden cabinets were Dad's punching bags. He was also a man to whom words
meant nothing. "JesusChristGoddamnSonofaBitch" was his catch-
phrase, and he'd use it as easily over something minor as something major. Of course, when you heard him yelling it, especially
if he was in the kitchen slamming the cabinets, you knew to stay
out of his way. And though I couldn't recall hearing him use the
word "faggot" before, it didn't surprise me—he did, after all, use
the *n* word casually.

All of this is to say that, even in that terrible moment, I knew
that he loved me. And like the rest of his kids, I knew that he loved
John, and Sabin, and that he was hopelessly devoted to Michael.
Hearing my dad say those awful, hateful words stung worse than
just about anything I'd ever experienced. But he was in the kitchen
slamming away, and I knew that meant he was working it out—
coming up with a plan as to how best to deal with it.

A little while later he called me into the living room. "Romaine,
I need to you tell me if what Bob told me is true." He was sitting
on the couch with a scrunched-up face, and it made me feel guilty.
I didn't want to be doing this to him, especially not now, but what
could I do? I wasn't going to lie.

"Yes, Dad, it is."

He nodded his head and looked away from me. He started
chewing on the inside of his cheeks and rolled his eyes up so high
in their sockets that all I could see was the whites. "OK," he said
finally. "We're not going to tell your mother because it will just
worry her. And I don't care what's going on, but I don't want to
hear another goddamn thing about it."

For Suzanne it was only a brief reprieve. A few weeks later her
mom found a couple of recent love notes from me in the pocket of

one of her vests. Under the guise of taking Suzanne and me to dinner one night, she unexpectedly drove us to a hotel and ushered us into a room where, she said with a sickening sweetness, we could all sit down and "have a little chat."

Once Suzanne and I had made ourselves comfortable on the bed, her mother locked the hotel room door, crossed her arms, and stood in front of it. She was wearing a baggy flannel shirt and a pair of jeans smattered with bleach stains. She was tall and busty like her daughter but without an ounce of her charm. She started tapping her foot, and the smile quickly disappeared from her face. I realized that she was looking at me only.

"Romaine," she said, then took a long pause. "Romaine, Romaine, Romaine... It has come to my attention that you think you love my daughter." She paced in front of the door, and I, eyes wide, shot a glance at Suzanne—who had, of course, started bawling. "Well, I'm here to tell you that you don't."

That one really pissed me off. I remember thinking, *She's a sturdy gal, but I could take her if I had to.*

"And I want you to know, young lady, that if I ever see you on my property again"—and I'll never forget what she did next: the way she, in one swift movement, ripped the curtains open so I could see through the windshield of her truck, the shotgun perched on its rack in the cab—"I. Will. Kill. You."

After that the constant pressure of feeling watched by parents, teachers, and classmates—not to mention the idea of being gunned down by Suzanne's mom—made things just a little bit difficult between Suzanne and me. We were on again, off again, and fighting all the time as we snuck around like spies. I kissed a girl from one of the other speech teams, a girl named Dani—who, it turned out, feigned interest in me in order to get to Suzanne. This love triangle came to a head in the Tongue River High parking lot one day after school when I got into it with Dani, who had come by to pick up Suzanne. I called her a fucking cunt; she responded by grabbing Suzanne and kissing her. I had to admit that I was duped, and I ended up getting so angry that I had to be taken to the doctor that afternoon with severe abdominal pain. After a battery of tests and the doctor's discovery that I had lost almost 40 pounds in six months, he determined I had a couple of nasty stomach ulcers.

Ultimately, Suzanne chose Dani over me, and that was the end. The last time I saw her was a few weeks later, when I drove up to her house (while Shotgun Mama was at the supermarket) to get my freedom rings back. That summer, as I predicted would happen if her mother found out about us, Suzanne was shipped off to Ohio to live with her grandparents.

14 | Adjusting to the Chaos

For a little while life felt normal. After a disappointing showing in the national speech competition in Fort Lauderdale, I headed straight back to Denver for the rest of the summer. It felt good to be back to my routine—morning shifts at Diedrich's, afternoons watching the soaps with Michael, and—with the use of my fake ID—evenings at my favorite bar, the Fox Hole.

By the middle of the summer Michael's health had deteriorated such that John and I felt uncomfortable about leaving him alone. One stir-crazy night we shut ourselves in a room to argue over who got to go out and who had to stay home. Michael overheard, of course, and flew into a rage. Storming into the room, wrapped wedding-dress-with-a-long-train-style in the parachute blanket, he shouted, "Listen up, bitches: I don't need a goddamn babysitter!" then, turning to leave, slammed the door on his train. Since he was trapped, we heard him yell "Shit!" from the hallway before he reopened the door to free his blanket, then slammed it again.

Then came the bouts of dementia. He'd call John or me by the wrong name or sing the wrong words to a song he'd loved for years…then he'd stop himself. With the innocent smile of a little kid discovering something for the first time, he'd sort of look off into the distance while forcing his brain around whatever it was he was trying to remember. Then he'd correct himself and move on. He would constantly lose the depressing books on AIDS he was obsessed with reading and became convinced that ghosts were hiding them from him. Those instances, though difficult for Michael, allowed me to see the little boy in him.

By the end of that summer so much of the Michael I had come to know and love was slowing down, but he wasn't gone yet. On his bad days, the days he just couldn't get off the couch, I'd remind myself that the doctors had initially given him six months. Now it had already been almost six years! I'd think of all the experimental drugs he was taking, the way he'd forced himself into medical trials that looked promising, and of how his determination to stay bitchy, vital, and funny had kept him alive for so long. It showed me just how much of a fighter and a survivor my brother was, and I loved him so much for it.

The idea of leaving at the end of the summer was made easier since I knew it would be my last year in Ranchester. My senior year wasn't nearly as difficult as I'd thought it would be. Not having a girlfriend meant that everyone left me alone, and being left alone gave me the freedom to focus on myself and explore new things. I became president of the art club when I realized how much I loved to sculpt, I made all-state choir for the first time, and, of course, I was an active member of the speech team.

As the year progressed, my health improved. Of course, my father was still sick and Michael was still dying, but I was learning how to deal with those realities (talking about them when I needed to, crying if I had to) rather than bottling up my emotions then becoming overwhelmed. By the end of the year I was thin but healthy-looking, my skin was back to its clear complexion, the bags under my eyes were gone, and I smiled a lot. I participated, and felt genuinely welcome, in all senior class activities. And I even, for my mother, took a guy to the prom.

Graduation was tough because Michael couldn't be there; he just wasn't well enough to travel. By then he'd convinced me to accept a full speech scholarship from Casper College in Casper, Wyo., and we both knew that, with all of the preparation it would take to get me there, he and I wouldn't see much of each other that summer.

And we didn't. I spent a few weeks in Denver—enough time to save a little cash—then Mom and I headed to Casper to hunt for an apartment.

Part Two

15 | The Fabulous Seven Becomes The Fabulous Eight

I moved into a big one-bedroom on Dergen Street at the end of August. It came fully furnished with damaged furniture that had either been crudely repaired or left broken. Lining the walls was a sort of contact paper that peeled in the corners. It was tacky and dingy, but it was mine, and I loved it.

I started to meet other gay students almost as soon as the school year began. Some were on the speech team with me, and others I met through a woman named Janet Devrees—who, as one of the only out faculty members, took on the personal task of identifying and bringing together out gay students. Every now then, as our little gay posse became more and more established, I'd get a call from Janet asking if she could send another student our way. We were always happy to make room.

One afternoon in September a young woman almost ran me over in the parking lot behind my apartment building. After slamming on the brakes and screeching to a stop, her front bumper inches from my knees, she stuck her head out the window and said she was sorry. She was a voluptuous girl with a round face and chestnut eyes that matched her long thick hair. A few days later I left a note on her car, asking if we could have coffee sometime. That same night—at around 1 A.M.—she showed up at my door in a miniskirt and a tight yellow sweater to invite me down to a party in her apartment on the level below. Her name was Roni, and she was stone drunk.

When I got down there, it turned out to be just her and her aunt, an exceptionally heavy woman with badly bleached blond hair and a couple of missing front teeth. They were sitting on the floor, drinking Jack Daniels and Coke from a 7-Eleven Big Gulp cup. The night culminated in Roni and me lugging her big aunt to bed as she passed in and out of consciousness, then Roni grilling me about my personal life.

"So do you have a boyfriend?" Roni sat Indian-style on the carpet in front of the couch, her eyes wide with anticipation.

"No," I said, laughing internally at the thought of *me* dating boys.

"Do you date boys?" she asked.

Was my dykiness not obvious? I was sure she was messing with me.

"No," I said with a chuckle.

"Do you date girls?"

"Yes," I said with a sigh of relief. "I'm a lesbian."

"Oh." She then tilted her head away from me while she considered that. Suddenly, with no warning, she lunged on top of me.

"What the fuck?" I laughed as she fumbled one hand up my shirt and tried to undo my belt with the other. It was a hilariously awkward moment because, though I can't imagine myself now ever pushing off me a hot straight girl in pursuit of exploratory sex, I didn't know what to do with that sort of thing back then. So, as politely as I could, I told her I wasn't into having sex with straight girls looking to experiment, so if she were really interested in me, she'd have to wait.

We hung out for the next week, and she attacked me every time. I finally gave in when she agreed to be my girlfriend.

With the addition of Roni to our group, there were seven of us. We were the Casper queers, a.k.a. The Fabulous Seven. Because I had the fake ID and didn't live in the dorm, my apartment became our party pad. My refrigerator was always stocked with beer and my freezer with vodka. We discovered a coffee shop called the Daily Grind that—when we weren't raising hell in the park across the street from my house—became our home base. It was a tiny place, the size of a living room, where they always had some kind of live band, poetry slam, or finger-painting event. The Grind, we all decided, was the perfect place to induct our eighth member.

Janet had called on a Monday afternoon and said that she had just received a call from a therapist. The therapist had a patient named Matthew Shepard who was about my age and was looking to meet other gay people. Janet had given him my phone number and told me to expect his call.

Matthew called a few days later to introduce himself. He spoke softly and his voice was a little shaky. I could tell he was nervous. I asked him to tell me a little bit about himself, and he said that he liked a lot of things.

"Like what?" I asked.

He thought about it for a second, like he was searching for the right answer. "Well, I like to watch the news and I like to talk about politics."

"Well, that's cool," I said, even though I didn't think it was. "What kind of clothes do you wear?"

"Usually button-up shirts and khakis."

"Any dog collars?" (I was really into spikes back then.)

"Yeah, sometimes," he said, which was a total lie.

I liked him immediately. He sounded innocent and corruptible. I told him a little bit about our group and how everyone was their own individual but that we had all sort of jelled together. I told him how we all hung out at the coffee shop in the afternoons and asked if he'd like to come down and join us the next day.

"I'll be there," he said.

The next day we all got to the coffee shop a little early. Around 3 P.M. the door opened and a boy walked in. He was small, around 5 foot 2, and skinny. He wore a blue button-down dress shirt underneath a light-tan jacket, a pair of khakis, and a pair of brown boots. He had wispy dirty-blond hair and sky-blue eyes. I knew right away that it was the same kid I'd spoken to the day before, if for no reason other than his terrified look as he stared at our table of freaks. I stood up and introduced myself, and when I did he smiled, and when he smiled the fear in his face was replaced with an innocent sort of expectation, as if thinking, *Well, here goes nothing.*

He pulled a chair over and the group parted to make room for him. Everyone had questions for the new kid, and he was obviously glad for the attention. He told us that he had lived in Casper when he was younger but had moved with his family to Saudi Arabia when his dad got a job in the oil industry there. He had gone to boarding school in Switzerland, then when it had come time to think about college he decided to come back to Casper and give Casper College a try. He lovingly referred to his mom as "overprotective" when he told us that she'd decided to come back with him. They were living in separate apartments in the same complex.

We all loved him immediately, especially Roni. It turned out they'd been in first grade together, and she used to pick on him for being "the skinny dork boy," and he had made fun of her for being "the big fat girl." Things had gotten especially ugly between them when he won the role of Peter Pan in the first-grade production. Apparently, she'd wanted it more than anything.

So we all met Matt, and our group became known as The Fabulous Eight. We were made up of a butch dyke (with a monster-size unrequited crush on me), a couple of femmes, a lanky cowboy, a fat drag queen, a cross-dresser who just couldn't get the makeup thing right, a drama queen wannabe activist (who covered every jacket he owned in lame-ass political buttons)—I hated that guy the most—and me, the ringleader. We were a motley crew if ever there were one, and Matt, the tiny guy whose sweet face and political knowledge betrayed nothing of his sometimes dirty little mind, seemed to be the element we were missing. Soon he began to trust and open up to us, and we learned that his sensitivity—more than his shyness—was his strongest characteristic. He brought an element of social awareness to the club, but he could also party with the best of us. And he was always up for anything...flying kites in the park at midnight or getting drunk and going to one of the local gay-themed dances he loved.

Those dances were hilarious. In a town with no gay bar, the dances were an attempt by the local gay community to provide itself with some place to meet and socialize. When enough money was raised to rent out a conference room in some run-down hotel, a DJ was hired and 30 or 40 people would show up. They always started out like an eighth-grade dance, with the boys on one side of the room and the girls on the other. But after a couple of beers people began to brave the dance floor and a drunken brouhaha ensued.

It was so funny to watch Matt at those events; for someone who was usually so aware of what people thought of him, he had an amazing ability to cut loose and dance. He had no rhythm whatsoever, but you had to love him as he swung his arms and be-bopped in place, his mouth open and his eyes wild. His usually perfect hair would be matted to his head with sweat and, if he was really feeling it, he'd undo a button or two of his shirt. He laughed a lot during that time; in fact, in my memories of him back then, he is always smiling. I think it had something to do with finally being part of a group, the security of belonging to something. Like Matt, we were all experiencing for the first time the phenomenon of being surrounded by other queer people and the sense of support and community that came along with it. It was an invaluable connection the eight of us shared, and I don't think a day went by that each of us wasn't grateful to have found each other.

16 | Memorized Moments

Roni and I broke up in December of '96, just before Christmas, because the Pentecostal Church wouldn't let her be a lesbian. I actually stormed into her church one day and confronted her pastor about it.

"How can God get mad about people loving each other?"

He responded by speaking in tongues and quoting the Bible. It wasn't the first time I'd come up against religious fanatics, and Lord knows it wouldn't be my last. But because it was Christmastime and I was going to lose my girlfriend to that man, it was an especially painful experience.

Mom picked me up a few days later and took me to Denver for Christmas with the family. Everyone came that year. We all kind of knew it was going to be our last opportunity to be with Michael, so we spent an embarrassing amount of time hovering near him in the kitchen, all trying to absorb as much of him as possible. He tried to be present but, every hour or so, would have to sneak up to his room to lie down. He and I, somehow, were still able to laugh together, but his energy was gone, and the rest of him was going.

I came back to Denver a few weeks later—on January 15, a few days before Michael's 36th birthday—to see *The Phantom of the Opera* at the same theater where Michael had taken us the first time. By that point, because it provided the most space for all his medical equipment, Michael had moved into the TV room. When I went in to see him that night before the show, he was sitting up in his chair, half covered by his parachute blanket, in a pair of sweats and a T-shirt. There was an oxygen tank nearby and a swirling mass of tubing that connected it to the mask on his face. I could tell as we talked—and as he gave me a hard time about not inviting him to the show—that he felt miserable to have me see him like that. "OK, I'm feeling a little tired," he said after a few minutes. "I think I better get some sleep."

The next morning we had a quick breakfast in the kitchen. Michael had rebounded and was on his way out to put in a few hours at the Colorado AIDS Project, and I was on my way back to Casper. I remember every detail of the moment we said goodbye. He was wearing a pair of jeans and his favorite shirt, a robin's-egg-blue polo. How many more times would I be compelled to memorize what could possibly be our last moment? How many times before there were none left to memorize? He stood in the doorway about to leave, and I asked him if there was anything I could get him before I left. He said, "Yeah, some Stouffer's macaroni and cheese."

"OK," I said. "I guess I'll see you in a few months. Have a happy birthday, OK?"

"OK," he said.

I stood there for a couple of seconds after he left. *How many times are you going to do this?* I thought. *How many times are you going to be convinced this is the last time you'll ever see him?* But I still couldn't help it: *Remember this moment,* I told myself. *Remember this moment, remember this moment…*

Before I left, I ran down to the store. I arranged the boxes of macaroni and cheese on the table around a *Phantom of the Opera* lapel pin. I left a note underneath the pin. "Happy birthday, Michael. I love you and I'll talk to you soon."

17 | *Pink Potpourri*

February, the month I always liked to forget about—as if somehow, having gotten through Wyoming's worst in January, the month's end meant that spring was in the air, my birthday would be here soon, and best of all, winter's slushy roads and dead-looking trees were over for another year. But that was never the case, and February, exacting its revenge for being the shortest, most overlooked month on the calendar, was always the worst.

Michael was very sick. Over the course of the first week of February 1997, as the family members made their way to the house in Denver, I checked in daily by phone. But I was not going to go. I told myself—and my family—that it was a momentum issue, that with school and the speech team I couldn't afford to slow down enough to be present for him. But the truth was that I couldn't see that there was anything beautiful or redeeming in just letting Michael go. How could I just stand over his bed and let it happen? It was better, I reasoned, to be powerless from afar.

When it came to handling the logistics, John was a superstar. He arranged for hospice care, and they brought a hospital bed that was set up in the formal living room. The doctors had determined that Michael was suffering from advanced liver cancer, his organs giving out thanks to years spent saturated with antiviral drugs.

Though his ability to communicate was minimal, it was also clear that he was in pain, so they started him on a morphine drip.

Though in constant contact with Mom, I spoke with Michael only once during the two weeks before he died. He was awake one afternoon when I called to check in, and when I finished talking to Mom she passed the phone to him. I was scared to hear his voice, afraid it would make his death too real and that all of a sudden I'd understand what a terrible mistake it was not to be there with him. He didn't sound like himself when he said hello.

"Hey, Michael, it's Romaine. How ya doin'?"

"Oh, not so good," he rasped.

"Well, you hang in there. It'll all be OK."

"I can't really talk. I'm sorry," he said, then he was gone.

Not long after, I called my mother to see how he was doing. She sounded like she was shaking when she said in a voice slightly louder than a whisper, "It won't be long now. It's started."

"What's started?" I asked.

"The death gurgle," she said, then started to sob. "That's what the doctors call it, the wheezing sound he makes when he tries to breathe. It's because his lungs are filling up…"

She broke down then, and John got on the phone. He told me to stay home and that they'd call as soon as anything happened. I knew I wouldn't be able to stand being alone just waiting for the news, so I gave him the number of a girl I'd been seeing. "If I'm not home, try me at Frankie's," I told him.

When I got to Frankie's I realized that the last thing I wanted was to be consoled. It would have meant being still, and I wasn't able to do that. I paced around her house for a little while. "Frankie," I said. "I can't take this. I think I need to go for a drive or something."

"Take my pager," said Frankie, her hair-sprayed mall bangs like a fortress protecting her head. She wore layered socks like a scene from *Flashdance* and was almost twice my age, a child of the '80s, and was fighting the maternal urge to hold and rock me in that moment only because she knew it would drive me nuts.

"Go on, get out of here," she said. "I can page you if your family calls."

I got in my car, sat silently at the wheel for moment, then drove down to St. Mark's, the local Catholic church. I'm not a religious person, but at the time it seemed appropriate. I walked in just as the service was ending and sat in the back pew. I sat there crying and feeling out of place as the churchgoers milled around then filed out.

"Excuse me," someone said a few minutes later. I looked up and saw a young priest walking toward me. He was dark, slender, and handsome—someone, I imagined, who in another life would have been a regular attendee at my brothers' parties at the brownstone in Denver. "I saw you when you came in," he said. "I don't mean to disturb you, but I'm wondering if I can help."

"My brother Michael has AIDS and he's dying," I said, feeling strange to have said "AIDS" in a church, like it was somehow sinful. "He's dying right now. And he's in a lot of pain, he's in horrible shape, and I don't know what to do." I was crying so hard it was difficult to get air.

"Would you like to pray about it?"

I didn't want to, but I didn't know what else to do, so I said yes.

He came over and sat next to me, held my hand, and began to pray.

"Dear Lord," he said as he gave my hand a gentle squeeze, "we ask that our brother Michael's death be painless. And when it is time to take him that he may go with ease..."

I listened for a few minutes, then stopped him.

"I'm angry," I said as I stood up.

"OK…" said the priest.

"I'm angry because God is taking my brother away and it's total bullshit."

The priest looked away for a second and considered what I had said. He folded his hands across his lap and sat back. "You know what?" he said. "I agree with you. It *is* shitty when God does these things and we don't understand why."

He didn't say anything else for a minute, then he took my hand again and I sat back down next to him. *Hey, he just swore in church*, I thought. *This is one cool priest.* We sat there for a few more minutes in silence, then he started to pray again.

"Help this family, dear Lord," he said, "give them guidance, courage, and understanding. And let them begin to heal…"

When I got home the light was blinking on my answering machine, and I knew what it meant before I even listened. It was my brother Patrick. "Romaine," he said, "you need to call Mom right away, OK?"

John picked up the plastic box containing Michael's ashes a few hours before the memorial service. I had gotten to Denver just as he was lugging it out of his Jeep and into the backyard. He gave me a big hug when he saw me then asked me to come out and help him transfer the ashes into the urn. I remembered reading somewhere, when I picked up the box and found it to be heavier than I expected, that a man's ashes weigh about the same as a newborn baby. Once outside, John presented me with his dilemma.

"OK, girl," he said. "We, obviously, have to line the vase with something, but the question is—Queen Soopers shopping bag, or pink trash bag *scented with potpourri*?"

"Pink potpourri," I said. "Obvious choice."

John nodded his approval and pulled the bag out of his pocket. We then opened the box and were about to begin transferring the ashes when a small gust of wind blew across the yard and swept a small handful of the ashes into the air. John and I both sort of gasped and instinctively held our breath, our eyes wide and our cheeks puffed out in an exaggerated display of shock.

We stood like that for a second or two before I scrambled for the box and began, frantically, to pour Michael into the vase. The cloud of ashes thickened between us. Though we both felt creepy about breathing in our brother, when John said with a smile, "We have to breathe, Romaine, or we'll never get through this," I knew he was right. So I took a breath through my nose—I couldn't imagine breathing through my mouth and actually tasting him—and as I started coughing I thought, *Hey, at least I can be sort of close to him this way.* And that helped me get through it.

The service was held in a rented mansion in downtown Denver. Everything went exactly as Michael had planned. My nephew Raif made sure everyone got a red ribbon. I made sure all the background music—RuPaul, Bette Midler, and a menagerie of show tunes—played at the appointed time. John and my sister Trish gave speeches, and Sabina gave a toast. Just before Sabina began we all pulled out our funky sunglasses decorated with sequins and feathers like the ones at her wedding. Then we raised a glass to his amazing life.

My parents drove me back to Casper early the next morning. Trish promised to deliver the 1990 white Pontiac convertible—the surprise gift that Michael, in addition to his leather jacket (which to this day is my favorite article of clothing) had willed me—once all the paperwork was taken care of. Before he left, my father, still depleted by his radiation treatments, gave me a hug and—for the first time in a long, long time—told me he loved me.

18 | A Plan We All Seemed Happy With...

As the days went on and I continued to grieve, I began to have many dreams about Michael. Usually he was in the kitchen cooking, and usually, no matter how many other family members were there, I was the only one who could see him. We'd stare at each other for a few seconds, then he'd give me a little wave and go back to what he was doing. For the first couple of nights I woke up crying, but as the dreams continued, I remember waking to a feeling of peace.

Roni called the week before my 19th birthday rolled around at the end of March.

"I miss you," she said, and the somberness in her voice was so out of character, it could have only meant one thing—she really did.

"I miss you too," I said, trying not to sound desperate. I wondered if she knew I had sort of been stalking her. (Nothing major, just driving a few blocks out of my way home to see if her light was on.)

"And I'm fucked-up about a lot of things," she said. "I love my church, and my family isn't going to understand this, but I love you too and I want to be with you. Do you think that's still possible?"

"Yeah," I said, trying to take some sort of pause, like I had to consider it for a second. "I think we can work something out."

Matt wanted to throw my birthday party at his apartment. "I'm gonna throw you a real rager," he told me, laughing. He put together a small decorating team that got to his place early to set up. I wasn't allowed to come by before 9 P.M.

Having never been to his building before but knowing he lived on the second floor, when I got there I went to the apartment directly above where I saw his car parked. I knocked on the door a couple of times, then waited. The woman who opened the door was wearing a nightgown and had clearly been sleeping. She did not look happy.

"Can I help you?"

"I'm sorry. I was looking for Matt Shepard's apartment."

"Oh, he's a few doors down," she said. "Who are you?"

"I'm Romaine," I said. "A friend of his."

"Yes, that would make you the birthday girl, wouldn't it?"

"Yeah, how'd you know?"

"I'm his mother," she said, then opened the screen door to shake my hand. "My name's Judy. It's nice to meet you, Romaine."

She went back inside and I thought to myself: *Of course that's his mother—they have the exact same eyes.*

I wandered down to the other end of the building and saw a door with a dozen or so purple balloons on it. Purple is my favorite color, so I knew that had to be the place. I knocked on the door then opened it.

Matt had outdone himself. There was purple stuff everywhere—paper bells and streamers hanging from the ceiling, stars hanging off the walls, and confetti and glitter all over the tables and floor. The bedroom was arrayed with purple candles and was to be the smoking section. I found Matt in the kitchen, putting the finishing touches on a tray of deviled eggs. We gave each other a quick hug before he was off, a serving tray in each hand, distributing treats to the seemingly endless number of guests.

That party was exactly what I needed, and Matt knew it. At times like that, I loved him so much. He knew not to push me to talk about Michael's death, that I would do that when I was ready. He also knew that, although I desperately needed a show of love and support from my friends, I would never have asked for it. By throwing my party, he created that show. That was the kind of friend he was.

The party also served as a wake-up call. Everyone I knew brought me a bottle of either Absolut or Skyy. Why? Because at that point I had no interest in anything but drinking. I'd given up on school and I hated Casper. In fact, Casper College was the last place I wanted to be. I'd only gone in the first place because it made Michael happy—and now I was on his former speech team *and* studying voice with his favorite teacher. Every aspect of my school life was a painful reminder of what I had just lost. Looking around at my numerous birthday booze bottles, I knew I was done there and that it was time for me to get back to Denver for good. I wanted to go out and participate in the real world—not just survive in it, but contribute to it. I was tired of spinning my wheels.

When I broke the news to The Fabulous Eight, they all wanted to come with me. But in the end, the only feasible two were Roni and Matt. The three of us came up with a strategy: I'd go in June and live with John while I worked at Diedrich's until I could find an apartment for Roni and me. In the meantime, Roni, who'd been kicked out of her house for getting back together with me, would live with Matt in Casper. When everything came together, they'd join me in Denver.

It was a plan we all seemed happy with.

19 | *The Snake Pit*

When Roni and Matt made it to Denver that July I still hadn't quite saved enough to get a place. Roni and I stayed on with John—who was glad for the company, since Sabin had moved to Aspen when Michael died—for a few more weeks, while Matt crashed with his aunt and uncle in a nearby suburb. Then we all began to hunt for an apartment.

I was killing myself working five or more opening shifts at Diedrich's every week—up by 4 A.M., at work by 5, and too exhausted when I finished to do anything but sleep. I was determined not to live off my brother, but with Roni only halfheartedly looking for a job and me making less than $800 a month, there weren't a lot of places we could afford. We finally settled on an apartment at 970 Downing St., a few blocks from John's and less than a block from Diedrich's, for $450 a month. It was a nice enough place, with a little kitchen, a decent-size living room, a bedroom, and a little outdoor porch area.

When we moved in we had nothing. For the first few weeks I slept on a blanket on the floor while Roni snored away on this beat-up old couch that had been donated by a neighbor. It was hard times, but we looked at it as an adventure.

Matt had already quit his job as a telemarketer for a vitamin company. The company's target demographic was elderly people living on Social Security or private retirement plans. The ever-ethical Matt often told his prospective customers that they could get the same products for half the cost at Walgreens but that they probably didn't need the vitamins at all. I remember him laughing hysterically as he told Roni and me the story of how his bosses started recording his calls for "quality assurance," then tried to fire him when they thought they caught him belching on the phone. The truth was that he couldn't figure out how to put the headset on right; the sounds they were hearing were not belches but rather his chin rubbing up against the receiver. After about two months he'd finally had enough and walked out.

He moved out of his aunt and uncle's house at the end of July, when he found a one-bedroom apartment on the corner of 13th Avenue and Clarkson Street. His mom had already begun packing up to move back to Saudi Arabia when Matt left for Denver but decided to come along with Matt's dad and his brother, Logan, to help Matt move into his new place.

While they were there they invited me to have coffee with them one afternoon at Diedrich's. I think his parents were a little nervous about Matt living on his own for the first time and, since I would be one of the only people he knew in Denver, wanted to get to know me a little bit. I was surprised at the differences in appearance between Matt and his younger brother, who was tall and broad-shouldered. But after a few minutes the ways in which they were alike became clear. Like Matt, Logan was very sweet and offered a quiet sort of intelligence to the conversation. As we sat and talked, I could understand why Matt saw his parents as a bit overprotective. But I could also understand their protectiveness, having felt it so strongly myself.

His parents were very attentive to him, and I could tell—with his dad especially, the way he sometimes cupped his hand on Matt's shoulder or looked him directly in the eye when they spoke—that they were very proud of the big step he was taking with this move. It was his first time living alone. My overriding impression when I left them that afternoon was that the Shepards were just an average family—and incredibly nice people.

Matt's new apartment was beautiful—especially compared to Roni's and mine. It had hardwood floors, high ceilings, and, because it faced the front of the building, a lot of natural light. Matt liked the place fine, but he *adored* his neighborhood. He lived across the street from a church and down the street from a public playground. Behind his house was a record store he loved called Wax Trax that specialized in hard-to-find music and old vinyl records. And down the street a little farther was Matt's favorite bar, the Snake Pit.

The Snake Pit, though mostly a gay bar, had a well-earned reputation for drawing a rough crowd. It was dark and dirty and, with its broken jukebox and 50-cent pool table, attracted a pretty seedy set. Matt, who fancied himself the world's most clean-cut, vanilla white boy, was fascinated by it. The people there were different from anyone he had ever known. Because he was unemployed at the time, he was free to go to the Snake Pit in the middle of the afternoon and sit with a beer or two for a couple of hours, watch people, and wait till someone struck up a conversation. He was so obsessed with the idea of meeting new and different people that he'd talk to anybody. After a while the regulars got to know him, and he loved that he'd come to fit in.

The longer Matt was unemployed, the more he began to slip into a sort of funk. At first I wasn't really worried about it because his history of depression was no secret. The better Roni and I had gotten to know him, the more he'd opened up on the subject.

During our late-night chats or post-shift cappuccinos at Diedrich's, if the subject came up, he'd talk about various antidepressants he'd taken or therapists he'd loved who had helped him get through dark times in his life. Occasionally one of us would push him to talk further about the problem, but he never wanted to go there. He'd say something vague like "The worst thing that can happen in life has already happened to me, so don't worry about it." It was a line Roni and I got used to hearing. "That's just Matt," we'd say to each other. We didn't take it all that seriously.

I started to worry when I noticed a decline in his physical upkeep. The Matt I'd known in Casper worked very hard on the way he looked. His hair was always dyed, streaked, and styled; his clothes were ironed; his smell was like that of a guy who just stepped out of the shower; and his unblemished skin glowed from the regular application of expensive sunscreen and moisturizers. But in Denver, as that summer faded into fall, it became obvious: He was starting to let himself go.

His hair grew out till his roots were visible; he stopped shaving; and though he seemed incapable of growing a full beard, little patches of fuzz dotted his cheeks. On the rare occasion he left his apartment, his clothes were wrinkled and had little stains on them. The changes were so obvious but so easy not to deal with. Ill-equipped and young as we were, I think we all, Matt included, hoped he'd just snap out of it.

One afternoon in late September, when I realized that we hadn't heard from Matt in a couple of days, I asked Roni to go over to his place and check on him while I was at work. When she got there she found him lying on his couch. He was stoned. The pot should have been our first clue—if he was depressed and not in therapy, where he would have had access to prescribed antidepressants, he used the pot to self-medicate, to get himself to a place outside of his head. The shades were drawn and the place stank like old garbage, dirty laundry, and stale marijuana. When she tried to talk to him, he just grunted like someone reluctant to be awakened from a nap, but when she insisted on him sitting up and talking to her, she saw that he was pale. "I have a stomachache," he groaned. "I haven't eaten all day." She went into the kitchen to fix him something and saw that he had no food, save a bottle of ketchup, anywhere in his apartment. She walked back into the living room. "Matt, what's up?"

"Nothing," he said.

"No, really, what's going on with you?"

After a minute he croaked out the words: "Look, I've got no food, my credit cards are maxed, and I can't get a hold of my parents to send me more money."

The situation was serious. "Matt, how long has it been since you've had a real meal?"

"I don't know…" He was lethargic and sounded like he really didn't care. That's when she called me.

"Romaine, hi. Listen, do you have $20? I need it for Matt—"

"For *Matt*?"

This call came in the middle of my shift at Diedrich's.

Let's just say that, even after she explained the situation, I was more than exasperated. Money had become a major bone of contention among the three of us. I worked nearly 50 hours a week to support Roni and myself on half the money Matt's parents *gave* him each month. It was hard not to resent him for taking that money— and even harder to watch how he spent it. In one afternoon at the mall he'd blow through all the cash in his wallet, then start pulling out the credit cards. It wasn't to show off or be flashy—that was never his style. He just seemed to lack common sense, like it never even occurred to him that his money could run out.

Was I surprised when Roni told me how desperate the situation had become? Not at all. Was I frustrated by the way he had—or, in this case, *had not*—handled it? No doubt. And the way he seemed to have just fallen apart...that scared me. It was so dramatic. If we hadn't checked in on him, would he have let himself starve to death? Why did it make more sense to get high and shut himself off from the world than to tell one of us he needed help? Was giving him money even the right thing to do? Shouldn't there have been an intervention, some sort of face-slapping, cold-shower-in-your-pajamas confrontation to let him know that this was not OK?

In the end, I didn't know what to do. I shied away from Matt's weakness because, back then, weakness—especially in someone I loved—was such a hard thing for me to deal with. Weakness was something I couldn't afford for myself.

Roni promised to use the $20 to go grocery shopping for him, that Matt would never touch it. "OK," I told her grudgingly. "But Roni, this can never happen again."

Then out of nowhere Matt was back to his normal self. As I came to understand his depression better, I saw that it came in waves: He'd have his downs, like in September, and he'd have his ups, like when I met him. During his ups he frequented the coffee shop.

My character has a monologue in *The Laramie Project* about how Matt would come in to see me at work and if there were somebody sitting in his favorite stool by the espresso bar, where I usually stood making drinks, he would stare at them until they got up and left. It was the funniest thing to see him do that: little Matt standing there trying to be intimidating, his arms crossed over his chest and his lips all scrunched up with intensity. That was about as mean-looking as he could pull off, and he couldn't at all pull it off.

He made a lot of friends at Diedrich's—not the kind he'd hang out with anywhere else, but they'd sit and chat at the coffee shop. There was an older man named Dave who absolutely loved talking politics with Matt over *The Denver Post*. And there was a homeless man whose name I never knew but who Matt always bought coffee for—and sometimes even lunch. He and Matt had these marathon conversations. I think Matt must've known his entire life story.

Around that time Matt's aunt Roxy, who also lived in town, was strongly encouraging him to "go out and get a job." When it became clear that she wasn't going to drop the issue, he fed her a lie that he'd gotten a job in the mall at a department store called Foley's. A few days later, Roxy, who loved Foley's, called Matt and told him that she had gotten a job there too—so that they could work together. She asked him what floors he worked on and which days. Not knowing what else to do, he made something up. Every day he had supposedly been at work, Aunt Roxy would call him up and say she'd looked for him, to which he'd respond, "We must just keep missing each other." It took him a couple of weeks to tell her the truth.

I never told him this, but I felt pretty sure she'd made up *her* story too.

As the holidays approached, Matt sank back into a slump, losing himself again in his vices. He took a lot of Klonopin during that time, a tranquilizer prescribed by his doctor to help take the edge off when he was feeling manic. He also used it to help himself fall asleep, and he sometimes took it more often than he needed to and at a higher dosage than was prescribed. And though it didn't seem to be doing any real damage at the time, it may have brought about a degree of lethargy that worsened his depressions.

But the drug Matt loved most was pot. He sometimes smoked two or three times a day, and because he hated to smoke alone, he'd call up Roni and ask her to join him.

It was no secret that back in Casper I'd been through my own pothead phase. But as I watched how much the drug was contributing to Matt's deterioration, I got worried. And when I saw that it was beginning to drag Roni down too—she had all but stopped looking for a job and was packing on the weight because of the amount of food she and Matt would binge on during their afternoon smoking sessions—I took a harsh stance against pot and drugs in general. I phoned Matt and asked him not to share his weed with Roni anymore—and of course I made clear to Roni that there was never to be drugs in our apartment and that I didn't want her to be smoking with Matt.

"That's fine, Romaine," she told me in her I-guess-I'll-tolerate-this-for-now tone of voice that I hated. "That's fine, no problem."

Because I knew she was lying, I naturally grew paranoid and would search the apartment upside down until I found her stash. In an attempt to redirect my fury, she'd tell me Matt had given it to her. I'd have a screaming match with her followed by a screaming match with Matt, and still nothing would change.

More than once I came home after a day of work to find Roni and Matt slouched on the living room sofa—ostensibly, "just talking"—but the entire place smelled like weed. Obviously, they'd sat around smoking all morning while I was busting my ass at the coffee shop. Once Roni and I went over to Matt's and they lit up a pipe right in front of me, thinking that because we were at his place it was OK. When they noticed I was upset, the line was: "You know, if you're uncomfortable, you can go home." This made me want to take the two of them and hang them upside down by their toes.

Still, I have to admit, I was jealous of their friendship. They'd grown so close since we moved to Denver, which I think had a lot to do with them being like little kids who got to have fun all the time while other people took care of them—Matt had his parents, and Roni had me. But also they were both in dark places emotionally. Roni, it turned out, hated living in Denver because of an attack she'd survived there when she was younger, and Matt was just always so depressed. The two would chat long into the afternoon, airing their deep, dark secrets to each other, and I always felt left out.

It wasn't that Matt never talked to me—he always wanted my input on whatever was going on in his life. But he seemed uncomfortable opening up to me about his past. I missed the Matt I had met in Casper, so I began making a concentrated effort to get closer. I initiated more personal conversations with him, opening up myself about Michael, about my dad being sick again, and about my experiences with Suzanne in high school. In return, Matt let it all out. He told me about coming out to his dad and how much energy he had put into the fear of disappointing him, only to be met with acceptance and approval when it finally happened. He talked about how he'd been bulimic when he was in boarding school, and how good it felt to be able to talk about it with Roni, who'd suffered off and on from the same eating disorder.

One afternoon as we sat on the back patio of Diedrich's after one of my shifts, Matt said the line I'd heard him say so many times: "The worst that can happen in life has already happened to me."

I said to him, "I hear you say that all the time—do you want to tell me what you mean by it?"

From where he sat in his plastic chair across the table, he took a long look at me, and I thought to myself, *Oh, my God, he's finally gonna tell me.* He took a hard pull off his cigarette then blew the smoke out through his nose. The dirty air hung over the little brown table between us. I hated that ashy smell, hated when he blew smoke in my direction, but I wasn't going to say anything then and take the chance of breaking the moment.

"When I was in high school," he said, "we took a class trip to Morocco." He took a short pause and nodded his head a little, as if encouraging himself to go on. "On the third or fourth day, I can't remember, I was waiting for my boyfriend Pedro in front of our hotel. I was standing there sort of just looking at the city. It was such a different city than any I had ever seen. Anyway," he said, quickening his pace, "this black limousine pulled up, and the back door opened, and before I knew what was happening, this man pulled me into the back of the car. There were three other guys back there and one of them said something about having seen me and Pedro together the day before. They drove out to this place where they stripped me and raped me."

The cigarette was still burning in his fingers when he stopped talking. He wasn't looking at me anymore. He wasn't really looking at anything, I noticed, as he took another long drag. Again he blew the smoke out his nose. "And you wanna know what the kicker is? When they were done," he looked back at me then, looked me right in the eye, then spoke in a softer tone, "when they were done, they took my shoes."

It was incredibly jarring to hear that story, and I didn't know how to react. I felt awkward; I didn't know what to say, or if I should say anything at all. I remember wanting to ask him what kind of shoes they were—the mid-ankle leather boots with the buckle I knew he loved? Or were they loafers? As if a question like that would have been comforting to him. In the end, I didn't say anything. I just sat there with him, and that seemed to be what he wanted.

What disturbs me the most about that story, even to this day, is the almost complete lack of emotion in his voice as he spoke. He added, almost as an epilogue, "And when they were done, they left me in the middle of nowhere."

Matt, Roni, and I spent Thanksgiving at John's house that year. We did our best to be cheery, but the holiday was not exactly a spirited one. Matt was thousands of miles away from his family, Roni's family still wasn't speaking to her, and I had to live all weekend with the sight of a kitchen without Michael in it to bark out orders. It was almost too much to bear. Thankfully, the whole "Matt and Roni vs. me" thing seemed to have settled down for the time being, and I felt comforted that the three of us were together.

Early in December, Matt called. He turned out to have met a guy he really liked and was sounding more excited than I'd heard him sound in weeks.

"Tell me about him," I said.

"Well, first of all, he's deaf and mute."

"What?" I said, unable to stop myself from laughing. "How do you guys communicate?"

"I bring a pad and a pen when we go out, and I write everything down. And you should see how he calls me...he's got this funny little phone with a keypad that connects to an operator. He types what he wants to say, and the operator reads it to me. Then I tell the operator my response, and she types it up for him. Sometimes we talk dirty just to freak her out."

Matt asked if Roni and I would have dinner with them the following night. "Of course," I said.

Matt chose a restaurant in a section of town called Cherry Creek, one of the most expensive neighborhoods in Denver. As soon as we got there I knew we couldn't afford it. It was the kind of place that has a leather-bound wine list and unlisted menu prices. When Matt and his date finally showed up, I recognized the guy immediately from the coffee shop. He was tall and blond with a medium build and icy-blue eyes. He had a reputation for having a lot of money and being a sort of wild child who did a lot of drugs and slept around. He was nice enough when we met him—despite his being obviously drunk already—but I hardly thought he'd be a good match for my friend. There was something about him I just didn't trust.

We were invited to sit at the owner's table. (Matt's date was a regular and well-known by the staff.) He, Matt, and Roni ordered a round of cocktails and a gigantic appetizer platter, while I limited myself to a Coke. All communication went through Matt and his pad and pencil. If the guy read lips, he didn't let on, and as everyone continued to drink, he and Matt seemed less and less interested in continuing the effort it took to ask and answer questions round the table. The bill came while Matt's date was in the bathroom, and after a full minute of incessant "Don't you love him? Isn't he great?" Matt told us not to worry about money. His date would pay for everything.

Of course, when the guy made it back to the table, he didn't have enough money to cover the check. The owner told us not to worry about it, that so-and-so was a regular and it was fine if he came back to take care of things the next day. That was my cue to get the hell out of there, and I was up and out the door before anyone else had even put on a coat.

Matt and his date were too drunk to drive, so I piled them into the back of the convertible and dropped them off at Matt's apartment. Despite my annoyance, it was nice to see Matt giggling.

A few days later he called to talk. He did that sometimes when he had something on his mind. He'd talk around whatever it was for a few minutes like he was testing the waters, then he'd jump in. Finally, he brought up the deaf-mute guy. "He stayed over last night and we had sex before we went to sleep. Then I woke up in the middle of the night because he was attacking me. He was on top of me then he was inside me and I didn't really want to but..." His voice trailed off.

"Was it protected?" I asked.

"No," he said. "I don't think so."

I had two reactions to that story. First, of course, was my concern for Matt—especially in light of what happened in Morocco. *Could this destroy him?* I thought. *Should I call his mother?* But he never used the word "rape" and he didn't want to press charges; rather, he seemed as though he just wanted to talk it out.

My second reaction was harder for me to own. I was angry with him. He couldn't have known that guy for more than a week or two. They couldn't have gone out more than a couple of times, and already he was spending the night. I remember wanting to scream into the phone, *"Why are you so trusting of people?"*

But I couldn't because that would be blaming the victim.

Matt's blind trust of strangers went hand in hand with his carelessness with money—he just didn't use common sense. More than once I struggled with whether I should point out that, given his size, he should be more discriminating about whom he trusted. In the end, I never had that talk with him.

To this day, I wish I had.

A few days after I got back from Wyoming, where I had been for Christmas, Matt called and said he was dating a new guy that he wanted Roni and me to meet. We met up at a bar in our neighborhood, and I was wary of this one from the first second I laid eyes on him. He wore a black T-shirt with cutoff sleeves, black vinyl pants, and black steel-toed boots laced to the top of his calf. His spiked dog collar with matching bracelet was so overkill, especially with the massive, poorly healed piercings in his nose, chin, eyebrow, and tongue. His hair was long, dark, and greasy.

The guy was a crystal meth dealer, and he talked about it openly. This worried me for a number of reasons. Aside from the obvious fact that what this man did for a living was dangerous and illegal, Matt told me he'd once had a problem with crystal at boarding school in Switzerland. I assumed he'd met this guy by way of a transaction and was starting up with the drug again. Roni and I hated him, and we told Matt as much. Thankfully, the relationship didn't last more than a couple of weeks.

20 | Something Way Too Familiar

By February, Matt was headed into another severe depression—then for two weeks we didn't hear from him at all. We called and left a couple of messages but were too busy dealing with our own problems to track him down. One afternoon we got a frantic call from his uncle, who said he hadn't heard from him in a couple of weeks either. Not a good sign. We assured him we'd go over to Matt's place to check up on him immediately.

We got to Matt's apartment and opened the door without knocking. The entire apartment stank of mildew. The first thing we saw when we walked in was a trail of Matt's damp and molding clothes that had been thrown down, God only knew how long ago, to sop up puddles of water. We followed this trail into the kitchen, where we discovered the radiator had burst.

Covering our noses and coughing, we staggered down the hallway and into the living room, where we found Matt sitting on the floor with his back against the couch and his knees pulled into his chest. The floor around him was cluttered with ashtrays full of old cigarettes, an empty carton of orange juice, and a couple of plates of half-eaten macaroni and cheese. The only sound in the place came from the closet, where he kept his TV, which was blaring CNN. He looked up at us as we walked into the room. His hair was ratty, and patches of scruff had grown in on his cheeks. He seemed a little confused.

Not wanting (or knowing, for that matter) how to deal, I looked at Roni as if to imply that it was she who would be doing the talking. Her eyes were wide with bewilderment, but that was all she was giving away as she stared down at our friend. She cleared her throat. "Hey, you. You know, nobody's heard from you in a while. We've all been pretty worried."

"Yeah?" Matt said, sounding surprised.

"Yeah," Roni said.

"I'm the worst." Matt flashed us a little smile, looking to Roni for a return smile that would let him know we weren't mad at him.

She let his words hang there for a second before rolling her eyes dramatically. "No you're not, you little queen," she said and went over to him. She sat on the floor, put her arm around his shoulder, and gave him a playful noogie.

I cased the rest of the apartment while they talked. His bedroom was as dark and dirty as the living room, and in the bathroom the toilet was full of piss and cigarette butts. His place was a disaster, and as I walked around it wondering how Matt the neat freak had let his apartment deteriorate to such an extent, I was really sad for him. I could hear him and Roni giggling in the living room, and I knew that he'd be OK. But still, there was something unsettling about how his low points, it seemed, were getting lower. Though I guessed he'd be up for a while after this incident, I was worried about how dramatic his next low point would be.

I walked back into the living room, where Roni and Matt were sitting. They both looked at me expectantly. "All right," I said, "let's clean it up."

In March, Matt disappeared again. It was only for a few days, but we couldn't find him anywhere. He resurfaced at the end of a weekend, walking into the coffee shop in the middle of my shift looking like a little hottie in his blue polo shirt. I stood—steaming espresso pump in hand—behind the coffee bar, where my little smile said *I'm willing to listen*, but my exaggerated eyebrow raise warned, *but it better be good*.

Plopping himself onto one of the empty stools, he said, "I checked myself into a hospital."

I was genuinely surprised. "Really?"

"Yeah, the depression was starting to get out of control."

"Wow, I'm really proud of you, Matt." I began making his medium skim latte, knowing he'd soon be so lost in conversation with another one of the regulars that I'd have to reheat it for him. "Did you tell your parents?" I asked him, as I pulled out one of his favorite cream cheese brownies and put it on a plate for him.

"Yeah," he said unconvincingly. "I called them. They said they're looking into making a trip."

A few weeks later Matt checked himself into another hospital, an overnight facility that encouraged its patients to take advantage of "open hours" during the day. Matt spent a lot of his open hours at the coffee shop, reading the paper or just hanging out with some of the other regulars. I knew he was getting better when he started caring about his appearance again. He was back to obsessing over his hair—spending hundreds of dollars every other week to get the perfect number of blond streaks and twisting, mussing, parting, and reparting it for at least an hour each day to get his bangs to fall right.

It seemed strange to me that through all of this the Shepards never showed up. Since then I've spent a lot of time thinking about it. It's possible, likely even, that Matt lied to me when he said he told them about his hospital stays. There was a lot at stake both for Matt and for his parents with his moving-out on his own in Denver. I think it was a test given to him by both parties, a sink-or-swim kind of thing that would be representative of how the rest of his life was going to go—he was either going to make it or he wasn't. It's also possible that Matt downplayed the kind of trouble he was in. Maybe, afraid to disappoint them, he even asked them *not* to come.

But still, after hearing their son had checked himself into a mental hospital, I wondered how they hadn't gotten on the next flight to Denver. It reminded me of my own family's denial when I was starving myself and had stomach ulcers in high school. I remember feeling so resentful of the Shepards back then because of the way Matt's care—constantly checking up on him, making sure he was eating, keeping an eye on the guys he was dating—had unfairly fallen upon my shoulders. Matt was a young man who needed some serious attention—and I was so angry it was me, and not them, who carried the majority of that burden.

About a month after Matt left the second hospital, he was feeling good about himself and was looking for new ways to improve his quality of life. He'd made attempts to embrace religion at various times in his life and wanted to give it another go in Denver. (Years later his mom would tell me about his misadventures in Casper, where he tried out various churches during their year there. In fact, the family chose the church where his memorial service was held because it had been the one he'd liked best, the one he'd tried to convince his entire family to attend.)

One day, knowing very little about the faith, he went into the Presbyterian Church across the street from his apartment and asked one of the rectory secretaries if there was someone he could speak to about how the church viewed homosexuality. "Why?" the woman asked him. "Are you gay?"

"Yes," he said. "I am."

The woman flew into a biblical tirade, ending with, "You're all a bunch of sinners! I hope you know you'll wind up in hell!"

He left the church, broke into a run, and headed straight for the coffee shop. When he came in I could see that he was terrified; he was shaking and had obviously been crying. "You should talk to my brother John," I suggested after listening to his story. "John spent a couple of years studying for the priesthood—before he came out, that is."

Matt looked at me and smiled. "John, the guy who passed out under a tree when he was supposed to be watching you at the pride festival?"

"Yeah," I said, "he's also the one who hung my other brother's toy duck with a coat hanger. Go figure."

Matt laughed. "Interesting guy, huh?"

"Call him up," I told him. "I'm serious."

After Matt was murdered, John and I talked about the conversation they had that afternoon. According to John, he'd had so many questions about who he could turn to for guidance and support. It struck me, as John and I talked about it, that this was a time when Matt was feeling healthy and strong. Even with his depression at bay, he was very emotionally fragile.

By the beginning of June, Matt was back to his old ways—spending money like crazy, still not working, and calling Roni every day to invite her over to smoke weed. I knew by then that I couldn't stop them, but as far as my friendship with Matt was concerned, I was throwing my hands up in the air. He and I didn't talk much during that time, and every time I saw him he looked less and less healthy. He had lost a good amount of weight—down to around 100 pounds—he was pale, and he never had any of that crazy Matt energy anymore. I was very concerned about his health, but I was tired of holding his hand. I decided to stop acting as his safety net. If he was going to crash and burn, so be it.

Matt called me at home one afternoon and said that he had checked himself into Rose Hospital—a medical facility where he'd gone because of severe stomach pain and vomiting. He sounded scared, and in a meek tone that implied *I know I have no right to ask this of you, but...* he asked if Roni and I would come visit him. I told him we'd come that day.

When we got to his room, he was sitting with his back to us on his bed. He turned when he heard us come in, and his face lit up when he saw us. Roni rushed over like a mother to a sick baby and took his hand as he lay back down. The two of them did most of the talking. I gazed down at him while he told us about how he'd been throwing up, that his stomach hurt all the time, how he couldn't eat, and that he didn't have any energy. There was a spot of dried blood on one of the gray plastic bed rails. I doubted it was Matt's—it doesn't matter whose it was, I guess—it just made me feel disgusting, and I couldn't wait to get out of there. I looked away from it and took in the rest of the scene: Matt looking terrible in the hospital bed, Roni stroking his hair, playing with his fingers as she held his hand. There was something way too familiar about it, and I finally realized what it was.

"Matt, have you had an HIV test?" I asked flatly. Matt didn't flinch, but Roni stopped petting him and looked over at me like I had just belched in the middle of a formal dinner party.

"Yeah," Matt said. "I had one done a few months ago. I'm fine."

"Really?" I said. "Because you should probably get tested if you haven't been."

"I said I'm fine, Romaine." But there was an edge to his voice.

After a few minutes Roni and I left together to use the restroom. Matt said he was waiting for his doctors to come in with some test results. "If they're in the room when you get back," he told us, "you might have to wait outside till they're done."

When we got outside the door, two doctors stood about five feet away. Chart in hand, one doctor said to the other in a hushed tone, "OK, we need to discuss with Mr. Shepard what kind of drug regimen we want to get him started on for the HIV." They continued to talk for a few more seconds while Roni and I exchanged a look. Did we really just hear that? I hung my head. I hadn't wanted to be right, but something had just told me.

The doctors went into the room, Roni went to find the bathroom and I, feeling absolutely devastated, stayed where I was. When she came back, she put an arm around my shoulder, and we waited for the doctors to finish. We went back into the room as the doctors were leaving and asked Matt if there was anything we could get him. "No, just take me out to dinner when I get out of here." We promised that we would.

In the days following the discovery of Matt's unconscious body tied to a prairie fence in Laramie, the hospital where he was taken would discover he was HIV-positive. When the media got hold of the story, they reported that because it was a relatively new infection, Matt was unaware of having HIV. Whether he ever told anybody, I have no idea, but for what it's worth, I know that he knew.

Less than 48 hours before he met his fate, I received a call from him in the middle of the night—when, I believe now, he tried to tell me. I waited for it as we talked. I felt him testing the waters, but he didn't jump in—I guess because he hadn't been ready.

21 | *Leaving Denver*

Our real problems began just a little before Christmas: greeting cards, tens of them, arriving every day. "Who's sending all these?" I asked Roni.

"Oh, just some old friends."

I thought it was great that she knew people who kept in touch so well, since I hardly kept in touch with anyone outside of family. I soon noticed, however, that she never wanted me to read these cards and that she never left them out. Instead, she'd scan their messages quickly, then run off and stash them somewhere. After Christmas came and went but the cards continued to arrive, she gave in and told me her mother had given our address to their entire congregation. They immediately began sending cards in a concerted effort to make Roni repent.

In addition, various family members of hers had made day-trip "missions" to Denver, where they begged her to forsake her "sinful lifestyle" and come home. Once her mother came down for the night to, ostensibly, begin rebuilding a relationship with Roni after months of refusing to speak to her. She was cold to me but, knowing she'd be spending the night at our house, was at least respectful. I went to bed early so mother and daughter could spend some time alone. I got up at one point to get some water and, as I passed the living room, heard her mother say, "I know you think you love her, but you have to leave her. This lifestyle is wrong. It's against God, and you have to save yourself."

Of course, I knew—because Roni had told me—that her mother had once been in a lesbian relationship for four years before she was "saved." Hearing her propagate that sort of fear and intolerance to her daughter, especially when she'd had her own lesbian experiences—and what's more, while she was staying under our roof—turned me ballistic. I stormed into the living room. "I just want you two to know that I just heard what you were talking about and I am really fucking furious!"

Roni jumped at the sound of my voice, but her mother was stoic. "Romaine," she said, her tone like that of a spell-conjuring witch. "I was just explaining to my daughter—"

"I heard what you were *just explaining to your daughter,* and it's bullshit! I'm sick of crazy mothers trying to brainwash my girlfriends into believing their love isn't real. Now, I'm going for a walk. I'll be gone for an hour. And when I get back, *you,* Crazy Woman," I said, pointing at Roni's mom, "better be gone."

Roni's mom looked to her, got nothing, and looked back at me. "Well," she started to say, but I didn't wait around for the rest of it. I grabbed my coat and was out the door.

After that Roni and I went through some severe ups and downs. The end came when her mother called with an ultimatum, me or her family; she had to choose immediately, and once she did, her mother said, there would be no taking it back. Roni chose her family. By the second week in July she had packed all her things, said goodbye to Matt, and was gone.

A week or so later I called Matt to check in. He sounded out of breath when he answered the phone.

I hold Sela, my new Dalmatian, with
Suzanne during junior year in high school

Top: Mom and Dad (Betty and Carl) visit Denver for a family holiday

Above: My father, Carl, and me; he called me his little frog lady

Above: My brother Michael
and me during our first
summer together in Denver

Above Right: Me at Tongue
River High School in my
junior year

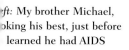

Left: My brother Michael,
looking his best, just before
I learned he had AIDS

Right: Matthew Shepard
snuggles with Eeyore; Matt
was a frequent and enthusi-
astic dog-sitter for me

Above: I help Ronnie Gustafson with his wings and halo in preparation for the Angel Action protest in Laramie.

Below: Angels wait outside my sister's store, preparing to head to the courthouse for the Angel Action protest against Fred Phelps

Right: A.J. Johnson of the university police department looks on as Fred Phelps, pastor of the Westboro Baptist Church in Topeka, Kan., protests during the trial of Russell Henderson.

Below: I read a statement I prepared on behalf of the Angels to members of the media outside the courthouse

From left: Nancy Sindelar, Kathie Beasley, and Jim Osborn walk to the University of Wyoming for the second half of the Angel Action protest against Fred Phelps.

At right: Ronnie Gustafson stands silently at the University of Wyoming during the protest

Angels head to the Laramie courthouse, where Aaron McKinney's trial is set to begin

Fred Phelps stands in protest outside the courthouse where the trial of Aaron McKinney is taking place in Laramie. *Next page:* A few of the Angels, *clockwise from top left:* Ladd Bosworth, Shannon Dalton (my girlfriend at the time of Aaron McKinney's trial), Dale Hottle, Kathie Beasley, Jim Osborn, and Nancy Sindelar

"What are you doing?" I asked.

"Packing," he said. "I'm leaving Denver too." He'd given it some serious thought and realized his life in Denver had contributed to his depression. He had finally had enough.

"I talked about it with my parents," he said, "and we all agree that the best thing would be to move to Laramie and start school again at my father's alma mater, the University of Wyoming. I'm going to study political science."

I asked him if we could meet for lunch that afternoon, and he agreed. I got to the restaurant a little before he did—it was one of our regular haunts, a place whose name I no longer remember but one that we loved for the milkshakes—and when he showed up it was in a U-Haul. Matt had packed up all his stuff that morning before I called and was planning to be on his way as soon as we were done. At first I was hurt because...well, what if I hadn't called him that morning? Would he have left without saying good-bye? It seemed so insensitive, especially after all the time I'd spent worrying about him and his disappearing acts. But then I relaxed and chuckled a little, because after all we'd been through, it seemed he still didn't realize how much I cared. And because his leaving, like just about everything he did, seemed so impulsive, so Matt.

We had a nice time as we ate, reliving some of the high points of the year. "Your poor Aunt Roxy," I teased, "spent like three weeks wandering around the ladies shoe department trying to find you."

Matt almost spit out his milkshake. "We must just keep missing each other," he laughed. "Oh, God, I don't know how I got away with it."

"Oh, honey," I told him, "I doubt you did."

And we talked about our futures. He was almost giddy when he talked about what he thought school was going to be like. He was so happy to be leaving, to be starting a new life somewhere else, that he kept shifting in his seat and smiling big. I'd almost forgotten he could get that way.

When we were finished, I walked him outside. It was warm in the parking lot—the heat rising from the pavement. And there was a freshness in the air, like a warm and cleansing summer rain had just ended. I gave him a hug.

"I love you," I said.

He blushed and laughed. "I love you too, Romaine."

Once Matt climbed into his truck and drove off, I thought about the high hopes I'd had for our friendship. What would become of us? Would we stay in touch as promised, or simply drift out of each other's lives?

22 | *Breaking News*

The phone sounded off around 2 A.M. Everyone who knew me knew I worked opening shifts at Diedrich's and had an unspoken don't-you-dare-call-me-after-midnight rule, so I answered the phone assuming it was someone with an emergency.

"Hello?"

"Hey, Romaine, it's Matt."

"Matt?" I said. "What's going on?" We hadn't spoken since he'd left in July. It was now October, and though it was good to hear from him, I felt cranky and annoyed. Didn't he care that I had to be up in less than three hours?

Matt cleared his throat. "I just wanted to call and see how things were going."

I was about to ask if I could call him back another time when it occurred to me how different he sounded—less mousy, more self-confident and happy than in quite a long time. "I'm fine, Matt. How are things in Laramie?"

He was thrilled to have been asked.

First, he told me about school and how excited he was about his decision to study political science. He said that he had gotten hooked up with a fantastic adviser who'd helped him pick out the perfect class schedule, then he told me details about all the classes he was taking. His only frustration was that some of his classes weren't moving quickly enough for him. He wanted to be learning more and he wanted to be learning faster.

Next, he told me about how he was turning around his lifestyle, cutting back on his meds, not going out as much. He'd joined the gay and lesbian group on campus and helped with the planning of both Gay Pride Week *and* National Coming Out Day. "It feels good to be a part of something positive," he said. "Part of a positive group like that—I don't know, I guess it makes me feel less lonely."

"You know," I said, "Halloween is coming up in a couple of weeks."

"Yeah, and?"

"Well, I've got this Xena costume that I'm gonna look so damn hot in that I'll probably need a bodyguard...interested in the job?"

"That would be fabulous," Matt said. "I'd love to."

"I'll find you the perfect costume," I said. "I'm thinking leather."

"And rhinestones," he added excitedly. "And I'll need a whip."

We laughed and talked about how fun it would be for the two of us to party together again.

"I'll definitely be there," he said. "I can't wait."

We also discussed his parents. They'd just returned to Saudi Arabia but had spent a great deal of time discussing Matt's plans for the future while they were helping him with his move. They wanted him to become a diplomat, which he thought was a good idea but perhaps a bit ambitious. Matt was sure he wanted to get into public service but that he might like to have a smaller focus—city-based politics, for example. "I just want to help people," he said. "I want to make the world a better place. And I know that I could have a big role or a small role in that. It doesn't really matter, just as long as I'm helping people."

I got off the phone with him that morning feeling good about our conversation and thinking how strange and wonderful it was to hear Matt, a guy whose aspirations were so often halted by his complacency and depression, say that he wanted to make the world a better place.

It was four days later, on the evening of Thursday, October 8, 1998, that Mike Sweeney, a Diedrich's regular, called there looking for me. Mike was an older gentleman, probably in his mid 50s, who spent a lot of time at the café and enjoyed Matt's company. Steve, one of the guys working that night, gave me the message when I stopped by for a cup of mint tea on my way home from dinner.

"Evidently," Steve said, "Mike saw something on the news tonight about a guy who'd been tied to fence and beat up. He said the guy's name was Matthew Shepard and that he lived in Laramie, Wyo. He wanted to know if you thought it was the same Matt who used to come in and visit you all the time."

It took me a few seconds to answer, probably because I was waiting for Steve to say he was only kidding. "I guess it would have to be," I said. "How many Matthew Shepards can there possibly be in Laramie?" There was a crescendo to my voice. "Did he say how bad he was beaten up?"

"No," Steve said slowly. "But he is in the hospital."

"OK…" There was an edge to my voice that I could see made Steve uncomfortable. He was just the messenger, but what a message! I wanted to throw my tea at him for not having more information.

I ran out of the coffee shop without saying another word. My heart pounded as I ran up Downing Street to my apartment. I began to rationalize the story. It had to have been just some sort of minor scuffle. But I couldn't imagine the circumstances under which Matt would engage in a fight. He was self-confident in some ways, but he hardly weighed 100 pounds and certainly knew his limitations.

Then I envisioned the scene almost comically: a bully holding his palm to Matt's forehead, antagonizing him, while Matt, his face scrunched up in frustration, swung his fists wildly. But *tied to a fence*? Clearly Steve had gotten that wrong. Or maybe the bully tied Matt to the fence just to smack him around a little bit—more to humiliate than to actually hurt him. *It has to be*, I thought as I picked up the phone to call Mike Sweeney. *Matt's in a hospital somewhere with a broken arm. It has to be that.*

As soon as Mike answered the phone, I knew something was very wrong. "I saw a story on the 6 o'clock news," he said, "about a boy in Laramie, Wyo., named Matthew Shepard who had been attacked and beaten pretty badly. They found him tied to a fence out in the plains and now he's in the hospital." It was the same story Steve told me at the coffee shop, but it was Mike's words— "attacked," "found," "badly," "the plains"—and the uncharacteristically soft way he spoke them, as if trying to explain a concept he knew I wouldn't understand. I was terrified.

My hand was over my mouth. *Oh my God, oh my God, oh my God.* I almost couldn't speak, but I knew I had to try, to start getting a grip on the whole picture. "OK," I said. "Well, how serious is it, because I can't even—"

Steve cut me off. "It didn't really say in the news report, but I'm sure it'll be on the 10 o'clock news, so make sure you watch it." He got off the phone before I was able to ask another question, though I felt there was so much more he could have said.

The 10 o'clock news wasn't going to start for another 20 minutes or so, and already my thoughts were beginning to churn. I felt dizzy and nauseous. My comprehension of what happened came and went in waves. What should I do now?

I grabbed the phone and dialed up my sister Trish. She lived in Laramie and owned a store there. If something had happened there, she'd have heard about it. When I got her on the phone I tried to not sound as desperate as I felt. I didn't tell her Matt was my friend for fear that she'd edit parts of the story—like Steve had. I said, "Tell me what you know about this kid who got beat up in Laramie."

"Well," she said, "it looks like two kids took him out, beat his brains in, essentially, and left him tied to a fence on the prairie out past Wal-Mart."

I concentrated on breathing to keep from breaking down. In through my nose, out through my mouth. "How bad is it?" I was near hysteria. "Is it a broken arm, a broken leg, is he going to be in the hospital for a while?"

"Oh, no, they went to town on this kid—with baseball bats. He's probably gonna die."

Time stopped. I noticed suddenly that my apartment smelled like pizza and that the white walls in the living room were dirty in spots and needed to be painted.

I'd been prepared to hear Trish confirm that Matt was injured, even badly injured, but the possibility of death, that *he was probably going to die,* hadn't even crossed my mind. I sat dumbstruck on the couch, the phone pressed against my ear.

"Why do you want to know all this anyway?"

"Because," I said, "Matt's a good friend of mine."

"Oh," she said, and I could almost hear the click of her edit function. "Well, he's in the hospital in Fort Collins now," which is in Colorado.

Strangely enough, I found out later that Matt and Trish actually knew each other. He'd come into her store and chatted with her a few times during his three months in Laramie, though neither one had ever connected the other back to me.

I got off the phone with Trish a few minutes before the news began. I remember thinking that I had to go be with Matt right then—I had to forget about everything else, get in my car, and find him. But my irrational need for it all not to be true stopped me. I wanted to watch the news and find out Mike and Trish had gotten some part of it wrong. I paced the living room full of nervous energy and felt, for the first time since Roni left, completely alone. *This cannot be real. They can't be talking about my Matt.* Then, as the theme to the 10 o'clock news played along, Matt's face appeared on my TV screen. It was the now famous picture of him, in profile, wearing a blue button-down shirt. I still don't know who took it, when it was taken, or where, but I'll never forget my first reaction to seeing it: pure horror. This *was* in fact *my* Matt. All hope that it had been somebody else, somebody I didn't know or love, was instantaneously wiped away. I couldn't sit, so I made myself stand in front of the TV. I don't think I blinked. I don't think I moved.

I draw a blank on certain details of those first newscasts. Who was reporting? I don't know. Where were they reporting from? No idea. But I do remember that they weren't in Laramie yet and that, though all the local Denver news programs were reporting on the attack, it hadn't yet become a national news story.

Right from the beginning it was reported that Matt was gay. He was referred to as "the gay student from the University of Wyoming" and the attack was called "a possible hate crime." Beyond that, so much of the reporting was speculative. He sustained a blow behind his right ear that "appeared" to have crushed his brain stem. He was beaten with a blunt object that was "assumed" to have been a baseball bat. They also talked about the welts, "possible burns" covering his body and his 18 hours spent alone in the cold, tied to the fence. Though different news reports that first night varied on certain details, they all agreed on two facts:

Matt had been tortured.

Matt was not expected to live.

I don't know exactly how I did it, but I must have somehow numbed myself. How else could I have watched the news? I had to find out all the facts that were available, even as a part of me struggled not to believe a single one. In the days that followed, the details of what transpired became more concrete: The blunt object Matt had been beaten with was actually the butt of a handgun, not a baseball bat. His welts had not been burns but the marks of a man who'd been pistol-whipped. But on that night I accepted the misinformation as fact, concocting the image that would haunt me through the morning.

I turned off the TV when I couldn't take it anymore. Again I thought about going to be with him. At that time I told myself that there were a hundred reasons why I shouldn't—I didn't know exactly where he was; I wouldn't be able to see him; I had to open the coffee shop first thing in the morning and wouldn't be able to reach any of my coworkers at that hour. Only now am I able to admit it, but the truth is, I just couldn't bear it. The idea of sitting in a waiting room, alone in the middle of the night, anticipating the news of my friend's imminent death, was too awful. Worse was the thought of being let in to confront the sight of his broken and tortured body, his obvious pain and suffering. Listening to the details on the news was bad enough, but having to be in the presence of it and being able to do nothing for him would have been impossible for me—just as it was when Michael was dying.

Staying in control was how I always got through things. Staying in control was how I was going to do it now. I needed to take an action—but what? The only thing I could think of was to call everybody I knew who cared about him. Why? Because I couldn't take the thought of anyone else finding out the way I had. Needing to be in motion, I paced as I dialed.

I got in touch with Matt's friends in Denver, then some of the members of The Fabulous Eight in Casper. Some had seen the story on the news, but most hadn't. As much as I could without breaking down, I told those who hadn't heard. And, of course, they had so many questions. I found myself stealing a line from Steve: "Watch the news, you'll get more information." Calling those people was one of the hardest things I've ever done in my life. How do you tell someone "Our friend is lying in a coma and is probably going to die—and if he doesn't die, he's going to live the rest of his life in a vegetative state"? How do you tell someone "Our friend, as we knew him, is gone forever"?

The hardest person to call was Roni. She and Matt had been so close when we all lived in Denver, and I knew that this would devastate her. We hadn't spoken since our breakup. Last I knew, she'd gone back to Casper and moved in with her mother. It was her mother who answered the phone when I called there a little after 11 P.M. "Roni's out," she told me. "Can I give her a message?"

"I have very important information I need to relay to her," I said. "I cannot stress enough how important it is that she call me back."

"If I see her, I'll let her know," she said before hanging up.

Then there was nothing left for me to do. I climbed into bed in a daze, hoping Roni would call back soon. I even brought the phone under the covers with me.

When I closed my eyes and tried to sleep I saw the disgusting scene played out in dark colors—dark reds, dark blues, dark blacks. My mind had glommed on to the most gruesome details from the news and created a picture that ran on a loop:

I'm an invisible presence on the prairie, set back from a scene shrouded in darkness. Matt's strung up on the fence, the truck's headlights on him like spotlights. He's tied crucifixion-style. There's blood everywhere—caked into his eyes and dried into his hair on the side of his caved-in head. Fresh wet blood rolls down his body over purple bruises and exposed bone. Just outside the light on either side of Matt I see the black outlines of two men, crouching beside him, each holding a lighter. Simultaneously they click their flames to life, press them to his flesh, and watch the skin curl.

My brain flashed, and I saw it from Matt's perspective: *The chafe against my wrists as I try to free myself, the crack of my bones with each blow of the bat.*

Then my brain flashed again, and I saw it from an attacker's perspective. I felt his rage and his sense of power as he looked on the body of that tiny little man: *I swing back my foot and kick him again and again, making him bleed, scream, and beg for his life.*

Suddenly I sat up and turned on the light, terrified of the dark. Then I collapsed and cried into my pillow. It was a violent cry, the kind that makes you feel like you're going to vomit. I prayed out loud, "God, please make it go away—whitewash my mind. Make it so I see nothing."

At least with the lights on, the images were gone. But still, so many worries were swimming around in my head. I worried if his parents knew yet, if someone had called Saudi Arabia. I worried about his younger brother, Logan, who I knew was somewhere in the States at school. What if he'd heard all the horrible details on the news the way I had? And if he hadn't, who was going to tell him? Then I thought about how this was a possible hate crime, that Matt might have been attacked simply because he was gay. Over and over again I asked myself, *Why him? Why not me?* It wasn't like I hadn't been gay in Wyoming—not to mention a zillion times more flamboyant about it. It wasn't like I hadn't made *my* fair share of enemies.

Only when Roni called me back—which was sometime around 1 A.M.—was I able to stop obsessing.

"My mom told me to call you," she said. "She said it was an emergency. What could possibly be so important?"

It was so good to hear her voice again. And even though she was being snippy, I was reminded of how much I missed her and wished she was there with me right then. For the rest of my life I will remember that conversation like it happened yesterday.

"Have you seen the news tonight?" I asked.

"No, I've been out to dinner with Jeremy. Why?"

"Roni, you need to sit down, I have something very important I need to tell you." I sensed her impatience at the other end of the phone, preferring it to what she'd be feeling very soon. "I'm really not sure how to say this, but something's happened to Matt."

"What happened to Matt?" she asked.

"Well," I said, "it appears that a couple of nights ago he was out at a bar in Laramie and a couple of guys kidnapped him, and drove him out to a prairie where they tied him to a fence and tortured and beat him—"

Roni cut me off, just as I had expected her to. "What do you mean? What do you mean!" When I heard her start to cry, I started to cry too.

"Just please let me finish," I said. "He's in a hospital in Fort Collins right now. I'm sorry, baby, but he's going to die."

She sobbed loudly and tried to say something, but I couldn't understand her.

When she'd calmed down a little, I finished: "I don't know how long they've given him to live. I wish I could tell you more, but this is all I know. It's all over the news, so if you can, you should watch it. You can get more information there."

We talked for a few more minutes after that. She told me that she and Matt hadn't seen each other since she left Denver. She'd been in Laramie a few weeks back and had wanted to see him but didn't have time to. I told her about how he and I had talked a few days prior; that we'd patched things up and were planning to spend Halloween together in Denver. She sounded a little jealous.

"You know, it's really nice," I said, "how we've been able to put the bad feelings between us aside and just be here for each other, even if it is only for a few minutes." Then I added, "You're not going to be alone tonight, are you?"

"Oh, no," she said. "I'm spending the night here at Jeremy's."

I assumed Jeremy was her new boyfriend—and that stung a bit.

"That's good," I told her. "I'm glad you're with someone—this might sound stupid, but I'm glad you're safe."

I got out of bed a few hours later after having dozed for no longer than 20 minutes. When I got to the coffee shop around 5:15 I tried to put myself on autopilot, thinking it was the only way to get through the day. I picked up *The Denver Post* bundle from the stoop outside before going in to set up for the morning rush. When I got inside I cut the papers open and flipped them over. There, on the front page, was Matt's name and a picture of *the fence*. This was where he'd been tied, beaten into a coma, and left to die. I was transfixed by it—it shocked me because it didn't look like a fence at all. And it wasn't chain-link like I'd imagined, but a bunch of wooden poles somehow fastened together, and because it was just one section and clearly hadn't been built to keep anything in or out, it seemed to serve no purpose. *What the hell was it there for?* I wondered. I was also transfixed by Matt's name. My eyes kept cutting back and forth across the page, trying to take in both the picture and the name. I couldn't believe how real it was.

Just then I heard a tapping on the window. Crazy-man Elias, one of the stranger regulars Matt loved to chat with, was (as usual) out front waiting for us to open. His soft gray hair was tousled by the early-morning breeze as he waved, the way he always did, hoping I'd let him come inside and read the paper while the first pot of coffee brewed.

I walked over to the door, opened it, and let him come in. Then I did, perhaps, the most evil thing I've ever done. "I'm going to give you the paper, Elias," I said, "but I'm going to need you to read it outside. There's an important story about Matt on the front page."

"Our Matt?" he said with such excitement that I immediately hated myself. But I knew I had to do it, that I needed more than anything to hear somebody else react violently to the news. Because *I* couldn't—I *had* to keep it together. I knew Elias would just erupt—and that, just for a minute, I could live vicariously through his pain.

"Yes, our Matt," I said, then I handed him the paper, pushed him back out the door, and locked it behind him.

I turned my back and waited. It took him a minute, but he found it. First, he screamed, then he was bawling and banging on the glass door.

I hoped it would break.

Most mornings I opened with a guy named Ted, a tall thin man whose trademark was his shaved head. When he got there I took him in the back and explained what had happened. Like everyone I worked with, Ted had gotten to know Matt well, and he was shaken by the story but more concerned with how I was doing. "Shouldn't you go home, Romaine?"

"Nah," I told him, dreading the idea of being alone. "There wouldn't really be much for me to do once I got there."

By 8 o'clock the café was full. The usual crowd of businessmen on their way to work and gay Denver bohemians who would linger over a small cup of coffee for most of the morning had packed the place. Almost all were clutching their copy of *The Denver Post*. The dialogue had begun; I heard it in fits and starts from where I stood making drinks at the espresso bar. People struggled to comprehend how such a thing could happen. They weren't outraged yet—that would come eventually. No, that day was spent in sympathy for the victim. "He had such a beautiful face," someone said. "Why would anyone do such a thing?" Almost none of them mentioned—or realized—that just a few months before, that same beautiful face had been among them, sharing their tables and swapping sections of the paper.

Every now and then someone would catch me when nobody else was around. They'd take my hand and murmur, "I just want you to know I'm thinking about you, Romaine. I know Matthew was a friend of yours. If there's anything I can do…" The sympathy was the hardest part. I'd listen politely then have to run to the back, where I'd break down again. It got to the point where I'd do anything to avoid a sympathetic-looking person coming my way. Their sincerity was just too hard to deal with—it underscored my misery too much.

I got off work at 2 and went home to watch the news. Jon Peacock, the CEO of Poudre Valley Hospital in Fort Collins, Colo., had held a press conference. This was replayed every hour, with no new information available, each time there was another story about the attack: Matt had suffered from hypothermia; he was in a coma from which he was not expected to wake up. Peacock also talked about the baskets of flowers and the cards that were already pouring in from all over the state. It was stated that his mother and father still hadn't arrived but that he did have some family with him. I assumed it was his Aunt Roxy and his uncle from Denver.

Everything felt so crazy. The brutality of this attack was still beyond my comprehension, but because I was learning details about it on TV ...*press conferences are being held... flowers are being sent to him from strangers...* the contradiction between what I knew to be true and what I needed to be true was dizzying.

I called my mother. She'd met Matt a few times during her weekend trips to Denver. She hadn't heard the story yet, so I told it to her and was expecting an "Oh, honey" sort of response, but what I got instead was: "You know, I always thought this sort of thing would happen to Matt." She didn't mean to be insensitive, and she got to the "Oh, honey" as soon as she realized how upset I was, but with a shocking sort of frankness, she brought up an idea about Matt that in the days that followed I would hear repeated by other people who had known him—*that he was the embodiment of a victim.*

I hated, and still hate, hearing Matthew described that way. And I still sometimes wonder where that "embodiment of a victim" description came from—if those people who had known him before I did had always seen him like that, or if their impression of him changed after he'd been raped in Morocco. It made me wonder in what ways the rape had changed him. What had he been like before? Had the rape so devastated his self-esteem that he had then become an easy target?

I called my brother John when I was finished talking to my mother. He was very sweet and supportive, but even that wasn't what I needed. More than anything I just wanted someone to give me a hug. Like the time with Suzanne looking down at the quilt, I needed the security of being held until I felt—if not better—at least that I could maybe face things better. I needed to be told "I love you and I've got you." But that option wasn't available just then, and I felt—more than I ever had in my life—so despairingly alone.

23 | The Whole World Was Watching

Over the next few days I continued to go to work. I didn't know what else to do. My coworkers, respectfully, didn't ask much of me and, seeing that I didn't feel like talking, let me do my job in silence. The best thing I did for myself during that time was listen to the way the conversations about Matt's attack began to evolve among the coffee shop regulars. What had begun as "How could this happen? I can't believe this happened!" was turning into "This should never have happened." And what amazed me was that all kinds of people were engaged in that conversation. Straight, gay, old, young, rich, poor: Everyone was talking about it as they stood in line to order or waited by the bar for their drinks. They were strangers, most of them, who saw one another every day but had never conversed until then. As the days passed, "This should never have happened" became "You know, hate crimes are actually quite common," and it seemed like these people were ready to act, like they were a force to be reckoned with now.

I've been asked hundreds of times why I think Matthew Shepard's story captured the world's attention the way it did. I think people's reactions in the coffee shop—a small sample of what the rest of the world was feeling—is part of it. The brutality of his murder brought people together in an unprecedented way, and once they saw that they were united in their shock, they realized it might be possible to do something about it, to stop it from ever happening again.

In addition to the local media blitz, the national media had begun to pick up the story. I saw Matt's picture and watched stories about him on CNN and MSNBC, his two favorite stations. Pieces about Matt ran in newspapers across the country. The hospital set up a hotline because their regular phone lines were so jammed with well-wishers, curious citizens, and international media. The hospital asked via the media that people stop sending flowers and gifts, as there was simply no space left to store them. On the local news I saw footage of truckloads of stuff rerouted to local shelters and charities. It felt so strange that my friend Matt, the shy little guy who was so self-conscious in front of strangers, had suddenly become the focus of so much attention.

It was hard for me to grasp what the story was turning into. I remember sitting on my couch after work those afternoons and knowing that I had my choice of networks for watching coverage of the story—they all were. I heard what his doctors were saying— that even if he didn't die from his injuries, he would probably never regain consciousness—but I was still holding on to the idea that he might pull through. Every free moment I had, I called the hotline. They promised to update it every three hours, but it was more like every five hours. Often the line was busy when I called, but I was persistent; even if I knew the message hadn't changed, I'd call until I got through just to feel connected. I was also waiting to hear whether his parents, Judy and Dennis, had arrived, because then, even though I still didn't want to go see him, I knew I could make plans to.

On Saturday afternoon, four days after Matt had gone into the hospital, Dede de Percin came to see me at the coffee shop: She was a spunky lesbian in her mid 30s with Equality Colorado, a local gay rights group that my brothers John and Michael had been involved with. She took me aside and very quietly said, "I know you were a friend of Matthew's because I used to see him in here with you all the time."

"Yeah," I said, dreading yet another painful bout of sympathy.

"We're putting together a vigil for him on Monday night at the capitol. We have a lot of politicians who've signed on to come and speak, but we don't know anyone who can talk about Matthew as a person. Except you. Would you consider coming to the vigil and speaking about Matthew?"

"I don't know," I said. I'd seen on the news the terrified and exhausted-looking people who had known Matt at school in Laramie—just ordinary people who since his death had become involuntary spokespeople for gay rights. Most of them looked like they hadn't slept in days, and all of them looked like they wished they'd just kept their mouths shut.

"You think about it," Dee Dee said, "and come down to the office and see me tomorrow if you want to."

I grappled with the idea for the rest of the day. On one hand, it seemed like a great opportunity to put a human face on my friend. Everyone I'd seen interviewed on TV had known him for less than four months and didn't really seem to know much about him. And on top of that, they were answering questions thrown by reporters who already knew the story *they* wanted to tell and who weren't afraid to twist words to tell it. Now I'd just been handed the opportunity to give a speech—which I already knew I was good at—and in that speech, uninterrupted, I could tell the world about who Matt was.

Still, I was afraid of how far it would go. To step forward was like opening Pandora's box. What if I became like those other kids I'd seen on TV, a person whose life was about being Matthew Shepard's friend?

Ultimately, I decided to do it. Matt was my friend, after all. He'd trusted me with his stories, and if his life was going to be made public domain, I at least owed it to him to make sure that it was done truthfully and in good taste.

I went home after work that day and watched the news as long as I could stand it. For the first time I saw Matt's attackers, Russell Henderson and Aaron McKinney. I'd been waiting for that moment. It was important to get an idea of what they looked like, and to realize that they didn't scare me. The local police had worked quickly and diligently to get a confession out of both guys, and the footage was of their arraignment. They wore orange prison jumpsuits and were both so small it shocked me. Neither kid could've been more than a few inches taller than Matt, nor could either one have weighed much more than he did. They were grungy and mean-looking, the kind of little guys who liked to pick on guys even littler than themselves.

My first thought was *Matt, why would you ever get into a car with them?* Then I answered my own question: *Because you put your trust in people ahead of your regard for your own safety.*

Watching the two of them, with their smug smiles—smiles that made you think that they were sure they were going to get away with it—made me sick and furious. I turned the TV off when I became overwhelmed with the desire to pound the living shit out of them.

I went out onto my back porch, the place I always went when I had something to discuss with Michael. *This is going to be a tough one*, I thought, as I began to walk in a circle around the deck. Night had fallen. I was still in my work T-shirt, and it was a little chilly out. I didn't mind the cold, though; it snapped me out of my news-watching trance, and it made me feel alert. I stopped walking when I became aware of how strangely still and silent the city was, like it had paused and was waiting for me to begin.

"Michael," I said softly, then took a long sigh. Across the way a neighbor turned off his back-porch light then, as if to give me privacy, closed his door. "In one way or another, I've felt you with me every day since you died. I've needed you and you've been here and I hope you know what that has meant for me. But I'm OK now and I think it might be time for me to let go of you for a little while. My friend Matt needs your spirit more than I do. He's in an unknowable amount of pain. He can't communicate with anybody, but I'm sure he's terrified. Please go and be with him and help him through this time. If it's his time to go, please help make that transition smooth for him. Let him know that he is loved, but that he should stop fighting if he wants to, that he should be at peace."

I stood on the porch for a while longer—and I swear, I felt Michael leave me. I was comforted that he was going to go be with Matt, but the comfort was bittersweet, because it meant I'd accepted that Matt was going to die.

I had a meeting with Equality Colorado's executive director the next day, Sunday, during which I was put at ease: We wanted the same thing. She was concerned that, with November's voting season just around the corner, the politicians who'd signed on to speak had done so mostly just to further their various political agendas. From me she wanted a three-minute speech that would be as personal as I could handle. "Give us the human side of Matthew Shepard."

I had 24 hours.

I went home after my meeting, grabbed a pen and a yellow

legal pad, and headed down to Cheesman Park. I sat under my favorite tree—the grand oak I imagined to be hundreds of years old that I'd hung out under in the afternoons during my summer trips to Denver—and thought about the daunting task of explaining, in three minutes, who Matthew Shepard was. I tapped my pen against the pad, not knowing where to begin.

"How can I describe Matthew and his life in a three-minute speech?" I wrote. "I can't. But I'll try to give you a glimpse into the life of the person I know and love."

After that the rest of it just poured out of me. For the next couple of hours I wrote furiously, scribbling draft after illegible draft. I conjured images of the Matt who loved to watch the news and the Matt who listened to Meredith Brooks's "Bitch" over and over until he knew all the words. I had to remind myself, as images of his unconscious body lying in a hospital bed somewhere tried to infiltrate my work, that this was not the Matt I was writing about. There was also another Matt I couldn't write about—the Matt who would go for days without leaving his apartment when depressed, and the Matt who might self-medicate when all else failed. While there might someday be a time to talk to the world about that Matt, it clearly wasn't right now. No, this speech was about rallying together. This speech was about inspiring hope in Matt's honor.

When I got to work on Monday the next morning, I felt that the speech was in good shape. I remember taking the bundle of newspapers into the coffee shop and, as had become my ritual, glancing through them as I set them out for the customers. If there was any mention of Matt's having passed during the night, I don't remember seeing it.

I don't remember the exact moment I found out. I know that it was from one of the first customers, who, unaware that Matt was a friend of mine, said something in passing while waiting for her drink. I also remember that I didn't believe it right away. I'd had a scare the day before, when a shopkeeper whose store was on the same block as Diedrich's told me as I was taking the trash out that "the parents of that Shepard boy pulled the plug." On the edge of hysteria, I dropped the trash and immediately ran back into the coffee shop, where I called the hospital hotline and found out it wasn't true.

But I didn't call the hotline that morning. I just couldn't bear it. And as the usual customers sauntered in and were all talking about it, I finally accepted Matt's death as fact.

My initial reaction, though in hindsight not surprising, was not at all what I expected it to be. I was tough about it, reasoning, *Yeah, it's sad. But I can't change it.* Of course, my toughness was a defense mechanism, a survival tactic. How could I not have been in a state of complete shock? My brother John and I had planned a trip to Fort Collins the next day to try to get in to see Matt, but I was relieved that now we wouldn't be able to, that the image of Matt covered in tubing and bandages, a machine breathing for him, was not going to be my last memory of him. And I hoped that now the Shepards, who had become the focus of so much media attention, would be able to grieve in peace. And I was glad now that I would not be intruding upon them.

I went home after work to watch the news. All the stations were replaying a press conference that had been held outside the hospital in the middle of the night. The CEO, standing in the pouring rain, told the world that Matt had died of natural causes a little before 1 A.M. on Monday. He had a message from Matt's parents: They wanted to "express their sincerest gratitude to the entire world for their overwhelming response for their son." He continued, "Matthew's mother said, 'Go home, give your kids a hug, and

don't let a day go by without telling them that you love them.' "
Then he broke down in tears.

I felt my real emotions, the sadness and anger, begin to creep
up as I watched that press conference. I wanted to cry and I wanted to scream. My first instinct was to call my mom and tell her that
I love her, because that's what Matt's mom had said. Suddenly I
was at a loss. I wanted someone to blame. I thought of Judy then.
"Where were you?" I shouted at the TV, furious with myself for
even thinking such a horrible thing. *Maybe if you had been there
giving Matt more hugs, this wouldn't have happened to him.*

I turned the TV off, swallowed hard, and tried to push the feelings back down into my stomach. To hell with my stupid ulcers—
I had work to do. I began to move, physically—fixing my hair,
changing my clothes, then going into the kitchen to wash the dirty
coffee mugs in the sink. I didn't let myself stop. As long as I was
in motion, I wouldn't have to feel. Knowing that I had to deliver
my speech in less than two hours, I picked it up and began, pen in
hand as I walked in circles around the couch, to rewrite it, changing everything about Matt's life from present to past tense.

When that was finished, I called around to various friends and
asked each of them to record a different news program that night,
knowing that the local TV stations would be covering the vigil. I
was buzzing with energy as I got myself ready and jumped into the
car. The traffic near the capitol was slow going and I was running
late. My stress level was high and I shook manically, like I'd drunk
too much coffee.

I found a parking space on the side of the capitol then broke
into a run to get to the front of the building on time. As I round-
ed the corner onto the lawn where the crowd gathered, I froze.
There, milling about in front of the stone steps, must have been
2,000 people—all waiting for the speakers to begin.

I had seen news stories about all the vigils for Matt in cities around the country. And though I was moved by the outpouring of emotion from people who had never met him, I felt comfortably distant from it, because the boy the people on TV were memorializing was not my friend Matt but rather a perfect and beautiful victim named Matthew Shepard.

As I stood there on the edge of the lawn, face-to-face with a crowd of people like the ones I'd seen on TV, I realized this moment was my last chance to remain anonymous, to not be a part of it. I could still walk away, get back in my car, and keep Matt for myself—or I could go ahead, speak out, and engage in the national dialogue. Making a mental note to change every "Matt" in my speech to "Matthew," I chose both.

When I started looking for someone who could tell me where to go, I saw the fence, a replica of the one Matt suffered on. It had been constructed on the steps near the speakers' podium and was draped in a rainbow pride flag. All around it were burning candles and piles of flowers. In the center was a picture of Matthew—the same one I'd seen on the news the night I found out about his murder. It had been enlarged to poster size. I focused on his face and again felt the sadness well up in me. Had it not been for the tug on my arm then the motion of being guided to the front of the crowd where the rest of the speakers were standing, I'd have broken down right there.

By the time it was my turn to address the crowd, I had listened to 40 minutes of politicians speaking of Matthew Shepard more as a concept than a person. They talked of agendas and said things like "We must work to ensure that there are no more Matthew Shepards in the world." They spoke of the power Matthew Shepard had to change the world.

I understood the sentiment, and I didn't necessarily think the

politicians were wrong, but I understood even more why human-
izing him was so important. I wanted to remind the crowd that
Matthew Shepard didn't walk on water, that he was a member of
their community, that they could practically see his old apartment
from where they stood, and that it would not do to deify him. He
was human, complete with his inherent flaws—just like everyone
else in that crowd.

I took my place on the steps and was handed a microphone. I
looked out over the sea of people—so many that it was impossible
to make anyone out. I took a deep breath and began my speech:

"Matthew Shepard was someone I was lucky enough to call a
friend. His heart beamed with love as he reached out to help those
who were not as fortunate as himself... Matthew always kept within him a unique and genuine hope for humanity. It was a hope he
brought into the lives of the many people who were fortunate
enough to know him.

"Politically, Matthew was a genius. He always stayed informed
as to what was happening worldwide, because in the long run he
wanted to affect those happenings. Matthew's memory now repre-
sents the job that faces us. That job is to reach out as Matthew
did, to teach those who are ignorant how to love unconditionally.

"Matthew took on the world with love and kindness. That is
why he was capable of showing his love for others in such an
unconditional way...

"I spoke with Matthew just days before his attack, and he told
me how important it was for him to do his part in ending discrimination and bettering the lives he touched. His most important
goal was to better humanity any way he could. I believe that
through this tragedy hope can be fulfilled through us."

"I stopped for a second to think about what I had just said, because as I stood there those words suddenly meant more. Matt's goal had been to help make the world a better place. And as I looked at those thousands of strangers he had brought together, I wished he could have seen through my eyes for just a second the love he had inspired. Almost absentmindedly, I said into the microphone, "If only Matthew could see all of you now."

There was a slight cool breeze that swept across the lawn, then somebody from the back of the crowd yelled, "He *can* see us now!"

I thought about it for a second. I closed my eyes and thought about Matt no longer being in that hospital bed, being free of whatever pain he had suffered. I blushed and said, "You're right, I guess he can see us." Then I finished my speech. "Thank you all for being here tonight to help Matthew take one more step toward his goals and dreams of a better and more caring humanity."

I walked back to the bottom of the steps. The Gay Men's Chorus of Denver went on after me and sang "We Shall Overcome." The crowd joined in, and I tried to sing along too, but by then I knew I didn't have to be strong any longer and I broke down and sobbed. I didn't try to stop. I wanted to cry hard, I wanted to feel it. Someone standing next to me, a stranger, put his arm around me, and I collapsed into his shoulder. Matthew was dead. My friend had been murdered in the most horrible way I could imagine, and I didn't want to be strong about it anymore.

When the vigil was over I went out to dinner with a couple of friends, then went home to watch the 10 o'clock news. By that point Matthew had lost the "gay University of Wyoming student" moniker; newscasters were now referring to him simply by his familiar full name. Since Matthew had died that day, the vigil was the lead story on almost every Denver news station—and many of them focused heavily on my speech.

Then I turned to CNN, which was showing an assemblage of

the vigils that had taken place around the country during the week Matthew was on life support. There had been one in every major city and many in small towns. Some of the clips I recognized, like the now famous one of Ellen DeGeneres in Washington, D.C. "This is what I was trying to stop," she said as the tears streaked her cheeks.

What startled me most was the footage of a demonstration held in New York City. It was dark out, and almost everyone held a candle and was crying. But the tone of the demonstration shifted as the attendees, unable to contain their anger, began to shake their fists and to rock the metal fences that kept them out of the street. As the police made arrests, the group, in unison, began to scream, "The whole world is watching! The whole world is watching! The whole world is watching!"

24 | Matthew's Memorial Service

The service would be held two days later on Wednesday, October 14, 1998, in Casper, the small city he was born in and the place where we had met. My brother John, his friend Frank (a cute, bubbly hairdresser he'd known, it seemed, forever), and I made the trip up together, not knowing if we'd even make it inside the church.

We left before 6 A.M. because the driving conditions were terrible. Growing up in Wyoming, you get used to a good heavy snowstorm by the last couple days of October, but a blizzard this size—still so early in the month—was almost completely unheard-of. As we approached the port of entry through the town of Cheyenne, I looked out the fogged-up window and saw six American flags, all flying at half-mast. I'd heard that the governor of Wyoming planned to do this throughout the state in memory of Matt, but I hadn't actually believed it would happen. It was a surreal moment, looking at those flags as we drove slowly, cautiously, past them. I think that was when I truly believed the world cared, that Matthew mattered to people.

Our plan was to stop by Roni's on the way to the service so she and I could ride together. I wasn't sure her mother would let her attend, but apparently the brutal murder of her good friend convinced her zealot family to stop thumping their Bibles in her ear for a day. When we got to her place around 9:30 in the morning, her mother was nowhere in sight—and that was fine by me, of course. While John and Frank changed into their suits, she and I sat in the kitchen and talked.

"How is it being back in Casper?" she asked, pouring herself what I imagined to be at least her third cup of coffee.

"Awkward," I said. *As awkward as this conversation*, I wanted to say.

She nodded like she'd expected me to say something like that. Her mug was steaming, and she held it with both hands in front of her face as if we were doing a Maxwell House commercial. "It's good to see you, Romaine. You look really good."

"Feels good to be here," I said. And it was true. It felt *so* damn good to be near her again. She was still so beautiful, but the events of the past week had taken their toll. Small purple circles had appeared under her eyes, and her face was puffy. She barely gestured when she spoke. And I hoped—as I sat there in her messy, kitschy kitchen with its multiple crucifixes and tacky religious plaques—that these changes were temporary, that she'd someday rediscover the air of spunkiness I loved so much.

When we got in the car Roni drove with one hand and turned the heat on with the other. I took her free hand in mine and she didn't resist. I wanted to wrap my entire body around hers. As the windows fogged up, I saw above the driver's seat, on the upper left-hand side of the window, initials beginning to form like a tattoo. It said R ❤ J FOREVER. I assumed the J was for Jeremy, her current boyfriend, and that one of them had written it with a finger. That hurt, but I decided not to think about it. She was mine for the day.

We parked in a small lot on the side of the church and pulled out our umbrellas. The snow had lightened up a little to reveal a bleak gray morning. There was no sun. The clouds were indiscernible. The still-leafy oak trees that towered over us as we walked around to the front of the church were inert under the weight of the snow. Here and there the solemn quiet was broken by a loud crack then a thud as a huge branch snapped off and fell to the ground.

The town of Casper had anticipated thousands of mourners. Despite the weather, people from all around the world descended upon that small town to pay their respects to the young man they'd gotten to know over the five days he spent on life support. In an effort to accommodate everyone, town officials set up two churches: one where the actual service would be held (which is where we were) and another where the service could be heard via closed-circuit PA. They also set up an area in the park across the street from the first church, where people who hadn't gotten into either service could gather and listen.

A group of protesters was also expected: Baptists from Kansas who, led by the so-called Reverend Fred Phelps, were coming to Casper to upstage Matt's funeral. It didn't make any sense to me until I did a little bit of research on Phelps, including a visit to his Web site: www.GodHatesFags.com. Phelps and his followers prided themselves on being preachers of God's hate. In the '80s they protested across the country at the funerals of gay men who'd died of AIDS. And because they always held their demonstrations on public property, it seemed there was nothing that could be done to stop them.

Roni, John, Frank, and I stood on the front lawn of the church for a few minutes looking from the media trucks, to the thousands of people lined up outside the church, to the Phelpsian protesters in the park. What caught my eye was their neon signs. On green and hot-pink poster board were pictures of Matt underneath declarations like MATT IN HELL and THE WAGES OF GAY SIN IS DEATH. There weren't a lot of these people—maybe 12, 15 max—and they'd been confined to a small fenced-in area, but they were getting exactly what they came for: Throngs of red-faced spectators stood yelling at them. The crowd got bigger and bigger as the ruckus surrounding the protesters intensified. At one point I worried it would turn into an all-out riot.* (*Footnote: I eventually became familiar with Fred's tactics. You see, violence is what they hope for. They fund their cross-country hate campaigns by filing lawsuits against people who blow a gasket and get physical.)

As the saying goes, the whole place was crawling with reporters that morning, men and women under see-through plastic umbrellas from every local and national news outlet, chatting up anyone willing to stand in front of a microphone or camera. As the call went up, and a herd of cameramen, reporters, and boom operators dashed across the lawn and into the park to get footage of all the shouting matches, I'd pretty much had enough. As if his murder wasn't bad enough, now Matthew's funeral had turned into a circus.

I moved in front of Roni and dropped my umbrella so that it rested it on my shoulder and blocked her view. I didn't want her to see those hateful signs. When she tried to step around me, I turned, put my arm around her shoulder, and led her back around to the other side of the church. John and Frank followed. The four of us stood there for a few minutes, discussing our options for getting into the service, when I felt a tap on my shoulder. "Excuse me, you're Romaine Patterson, correct?"

I turned and saw a tall and kind of skinny guy, probably in his early 50s, peering at me with a smile on his face. He had a Human

Rights Campaign button—a yellow "=" glyph on a blue back-ground—pinned to his suit lapel, so I decided he could be trusted. "Yeah, I'm Romaine," I said, extending my hand. "I'm sorry, do I know you?"

"No," he said. "I'm Dennis Doherty. I saw you on TV at the vigil on Monday. But what are you doing out here? Shouldn't you be inside?"

"We just drove in from Denver," I said. "There was a pretty bad snowstorm so we were running late, and now, with all these peo-ple here, we're not sure how to get in."

Dennis squinted his eyes and looked around as if gauging how softly to tell me a secret. He then cocked a half smile and jerked his thumb over his left shoulder. "Why don't you follow me and I'll handle that."

John and Frank, deciding Roni and I had a better chance of getting in if they didn't come too, said they'd meet us after the service. I took Roni's hand and we followed Dennis around a cor-ner where, between two large bushes, there was a wooden door. In front of the door stood three men in sunglasses and long black coats. They looked like Secret Service agents. Dennis went over and spoke softly to one of them, then, as he opened the door, waved us in.

We followed Dennis down a flight of stairs and into a fairly spa-cious basement. There were probably 15 other people down there, who took no notice of us as they primped their hair and fixed their ties. Four little kids in their Sunday clothes played with Matchbox cars on the floor. An untouched platter of cold cuts had been left out on a table.

"This must be Matt's extended family," Roni whispered, as she took my arm. Dennis led us across the room to another staircase. This one led up to the church banquet room, where there was a commotion taking place near the farthest wall: a group of people huddled around an older gentleman who lay on the floor. The EMTs had just arrived and were preparing to take him out. We'd find out later that this was one of Matt's uncles, who'd just had a heart attack. He died a few days later.

"Would you mind waiting here for just a moment?" asked Dennis. "I think I need to go over and see if there's anything I can do." As we stood there, I noticed that standing alone in a doorway against the back wall, wearing a navy-blue suit and looking nowhere in particular, was Logan, Matt's brother. I'd only met him once before, but I recognized him immediately. He looked exhausted, like he couldn't wait for all this stupid craziness to be over. "Hang tight for a minute," I told Roni. "I'll be right back."

He noticed me as I walked toward him and straightened up a little as if bracing for another "I'm so sorry for your loss."

"Hey, Logan," I said. "You might not remember me—I'm Matt's friend Romaine."

"Hi," he said politely.

"I just wanted you to know that we're all going to miss him. But also, I lost a brother not so long ago too, so I kind of know how it feels. If you ever want to talk about it, please feel free to give me a call, because I really do understand."

He nodded his head for a few seconds then said, "Thank you."

When I got back to Roni, Dennis was waiting. "Follow me," he said, "I'll take you into the church so you two can find seats."

We followed him out of the banquet room, squeezing ourselves into the crowded antechamber of the church. Dennis stopped abruptly and put his hand on a woman's shoulder. "Look who I found," he said softly, indicating Roni and myself. Judy Shepard and I gasped simultaneously.

"Oh, Romaine," she said as she pulled me into a hug. "I'm so glad you're here, I didn't think you'd make it."

"Nothing in the world could have kept me from this."

In that instant, a bond was formed between Judy and me that would become one of the most cherished things in my life. This was the hug I'd needed all along. She was warm and soft, and she continued to hold my hand as we talked. She called over her husband, Dennis, and he hugged me too. They both smiled and hugged Roni when I introduced her. "So this is Roni," said Dennis. "You know, Matt used to talk about you all the time." Roni squeezed my hand—and I knew she was fighting back tears.

For two people who'd just been through the worst week of their lives, Judy and Dennis Shepard were the embodiment of strength. They were sad and they were tired, but they smiled through it. They were so gracious to Roni and me, repeating over and over how nice it was to see us, as if more concerned for us than for themselves. Before Roni and I went into the church, Dennis Shepard went back to the receiving line. "Judy," I said, "can I ask you a question?"

"Of course you can."

"I spoke at a vigil for Matt in Denver a few days ago and kind of identified myself as a friend of his. With all of the media stuff that's going on right now, I have a feeling that some reporters are going to want to talk to me. How would you feel about that?"

She thought about it for a few seconds. "If you do, just be honest. Don't lie about who Matt was."

"Thank you," I said. "I won't."

Roni and I entered the church and found a space in a pew about halfway down the center aisle. The room, with its high arched ceiling, was cold and quiet, its somber mood intensified by the darkness. The lights had been dimmed, and only the smallest trickle of natural light came in through the stained-glass windows. Looking around at those already seated and the others still making their way in, I recognized some faces from my time in Casper— Marc Scheguart, and Danielle, from The Fabulous Eight, and Jane from the Daily Grind. We nodded if we caught each other's eye. Our shared sadness was palpable.

I slipped back into my coat and took Roni's hand again. We were both trembling. It was clear that we weren't going to speak once we were seated, so I closed my eyes and let my mind wander. My thoughts landed on Michael and a memory of the day we spread his ashes the previous summer. He'd chosen a specific spot by a creek on a mountain outside Denver, so we'd waited for the perfect August afternoon. The sun was shining, the day bright and warm, as we drove with his urn. Most of the family was there, all in great moods. We had a quick picnic near the car then, with Michael and a boom box set to play the song Michael had chosen—an obscure rendition of "Amazing Grace" by a woman whose name I don't think I ever knew—we set off down a dirt road that led to the creek.

Once there, the discussion began about what would be the perfect resting place. The most beautiful location was the opposite bank of the creek, but that meant having to wade through the knee-deep icy water, which seemed totally out of the question. Mom didn't like the idea of spreading Michael on the nearest bank, because she thought people would walk all over him. Then someone raised the idea of hiding him behind a tree, and before we knew it we were all trying to outshout each other.

It took us all about five minutes to realize that someone's voice was noticeably missing. We turned to look for our father, then spotted him, soaked to the knee, trudging through the creek with the urn in one hand and a shovel in the other. All conversation stopped. Quickly we all took off our shoes, rolled up our pants, and ran into the water after him. "We're going to put him on the other side like your mother wanted," he said. Roni stayed on the shore with the boom box, and I told her I'd point at her when it was time to hit the "play" button. We all reached the other side together and waited as my dad dug a small hole. When he was finished, I nodded to Roni and the music began to play. As my dad poured Michael's ashes, I put an arm around Mom and closed my eyes. I felt the heat of the sun on my back, and a slight warm breeze flowed lazily through our circle. Over my mother's sobs came the gentle, angelic vibrato of "Amazing Grace" and the tumbling current of the water in the creek.

I was jolted from my memory as the people in the dark church stood for the service. The Shepards, as a family, walked down the center aisle and took their places in the front pew. I couldn't take my eyes off them, and I don't think anyone else could either. I watched Dennis slip his arm around Judy's shoulder, then I took a look around. The place was full of bouquets and arrangements whose floral aroma included the dirty wet snow tracked in by mourners. When I looked back at the family, Logan had moved closer to his mother, and after a minute Judy put her arm around him and held him. She did that on and off throughout the service—she'd hold onto him for a few minutes, then let him go.

The lights in the church flickered throughout the service. At one point they went out all together, and we sat in darkness for a few seconds before the emergency generator kicked in. In moments of silence one could hear the echo of the speakers in the park and the occasional crack of a tree branch as the snowstorm continued to rage outside. Many of Matthew's family members spoke. One of his cousins read a poem. When it came time for Communion, Roni didn't want to go up, so I went alone. Like many in the sorrow-filled line approaching the altar, I had no interest in participating in that aspect of the Mass—I was going up to see Matthew, to say my final goodbye. He'd been cremated, and his ashes lay in a beautiful cedar box painted with a mountain scene that sat on a little table to the right of the priest. Several people touched it as they passed, but I did not. Instead, I stood for a few seconds, looking at it, then I closed my eyes. I saw my Matthew on the day we met, that squeamish little guy in the blue button-down shirt who'd walked in at the coffee shop in Casper, terrified the group waiting for him at the table was going to eat him alive. He smiled then, the smile I'll always remember, that said, *You're going to love me—you just don't know it yet.*

"Bye Matt," I said. Then I went back to my seat. I cried through the rest of the Mass, and Roni held me. I wanted to get all my emotion out, to grieve right then and have it be over with. I'd been living with tragedy and death for so long. But months later, in the midst of the media frenzy, I'd reflect upon that moment in the church with Roni and my need to let it all go as foresight—that with all the work to be done for the sake of Matthew's memory, there would be little time for grief.

Roni and I didn't try to see the Shepards again before we left the church; they'd been whisked away anyhow, as soon as the service ended. We went out front and stood on the steps and waited for John. The crowd outside seemed to have doubled, and the rally in the park sounded as though it had gained momentum too. Reporters and cameramen were everywhere, jockeying for interviews and setting up shots. Roni and I recognized some of the people around us but turned away. We just didn't feel like talking. Instead, we fell back into a hug and sang "You Are My Sunshine," our favorite comfort song.

It was hard for us to say goodbye that afternoon because we

didn't know how we were leaving things. We had had a quick lunch at Denny's with John and Frank, during which we snuck off to the bathroom to make out, and I realized I was still in love with her. I would have gotten on my knees and begged her to come back to Denver with me if I thought there were even a chance.

Feeling like it had all been a surreal dream, that the three of us now were back on the road to Denver in no time, I sat in the backseat, with John and Frank in front. I felt heartbroken for a hundred reasons. The snow fell in huge clumps, harder and thicker than on the ride up. I was settling myself in for a nice long sulk when John turned on the radio and I heard a female voice grind out the words *"I'm a child, I'm a lover, I'm your angel undercover...."* At first I started to giggle, and in seconds I was doubled over with laughter.

John turned down the radio. "What's so funny?"

"This song is 'Bitch' by Meredith Brooks," I said. "It's Matthew's favorite song."

"Yeah?" John said.

I went on like a madwoman: "At first I just took it as a 'hello' from him. But then I got this image of him up in heaven, waving his arms around all dramatic like to make this storm happen, and in a deep, booming voice that echoes throughout the universe saying, *'LET THEM ALL REMEMBER ME... IT WAS THE DAY OF THE GREAT SNOWSTORM...'*"

John turned the radio back up, and we belted out the rest of the song at the top of our lungs. We laughed and cried as much as we could as we continued to drive through Matthew's storm. John dropped me off at my place sometime after 9, and I immediately walked over to the answering machine. The red light was flashing, and I hoped it was Roni. I was about to hit the "play" button when I noticed the number of new messages: 31. I was sure it was a mistake. I didn't think I even *knew* 31 people. I sat down next to the machine with a pencil and a piece of paper so I could write down any important information as the tape began to play. All 31 messages were a variation on the same theme.

"Hi, Romaine. I'm calling from *People Magazine... Newsweek... The Denver Post... Nightline...* The NBC affiliate here in Denver... The *Laramie Boomerang...* The *Casper Star-Tribune...* Court TV...*The Washington Post... Out* magazine... The *San Francisco Chronicle...* I saw you on TV at the vigil for Matthew Shepard in Denver...seems you were a friend of his...wondering if it might be possible to set up a time for a formal interview...can call me back at..."

Part Three

25 | The Media

I spent the rest of the night trying to decide what to do. A few things were clear. First of all, the press had not been able to find anyone else who'd had any extended history with Matthew. Most stories up to that point, both in print and on TV, centered on what had happened to him and various communities' responses. But there was no one, save his parents, who could speak with any real authority on who this Matthew Shepard was—and his parents simply weren't talking. In fact, Judy and Dennis had gone so far as to make a public statement asking the press to leave them alone. Roni and I were Matthew's closest friends and the only two people in the world who spent virtually every day with him in the two-and-a-half years before his death—and Roni definitely wasn't talking. On top of the fact that publicly associating herself with a gay hate-crime victim would probably have been grounds for familial excommunication, she loathed what the press was doing to Matthew. She truly believed that every story printed and every vigil held in his name was exploiting the murder of her friend. She also felt that anyone who knew Matthew and came forward to talk publicly about him was doing so out of a perverted desire to claim their 15 minutes of fame. "This is bullshit," she'd say. "What a bunch of media whores."

She'd even been furious with *me* when she found out I'd spoken at the vigil in Denver. "I just think it's a betrayal of the friendship," she'd muttered.

I, of course, didn't see it that way.

The way I saw it, the world ought to have known who he was.
What made me angry about the press coverage of Matthew was
the same thing that had gotten me worked up listening to the
politicians talk about him at the Denver vigil. It was like there was
this warped need for him to have been flawless—as if that made
his death more tragic. Already comparisons were being drawn
between the way Matthew had been tied to the fence and the crucifixion of Christ.*

(*Footnote: He was not strung up like a scarecrow or Jesus
Christ. He'd been kneeling—or sitting—when Henderson and
McKinney tied his hands behind his back to the bottom of one of
the fence posts. But like everyone else in the world, I believed the
misleading, and sometimes blatantly untrue, stories when I read
them in the paper or saw them on TV.)

The words of Judy Shepard rang in my ears. *Tell the truth.
Don't lie about who Matt was.*

What happened to Matthew was horrifying and terrible
because it was horrifying and terrible, not because it happened to
a saint—or even a sinless, perfect, beautiful boy next door.
Matthew Shepard was a flawed human being. His death was horrible because it could have happened to anyone. I really believed
that if I spoke up by granting some or all of those interviews, I
could help deliver that point.

The next afternoon I sat down with my pad and pencil and
called the reporters back. I started with *People* magazine because
it was my favorite when I was a kid, then went down the list. Some
of the interviews were short, and some lasted longer than 45 min-

utes, but they all asked the same questions:

"Tell me about Matthew."

"What kinds of things did Matthew like to do?"

"Why do you think Matthew left with those boys?"

Most of the questions were easy, and I could tell the reporters were eager for any new information. Of course, they wanted me to tell them stories about Matthew, quirky things that would make their pieces stand out. I wanted to provide those stories—why else do an interview?—but I also wanted to be careful. I wasn't sure about providing details of Matthew's hospital stays or his drug use. Luckily, any questions that might have led me there were rarely, if ever, asked. I talked about his depression only when I was asked about it, and believed it did—and still does—help paint a more humanly accurate picture of him. But mostly I stuck to a script. I picked my favorite stories, like how he loved collecting glass bottles and how we used to spend entire days in Denver searching for unique ones; or the time he threw me my 19th birthday party; or how he'd visit me all the time at the coffee shop and how he became friends with all the regulars. I told different aspects of the stories to different reporters so none would feel like they'd gotten scooped.

And the reporters all got the message out—Matthew was a good and decent young man who enjoyed certain things in life that were ordinary and simple.

That was how it went for the first couple of weeks. The more I talked and my name was used, the more interview requests I got. I'd come home from work in the early afternoon and there'd be 20 to 30 messages on my answering machine. I'd get my pad and pencil, write down pertinent information, call everyone back, and answer their questions. Only once was I offered payment for an interview—*Hard Copy* gave me $1,000 for about a half hour of my

time. I wrestled with that one for a while. Did my taking the
money make Roni right? Was I also a media whore? Exploiting my
friendship with Matthew for personal gain? I justified it to myself
by reasoning that the amount of interviews I was doing was equivalent to having a second full-time job, and so, because I was so
financially desperate, taking the money was OK. And besides, I
really didn't think Matthew would mind. But still, a certain
amount of guilt came along with the cashing of that check—I was
glad to find out the segment I'd been interviewed for was never
going to air.

I learned so much through that process. For example: Emotion
is good, but diplomacy is better. One question I got all the time
was "How do you feel about Russell Henderson or Aaron
McKinney?" And while I would have loved to say "I hope those
fuckers fry in hell," I quickly learned to say "I'm glad they are going
to have their day in court, and I have full faith that the system will
bring them to justice." Another question I got a lot was "Do you
think Matthew Shepard was out cruising for sex on the night he
met Henderson and McKinney?" I always wanted to say, "First of
all, no, I don't. *Cruising* for sex anywhere, but especially at straight
bars, just wasn't something Matthew did. Second of all, who the
hell cares if he was? People have sex—some people go looking for
it at bars. If Matthew had been cruising for sex that night, does it
make tying him to a fence and beating him to death OK?" Instead,
I would say, "No, I don't believe he was doing that; it wasn't something he did." I always kept in mind that if I lost my cool, I'd be
seen as a reactionary and lose my credibility.

I'd never had any formal media training, but I learned the ropes
very quickly. Always listen carefully to the question, and answer
only what you are asked: This prevents your rambling into an area
you'll later wish you hadn't talked about. Short answers—often

called "sound bites"—provide the best opportunity to be quoted directly. Read every story you've been interviewed for and you will know which reporters can be trusted in the future.

In the beginning the reporters were fairly respectful. As I fumbled my way through learning how to be interviewed, they let me talk. It was good for all parties involved—for them because they got their story then some, and for me because I was able to hone, shape, and really come to an understanding of what I was trying to say. I realized over the course of those weeks that talking about Matthew or his attack or hate crimes was too narrow; that, in fact, what I wanted to be talking about was hatred itself. Hatred, I realized by doing interview after interview, was, and still is, the core of the issue. Hatred is why my friend died.

Not long after I gave my first interview, things began to get out of control. Because Laramie doesn't have a large international airport, reporters from all over the world were flying into Denver en route to Laramie, and it seemed as though they *all* wanted to talk to me. By then I'd made myself way too available, returning literally every media call or e-mail. I set no boundaries—it hadn't seemed necessary. And without an adviser or agent to protect me, I was like meat thrown to the sharks.

It had been written somewhere that I worked at Diedrich's, and as soon as that story broke, reporters started showing up there looking for me. They'd march right up to the counter and ask if Romaine Patterson was there. I'd skeptically identify myself, then, with a line of paying, coffee-deprived customers forming behind, they'd say as they whipped out their little notebooks, "I have a few questions for you about your friendship with Matthew Shepard."

At first I couldn't believe they thought it was just OK for them to invade my place of work. But soon I came to understand that for them, when it comes to getting a story there is virtually no code of ethics. Thank God for my coworkers at Diedrich's and my boss, Ken Rutiberries, who would always just smile and say, "Don't worry about it, Romaine. Go do your interview." Even when I made it clear that I was working and wouldn't be available for an interview until my shift was over, the print media made it clear that they would wait.

Television journalists were another story. That November I'd agreed to do an interview with MSNBC—though a time and date had not been determined. I came home from work one evening and in the lobby of my building I found that an entire set had been erected by the MSNBC people. There were lights, a backdrop, a sound technician, two cameramen, and a reporter waiting for me. Not only had I not planned on doing an interview that day, I was exhausted. I felt and looked like shit. But when they asked if I could be ready in 10 minutes, saying no seemed like a non-option.

Another time *Court TV* stopped by to do an interview (at least that one had been scheduled long in advance). When they arrived at my apartment and looked around, they decided the setting didn't provide enough "atmosphere" and asked if there was anywhere else we could go do it. I suggested my brother John's house, and before I knew it their crew was removing all the furniture from his formal living room and setting up shop. It took up John's entire night, but being his usual good-sport self, he put on a pot of coffee for the crew, made room for the couch in the kitchen, then stood around to see if he could be of any further help.

Michael would have had a fit.

Television journalists were a lot pushier about getting an emotional response. I got pretty good at hardening myself to obvious attempts at button-pushing, but as time progressed they seemed willing to try anything to get me to break down. Nothing, and I mean *nothing*, was off-limits. They'd describe in great gory detail the image of Matthew in his hospital bed—bruised, intubated, covered with bandages—then ask, "Does this at all resemble the Matthew Shepard you knew?" One spoke at length, as if I didn't know, about what "those boys did to Matthew" that night and how he "sat out there in the cold for 18 hours," then, putting on an earnest, psychotherapeutic expression, asked, "How does hearing that make you feel?" I learned to insert a dramatic pause before I answered, to take a deep breath as if I had just had that question framed this way for the very first time—then provide a variation on my stock answer.

Of course, I wanted to give them all what they wanted. The trouble was that it was too easy to get swallowed up in the emotion of what happened. No matter how much I talked about it or tried to harden myself against the horror of it, it never got any easier to deal with. The sadness never diminished. The more interviews I did, the more I realized how the media fed on that sadness—how their stories lived or died based on how sad their questions could make me. As I continued to grant them, every interview came to feel like the violent reopening of a wound. But I knew I had to continue, that stopping was not an option. Call it survivor's guilt maybe, but I just couldn't stop thinking to myself, *No matter how much of a sacrifice I'm making or how much pain it's causing me, it is nothing compared to what Matthew went through...*

I soon grew to hate the media. It was the kind of hate that often made getting out of bed in the morning seemingly an insurmountable challenge because I knew that no matter what I did with my day I'd be coming home to interview after interview, conducted by people with little sensitivity to the subject matter—and none at all to me. I knew that it was a trade: I gave them the emotion that made their stories interesting, and in return they gave me a platform, a means to fulfill what would have undoubtedly been Matt's wishes. But as I ground my teeth and bit my tongue in the face of their condescension, I came to wonder if that trade was even.

One particular interview stands out in my mind, only because I really liked my interviewers. Their names were Leigh Fondakowski and Greg Pierotti. They were with the Tectonic Theater Project from New York City and had been to Laramie for a few days before passing through Denver on the way home. They'd interviewed my sister Trish at her store in Laramie, and she'd told them all about me and gave them my number. After speaking briefly with Leigh on the phone, I agreed to meet them for dinner next to their hotel at Chili's restaurant. They recognized me immediately because of my leather jacket—whenever I was meeting a reporter I didn't know, I always told them to look for a girl in a leather jacket.

We talked for over an hour. They placed a giant tape recorder in the middle of the table and wanted to know everything about my friendship with Matt. So I told them all the stories I had scripted for interviews like that. When they finished their questions, I asked them to tell me about their project. Leigh, a petite blond girl whose hair was in a ponytail and pulled through the back of her hat, was holding her ear to the tape recorder. Her face was scrunched up, and I could tell she was straining to hear our recorded conversation over the restaurant's background noise. "Well," she said as she lifted her head, "we're writing a play about the people of Laramie, and eventually we want to bring it back there to perform for the people we've interviewed."

It sounded like a nice idea, but I didn't really get it.

The next day, on their way to the airport, Leigh and Greg

stopped to visit me at the coffee shop. Leigh liked my Diedrich Coffee hat and asked if she could have one. I searched the place high and low (I thought she was cute) but to no avail. They each gave me a hug before they left, and I wished them luck with their play, sure that I'd never hear of them again.

26 | *Jim*

The first time I met Jim Osborn was at the state speech competition in Wyoming. He was a judge, and I was a student competitor in my senior year of high school. Just two years out of high
school and a former speech competitor himself, he had earned a
reputation that season as being one of the most stoic judges on the
circuit. I remember walking into the assigned room and finding it
to be a seminar-style classroom, the kind that rises up like a college amphitheater. I saw Jim in the very last row, wearing a pair of
sunglasses. I yelled up to him, "Would you mind if I stood on that
table?", indicating a tall wooden table that seemed out of place,
like it belonged in a wood shop—and got no response. Again I
shouted, "Excuse me, I just want to make sure that you're going to
be able to see me back there! Would you mind if I stood on that
table?"

He pulled his sunglasses down on his nose—annoyed or
amused—and said, "Don't fall off."

He was enormous, I noticed, and queeny. I loved him immediately.

I followed him around in between judging sessions for the rest
of the day. We talked about what it was like to grow up gay in
Wyoming. At the end of the day we exchanged phone numbers and

e-mail addresses and became friends. He went on to the University of Wyoming in Laramie, where he became the president of the gay, lesbian, bisexual, and transgender (GLBT) group on campus, and for a little while we fell out of touch.

After Matt died I started seeing Jim on TV. Of course, as president of the GLBT group, he'd have known him. Small world. As the media tidal wave hit Laramie, Jim became sort of "the face of gay and lesbian University of Wyoming students." He held press conference after press conference and was constantly being interviewed by news outlets, newspapers, and magazines. Every time I saw a picture of him he looked exhausted—and I knew we were living parallel lives.

Late in November of '98 I dug through some old address books until I found his e-mail address and, hoping he still checked that account, I sent him an e-mail. He called me the next day, and we talked for over an hour. It was anything but the usual sort of catching-up. He'd seen me on TV too and had the same thought: *How did she know Matt?* He wanted to know the name of every reporter I'd talked to, what sorts of things we'd talked about, and which ones I liked and trusted. We each got out notebooks and scribbled notes.

After that Jim and I kept in regular touch. If I met a reporter I liked in Denver who was on her way to Laramie, I'd pass her on to Jim, and Jim would do the same for a reporter on his way to Denver. If one of us met a reporter we didn't like, we'd let the other one know to steer clear. Being the best media contacts in our respective cities, we made it easy for reporters if we liked their message. If we felt a reporter was exploitive or insensitive, we were able to make her job quite difficult.

At the end of November, Jim called to tell me that the National Gay and Lesbian Task Force had asked him to invite 10 people from Laramie to attend its national conference in Pittsburgh. He wanted me to be one of the 10. It was a four-day event for which all expenses were covered, so I thought, *Why not?*

From the beginning of the trip it was clear that Jim and I took the event more seriously than any of the other eight from Laramie. While they were off drinking and shopping, Jim and I were getting ourselves checked in at the conference. As we stood in line at the orientation table I realized that Matthew Shepard was the unofficial theme that year. There were pictures of him everywhere—on the walls, on poster board displays, even on the cover of our orientation folders. Most of the pictures were black-and-white and had been taken on a trip he made to Alcatraz sometime before he and I met. The one I couldn't take my eyes off was of Matt lying in the middle of what looked like the desert, digging his hands into the sand. He looked so young, so innocent—and though looking away from the camera, I could see he had a huge smile on his face. Everyone around us was looking at the pictures too as they picked up buttons that said things like MATTHEW SHEPARD IS MY BROTHER. Their mouths hung open at the sight of him. They were mesmerized the way some people are by pictures of Madonna or Bruce Springsteen. Watching them look at him made me want him back.

Once we checked in, Jim took me over to meet Cathy Renna. She was a petite boyish-looking woman wearing a white button-down shirt and a pair of jeans. She shook my hand firmly when Jim introduced us, then explained that she worked for an organization called the Gay and Lesbian Alliance Against Defamation—GLAAD. The organization had been created to ensure that gay, lesbian, bisexual, and transgender people were represented accurately, fairly, and inclusively within the media. "Cathy," Jim said, "called me a few days after Matt's attack when she saw how inundated I was with press at the university. She said 'How can I help?' and I said

'Get on a plane.' She was in Laramie the next day."

Cathy was obviously very serious about her job. She wanted to know what kind of media I had talked to and what I was saying.

"I've created sort of a script I use when I'm talking to reporters," I said. "That way I can stay on-message and I don't ramble into areas I don't want to talk about."

Cathy didn't blink. She bit her lower lip and nodded her head. She was either impressed or concerned; I couldn't tell.

"And Jim and I have created an unofficial database of reporters we like and don't like. That way we can keep track of who has said what to whom, who we liked talking to, who we hated, and so on."

"Very good," Cathy said. "Very, very good."

On the second day of the event the NGLTF held a press conference. Jim, as the president of the GLBT group from the university, had been asked to participate in the portion that dealt with Matt. It was hard for me to sit on the sidelines and watch Jim—someone who hadn't really know Matt that well—speak about him. Though in the years since Matt's attack Jim has stayed so true to Matt and proved himself, with the personal sacrifices he has made, to be one of the best friends Matt ever had, I think that was the moment I came to realize how protective, maybe even possessive, I had become of Matt since his murder.

That night the NGLTF held a vigil for Matt outside on the steps of the conference center. At Jim's request to the organizers, I was asked to speak at the event, though it wasn't until literally five minutes before the vigil started that the event planner found me and asked me to do it. "We were hoping you would open the vigil with a speech about Matthew," he said rather frantically, "and that you would light your candle then help everyone else light theirs." He shoved a candle in my hand, pointed me in the direction of the microphone, and said, "You're on in five minutes."

Terrified, and with absolutely no idea what to say, I walked away from Jim and the group I had been standing with. The people I was about to address, the NGLTF, were the movers and shakers of the gay community, so I was scared shitless. What could I say to these people that would move them beyond what they already knew? I closed my eyes for a few minutes and focused on Matthew—not on memories of him, necessarily, but on his spirit, how he felt. I needed to get into his head, to try to understand what he would say to a community of people who'd been galvanized by his death but were unsure of what course of action to take. Standing by myself, I said in a low voice, "OK, Matthew, what do you want to say?"

I walked up the steps after I was introduced. I took a deep breath and looked at the crowd. Night had fallen by then, so faces were not discernible, but the crowd was large. Everyone was bundled up in parkas, hats, and scarves. Some bobbed up and down to keep warm in the frigid evening breeze. I felt different than I had at the Denver vigil—less nervous and less sad. Anger, though still present, was no longer my prevailing emotion. I felt energized by the crowd, comforted even. There was a constructive buzz in the air, and there was hope, as if some great change was going to take place in the wake of this senseless tragedy. And that was what I addressed: "People are talking less about the brutality of the attack and are talking more about what we can do to prevent these things from happening—how can I prevent something like this from ever happening to my children?"

I ended my talk with: "So, as we light our candles tonight for Matthew, each one of those lights will be a little light of hope that Matthew has cast for each of us, that we may go on continuing to talk, educate, and, most important, learn about these issues."

I sincerely hoped we would.

27 | *Please Don't Make Me Explain*

Winter seemed to have flown by. There were days, maybe even a week from time to time, when Matthew's name didn't appear in print and my phone would stop ringing off the hook, but then something would happen—like in December, Albany County District Attorney Cal Rerucha announced that he would seek the death penalty for both Henderson and McKinney—and for me it would start all over again. "Wasn't Matthew against the death penalty?" reporters would ask. "Do you think he'd want those boys to be put to death?" And "What do you think, Romaine? Do you want those boys to die?"

I was also bombarded with questions about Judy and Dennis, who had recently been interviewed by Katie Couric for a prime-time special on NBC. "Are Matthew's parents doing enough?" the press wanted to know. I had never spoken publicly about my frustrations with Matthew's parents for having been so far away from him during his miserable year in Denver, but I was eager to talk about my response to their interview. It amazed me to hear how lovingly they spoke of their son and how unconditionally accepting they were of him. It would have been music to Matt's ears.

In the early part of March I picked up a copy of *Vanity Fair* to read an article about Matthew for which I had been interviewed. I was nervous about what it was going to say, not because I felt that I had misspoken in any way but because the reporter, a skinny bleach-blond twit of a woman, had barely been able to form questions while she was interviewing me. Her name was Melanie Thernstrom, and she had shown up at my apartment in the middle of the afternoon one day in December and, uninvited, helped herself to a slice of pizza I'd just reheated before fumbling her way through an interview she clearly wasn't prepared for.

At the request of the editor, I had also sold a picture of Matthew—the only one Roni hadn't taken with her when she moved out—to the magazine for the piece. It was one I had taken at the McDonald's in Casper just before the move to Denver. He's wearing his trademark blue button-down shirt, and he's got his sunglasses on his head. With his elbow resting on the table, he's holding a cigarette in his right hand a few inches from his face. Because of the light in the picture, the cigarette, blending into the sky behind it, is almost invisible, which, with his hand raised the way it is, makes it look like Matthew is waving hello. Pictures of Matthew—because there seemed to be so few in existence—were a very hot item. *Vanity Fair* gave me $1,000 for mine. As with the money for the *Hard Copy* interview, I was able to convince myself that I could take the money in good conscience because I had missed work at the coffee shop on many occasions due to the work I was doing in Matthew's memory. And again, the guilt set in quickly thereafter. (I never took the money again.)

Seeing the title of the piece, "The Crucifixion of Matthew Shepard," didn't make me feel any better. In fact, it made me furious. I almost didn't read the article, but figuring it would be the most widely circulated piece of anything I had been interviewed for to date, I decided that I should at least know what quotes of mine had been used. I have to say that though I didn't (and still don't) necessarily like the article, I was shocked by how well the piece was put together. It seemed that there wasn't a single person, including Judy Shepard as well as Henderson's and McKinney's girlfriends, whom Thernstrom hadn't interviewed.

The piece sat with me. There was something about what I had read that nagged at me, but I wasn't able to put my finger on it. That is, until two days later, when I woke in the middle of the night to a realization. The article reminded me of something I'd known since Matthew's final hospital stay in Denver: that he was HIV-positive. For some reason, until that very moment, the moment I woke up, I had forgotten what happened on a night two summers before, about a week after Matthew moved into his place in Denver. He had wanted to decorate his new place and had called me to see if I would go on a shopping spree with him. Our last stop was a store called Hobby-Lobby that sold knickknacks and room accessories. He was looking for glass bottles, yellow ones in particular, to put on shelves he was planning to build in his living room. He found a couple he really liked and was putting them down by a cash register when a four-inch cut on the palm of his hand reopened. All of a sudden there was blood everywhere. Matt, panicking, squeezed his wrist and, to the horror of the girl behind the register, pressed his hand down against the counter. It all happened so fast that I just reacted. With blood from Matt's hand starting to flow out onto the counter, I yelled to the salesgirl to throw me a roll of paper towels. When she did, I took Matt's hand, lifted it straight up in the air to get it above his heart, and started to wrap it. By the time I got him to calm down and to hold his own hand so I could clean up the mess on the counter, my hand and arm was covered in his blood.

For the rest of the night I tossed and turned and went over and over in my head the events of that night almost two years before. The next morning I went down to the local family planning clinic and had an HIV test. I was terrified as I was led by a little old white-haired lady into a room in the back of the building. I sat on the examining table, crinkling the white sheet of sterile paper that had been laid out over it, while she got out a folder. "I have to ask you a couple of questions before I draw your blood," she said. "Have you ever had sex?"

"Yes," I told her.

"Do you have sex with men?"

"No."

"Do you have sex with women?"

"Yes."

"Have you ever had vaginal sex?"

"Yes."

"Have you ever had oral sex?"

"Yes."

"Have you had anal sex?"

"Yes."

The nurse was incredulous. She peered up at me over the questionnaire. "You've had anal sex, but you don't have sex with men?"

"Yes."

"Well, how is *that* possible?"

"I'm a lesbian. If you can imagine it, I can do it. Please don't make me explain the intricacies of lesbian sex to you right now."

"Fair enough," she said. "One last question: Why are you here today?"

"I've come in direct contact with the blood of an HIV-infected person," I said. I had decided not to tell her that it was Matthew Shepard's blood. I told her how badly he'd been cut, how I had been covered in his blood, and because I worked at the coffee shop and was always cutting myself, I always had little open wounds on my hands.

After that she drew my blood, then told me to come back in two weeks for the results. When I asked her if I could call in for them, she said, "No, actually, because you've had direct contact with infected blood I'd like it if you came down. We have on-site counseling—just in case."

By the time I came back I had lived through two of the most agonizing weeks of my life. Once the story of Matthew's HIV status had broken in the *Vanity Fair* article, almost every reporter I talked to had a question about it. AIDS and the possibility of my having it was all I thought about. I'd stare at the veins in my forearm and wonder if the virus was multiplying inside them. Would I be condemned to the same fate as Michael?

When I returned for my results, I was ready for the worst. That time it was a young, good-looking doctor who took me back to an examining room. He held my folder in his hand, and I knew it contained my results. He talked a little about safe sex and I half listened, my eyes never off the folder.

"Do you have any family we can call for you should you have tested positive?"

"Yes," I lied. I never would have told my family.

"OK then," he said as he slid his finger across the open edge of the folder and broke its seal. In that second I felt the powerless anticipation of being in the front car of a roller coaster the instant it peaks at the top.

"You're negative," he said.

I felt weightless for a second, then dizzy.

"It's been well over six months since you had this contact," the doctor said, "so there's no need for a follow-up."

I couldn't help myself; I stood up and hugged the man.

28 | Preparing for the Return of Phelps

At the end of March, Jim and I were invited out to be guest speakers at a rally during Pennsylvania State University's Gay Pride Week. With the mounting number of interviews I was being asked to do and having just survived the intensity of my HIV scare, I couldn't get out of town fast enough.

It was at a party at the lesbian sorority house on my second night there that I met Shannon. She was a slender girl with bone-white skin and billowing locks of fire-red hair. She had a sharp wit and an innocent smile, which she used in tandem like a one-two punch.

We joined the other girls in front of the TV for the "Jerry Springer Drinking Game"* (Footnote:* The rules are simple: Everyone does a shot when there's a mullet on the screen and when the audience yells "Jerry! Jerry!") then, sufficiently toasted, snuck off to a couch somewhere in the back of the house and stayed up the entire night talking. We talked about philosophy and religion— strange topics of conversation, we noted, for a sorority party.

"I was a pagan for a while," she said with a proud smile after I told her about my painfully Catholic upbringing.

"Really?" I tried, as I inched a little closer to her to sound like I found this fascinating—even though I wasn't entirely sure what a pagan was.

Minutes later, as we were competing to see who best loved the work of Michelangelo, a magical thing happened: Our naked toes touched.

"Romaine," she said a few seconds later as she gently pushed on my shoulder, "did you hear me?"

"No, sorry, what?"

"I said, have you ever read *The Agony and the Ecstasy*?"

"Uh-uh," I said.

She gasped exaggeratedly, then, rolling her eyes as far into her head as she could, she grabbed her T-shirt just above the spot where her heart was. "Tsk, tsk," she said. "It's all about our boy Michelangelo...and you call yourself a fan." She pinched my pinkie toe affectionately, and I tried not to flinch or pull it away. "Well, I guess that's all right," she said. "I'll just have to get you my copy before you leave."

Back in Denver I'd become somewhat of a recluse in my determination to start thinking about what I wanted to do with my life. I bought a new computer, plus software that enabled me to make and record music, then moved all the furniture out of my bedroom and turned it into a "recording studio." I spent hours on the phone with Shannon then online, sending her instant messages and e-mails. As we got to know each other I found her to be one of the best listeners I had ever met. She always wanted to know how I was and—unlike so many others—was neither satisfied nor fooled by the whole "I'm fine and nothing bothers me" routine I thought I'd become so good at.

Shannon saw that I was getting depressed—that in leaving my apartment to go only to work and to do in-person interviews, I was locking myself away from the outside world. And she cared. She asked questions that nobody—not even my family—had asked, and it was through my conversations with her that I realized how much anger I was carrying around.

She wanted to know about it, so I told her. I talked about how I felt about the people in Laramie who'd gone running to the press, pretending to have known something about Matthew after he died; I talked about how much I hated the politicians who used Matthew's death as an advancement tool for their careers; I talked about my family's inability to show support for me—the way they seemed so afraid simply to ask how I was doing. "And they're so sick of hearing about the press," I told Shannon during one of our late-night phone conversations. "I don't know," I sighed. "I get the distinct impression that they think I'm doing all of this for the attention."

"Oh, honey" was her response. Then after taking a deep breath she said, "I'm so sorry to hear that. I wish I could be there with you right now."

She did eventually come out to see me a couple of times in Denver before her school year was over. The sex was great, the conversation was better. Clearly we were falling in love.

I look back on that time now and realize it was my connection with Shannon that revitalized me, and as the trial of Henderson approached, it helped put me in an emotional state to be able to do the work that lay ahead.

That April, Jim Osborn called from Laramie with bad news. "Phelps is coming back for the trial on April 5. He's going to protest at the courthouse then up at the University of Wyoming. Can you believe that shit?"

"How do you know?" I asked.

"We just got a fax from him."

"You're kidding me." I rolled my eyes. "And I'm sure he's sent the same fax to every major media outlet he expects to be there."

Jim told me how it was going to be set up. The police department, knowing what a circus that day would inevitably be, had fenced the lawn of the courthouse into various sections. Members of the media would be allowed to park their satellite trucks on Grand Street next to the courthouse and in the parking lot across the street. Certain areas of the lawn would also be fenced off to provide as few interruptions in coverage as possible. Also near the courthouse, a three-sided bullpen had been built to contain Phelps and his group. About three feet in front of that was a smaller bullpen in which the police would stand, in order to keep distance between Phelps and the general public. There was definitely a fear of violence, that either an onlooker would jump over Phelps's barricade and beat the hell out of him or just shoot him—this was, after all, Wyoming.

The unfortunate thing about Phelps's position, Jim said, was that they were near the side door where Judy and Dennis Shepard were going to be brought in. If Phelps was set up before the Shepards were inside, there was no way to prevent them from seeing his ugly show.

Jim hadn't been at Matthew's memorial service. He'd been at a vigil held for Matthew in Laramie that day.

"It was bad enough dealing with this asshole at the funeral," I said. "And wait until you see their signs. They have Matt's picture on them, and they say things like 'Matt in Hell' and 'AIDS Cures Fags.' " I took a deep breath. "I can't imagine what it'll be like for Matthew's parents to have to see that—then have to go into the trial and listen to the brutal details of his murder all over again."

How is it, I wondered, *that Phelps's protests are just allowed to happen?* It made me furious that our civil right to freedom of speech could be bastardized in such a way—that nobody could do anything to stop it. "He's going to be utilizing every piece of media he can get his hands on," I said. "His story is going to be told all over the country that night."

"You told me that at Matt's memorial service people had sort of stood in front of them to try to block them out with their bodies," Jim said.

"Yeah, but that was only kind of effective," I said, "because his signs are huge and they hold them way up over their heads. So even if you block them out, people can still see the signs."

Jim stewed silently for a moment. "There's got to be something we can do."

"Hey," I said. "You know what would be amazing?"

"What's that?"

"You know how he's all about 'God hates fags' and all that? Well, I think God is about love and respect and peace. Wouldn't it be amazing if someone could find a way to turn the Bible around on him and show those qualities?"

"Oh, my God, that *would* be amazing."

Almost immediately the idea of the angels was born.

"They could be, like, huge and made out of cardboard or something," I said.

"And they could block out all those signs," Jim said.

"Someone totally has to do that," I said. "It's such a good idea. I can't do it, but I wish I could. I've just got too much going on." By then I had taken on a second job, scanning images for the Web site of a small comic book company. That, on top of Diedrich's and interviews, made the idea seem impossible.

"Don't I hear that, sister," he said. His mountain of interview requests in Laramie had doubled in the weeks before the trial.

"Jim, maybe you should talk to some people in Laramie; see if anyone up there wants to take it on."

Jim sighed into the phone. "I'll give it a shot, but you know the people in Laramie. They're kinda hard to get motivated."

That day I got to work at the comic book company at 5 P.M. and by 7 P.M. had told just about everybody there about our idea. Everyone had the same response to it: "That would be incredible."

Sitting at my desk, scanning angry red faces of cartoon musclemen, I wondered, *Would it really be so impossible?* Then, and I've come to think of this moment as a swift kick in the ass from Matthew, I got a shiver down my spine and my mind started reeling. I grabbed a piece of paper and drew a line down its center. On one side I wrote my name; on the other I wrote Jim's. Then, in each column, I created a bullet-point list of what each of us would have to do in order to make it work.

I called Jim back as soon as I got home. "Listen," I said, "I've had some time to think about it. When the news from the trial comes out Monday night, I want there to be a message of love, not hate, and respect instead of ignorance. We have to do this angel thing."

"OK," Jim said ferociously. "What can I do?"

"A couple of things," I said. "First, I need you to get in touch with whatever contacts you have at the Laramie police department and find out if it would even be legal for us to do this. After that, your job is to find some people in Laramie who'd be willing to be angels—like 20 or so. The most important thing is that we get as much diversity in the mix as possible, so we need gay, straight, black, Asian, guys, girls, everything. We need this group to not just represent gay people but humankind, to show that hate affects everyone."

"All right," Jim said. "Sounds good. What are you going to do?"

"I'm going to figure out how to build these motherfuckers."

The next morning at the coffee shop I was all hyped up on adrenaline. As the regulars trickled in, many of whom were discussing the upcoming trial, I told them about the plan. Like my coworkers at the comic book company, they were immediately fascinated, and a lot of them offered to help.

A gentleman by the name of Ron Wilcoxen, who was in the process of refurbishing his house, approached the counter and said he'd overheard my idea. He was a lanky, unassuming man with salt-and-pepper hair, and he asked in his most unobtrusive voice, "How are you planning to build the costumes?"

"I'm going to get big sheets of cardboard," I said, "and cut them down into the shape of wings. Then I'm going to spray-paint them white then sprinkle some feathers and glitter on them that will be held down with glue."

"That sounds interesting," he said, "but I have an idea that might work better. Let me think about it overnight and I'll bring in a prototype for you tomorrow."

The next morning Ron walked into the coffee shop proudly holding what looked like the skeletal remains of pterodactyl wings. Despite my puzzled look, he showed me the shoulder harness, then put the contraption on. When worn like a backpack, the bony wings, made out of the thin plastic piping he used to fix the plumbing in his bathroom climbed at a 45-degree angle, above both shoulders. At a foot or so above his head, the piping was connected by a plastic joint to more piping that stretched out horizontally for about three-and-a-half feet in each direction. I stared for a few seconds but still didn't quite get it.

"Don't you see?" he said. "If you drape some sort of white fabric down from the piping, you have wings. Angel wings!"

"Brilliant!" I shouted. "Oh, my God, Ron—it's just brilliant. Any idea how much of that piping stuff we're going to need to make, like, 20 of these?"

"Leave that to me." His smile was enormous, and he was trembling a little. "I'll get the piping; you get the fabric and enough people together to build 20 of these babies."

"Great," I said, "let's meet at my place tomorrow night around 7."

I began my search for 45 white bedsheets after work that Friday afternoon, raiding the linen section of every Wal-Mart, Target, and Bed Bath & Beyond within 30 miles of Denver. I had roughly $350 left from the $1,000 *Vanity Fair* had paid me, and I was going to spend every last dime of it on the angels.

Dave Cullen, a reporter for Salon.com, has a mild-mannered stubbornness about him that makes for pleasant company. So I was happy to oblige when he called that Saturday before Easter to request an interview about the upcoming Henderson trial. However, I told him, I would be in the middle of a project while we talked. He promised not to get in the way.

Ron dropped off the plastic piping and other costume materials at my apartment late that afternoon just as Dave and I were beginning the interview. Having been shown how to measure and cut the piping, I set to work in hopes of getting a jump start on things before Ron came back with my friends Chris, Ladd, and Roland. They all wanted to help make the angels then come to Laramie with me to be part of the counterprotest. It was slow going in the beginning as I tried to thoughtfully answer Dave's questions while working the plastic pipes with a cutter that clearly wasn't working. In a fit of frustration I threw the piping on the floor and called Ron. Twenty minutes later he and the rest of the group—the founding angels—were at my door with a power saw.

All of a sudden my apartment was aflutter with activity. I measured the pieces to be cut, Ron worked the saw, Chris and Ladd glued and jointed the things together, and Roland ran around making sure everyone's beer glass was full. At one point Dave set down his tape recorder and pad and jumped in to help. It was a beautiful thing to watch an "unbiased" reporter totally lose his composure and get caught up in the moment. I remember standing back for a minute to take in the scene. We were like little elves in Santa's workshop, all smiling and giddy with the knowledge that we were about to do something good. As I watched those angels being born, I realized their full power—not only in their ability to block out Phelps and his group but also in what they would symbolize: compassion, hope, and love.

We finished after midnight, tied the costumes together, and loaded them into Ron's truck. With the trial set to begin Monday afternoon, we were leaving for Laramie the following morning, Sunday, in order to give ourselves a full day of preparation. On his way out, Dave asked me if I'd prepared a release.

"A what?"

"A press release," he said, "to let the media know why you're there."

"No," I said, "I had no idea I needed one."

He looked at me with affection. "Well, you do. It's important. Come to my house before you leave tomorrow and we'll write one up."

We got to Jim's house in Laramie around 5 P.M., on Easter Sunday. He had assembled a group of local activists and friends who wanted to be angels and laid out a table full of refreshments for the meeting.

By that point Matthew's parents and I had separately agreed to work with a company called New Light Media that was putting together a documentary called *Journey to a Hate Free Millennium*, with Matthew's murder at the center of it. They'd caught wind of the angels and asked me if they could film the meeting at Jim's house, our preparations the following morning, and our costumed walk to the courthouse. I agreed.

Watching myself on that tape now, five years later, is amazing. I had such energy, such determination, as I zipped around the house, gathering would-be angels into the living room, where I was about to go over the rules.

As I saw the apprehension on their faces, I thought about the conversation I'd had with my mother that day, a sort of bubble-bursting reality check. I'd been so focused on putting the angels together that I forgot to call her and tell her what was going on. When I finally got her on the phone and told her, she said, almost without skipping a beat, "Why don't you just paint a big target on yourself that says SHOOT ME?"

"What?" I said, shaking my head.

"You've got to stop going out there and telling people that you're gay," she went on. "Didn't you learn anything from Matthew? People don't like gay people, and I'm worried it's going to happen to you too."

That blew me away. "Mom," I said. "We're going to do something good here."

"I don't see how it's doing any good. You're putting yourself in harm's way, and for what reason?"

I wished my mother could have been there with me in Jim's living room. Among those people, with all of their nervousness and fear, the reason for doing the angels was as clear as it ever would be—because it was the right thing to do. They understood as I understood: that so often people are faced with the opportunity to do the right thing and, for whatever reason, don't. This was our chance to take that opportunity—and we all felt terrific about it.

I wanted so much to inspire and energize them and to make

them believe as strongly as I did in what we were about to do. Almost everyone was sitting on Jim's beat-up couch, a couple of people were standing next to it, and they all nodded their heads in unison. I could tell as they stared at me—some blankly, some excitedly—that they were waiting to hear me say the words that would let them know this was going to work. "We are going to bring a visual image to the nation that is really important," I said. "This is the message that *should* come across. I'm really excited about this, and I think it will be powerful beyond our control. But in order to carry this off, there are a few rules we have to follow.

"First, we are allowed to surround Phelps, but we are not allowed to hold hands—that's a legal issue. This man, it turns out, was a lawyer at one point. He knows the law, and he will use it against us, so keep your hands to yourself.

"Second, if you hit or touch them in any way, they will sue you. That's one of the ways they raise funds for themselves, so keep your wits, and remember, we are there as a display of love, peace, and compassion.

"Third, we are a counterprotest, so we aren't allowed to say any-thing—one word to any crowd that gathers will get us thrown out of there.

"Fourth, I will act as the spokesperson for the group, so if the press speaks to any of you, just send them my way. One person speak-ing for the group will ensure that our message doesn't get blurred.

"Finally, I want you all to go home tonight and think of a happy thought. You are going to need to call on that probably many times as you are standing in front of that son of a bitch tomorrow, so make it a really good one."

29 | *The Power of Angels*

The morning of the trial, my sister Trish let the angels meet at her store, the Jaded Lair, in downtown Laramie, a New Age place that sold crystals, dream catchers, and miniature fountains. Though the Henderson trial wasn't set to begin until mid afternoon, Phelps and his group were going to begin their protest on the lawn of the courthouse at 7 A.M. The angels agreed to meet at 6, so Ron, Roland, Chris, Ladd, Jim, and I got there at 5:30. The documentary crew for *Journey to a Hate Free Millennium* was set up and waiting for us by the time we got there. The five of us had assembled all of the costumes the night before, including golden heart-speckled halos, so that as the angels arrived, all they would need to do is slip into their harnesses and have the sheets draped over them.

As the angels trickled in, I flitted around making sure harnesses were securely fastened and helping Jim bobby-pin halos. What a charge! Whatever fear had existed among us the day before had been transformed into excitement. We all laughed when someone discovered a lopsided wing or a harness that just wouldn't fit on a shoulder, but there was a sense of reflection too, a sense that we all were doing something big.

In the documentary, as the angels are beginning to file out of the cramped storeroom of the Jaded Lair, someone is draping the middle part of the costume over me as I'm talking to the camera. On the verge of tears, I say, "When I first thought this up, I didn't *know* that I'd be seeing this. This really is something. They're beautiful and they're wonderful. They're angelic."

The doors opened and the documentary cameras followed us into the alley next to the store. The light from outside hit the lens in a way that created, at least on the video, such a stark contrast to the dark indoors that as the angels turned to fit through the door and walk out, it really did look as though they were walking sideways into a great white light. The angels, all of us in full costume by then, arranged ourselves in a circle. Smiling at my ingenious trick, I then pulled out a box filled with earplugs that I handed around. "You can put them in now," I said, "or wait till you feel like you need them. Look at the heavens and remember your happy thought if you get angry or sad or your emotions start to overcome you. Remember, you are silent, you are a visual, you are a message."

We all stood silently for a moment and collected our thoughts. "Anyone who wants to share their happy thought can do so now," I then said. "I'll start. Matthew, be with us today to continue your light, to continue your path. I know in my heart of hearts that I do this for you and I do this for my beliefs. I can't thank you enough for the gifts you have given me."

Next to me was Sue, who almost constantly had one hand on her halo because she was sure it was going to fall off; as the oldest in our group, she said, "I'm here for my children. I'm here for all children and I'm here for all families."

The woman next to her, Niki, the most bundled-up of all of us in her turtleneck, sweater, jacket, and thick wool gloves, said as she too fought back tears, "I'm doing this for my daughter, her name is Alana. I hope that in the future she has a beautiful world to live in, where we don't have to do this anymore."

Next to her stood a short young girl named Katie. She was probably my favorite of the original angels because of her quiet innocence. She had a shaved head and a wonderfully childlike voice. Her ears and cheeks were turning red in the frosty air of that morning. She said, "I'm not going to say anything except for..." then she put her hand over her mouth and blew a kiss at the sky.

Jim stood next to her. He took a minute to think before he spoke, and when he did, his voice was soft. "One of the things that bothers me most about Matt's death," he said, "is that he's silent now. He doesn't have a voice to speak out. So now I feel like it's my duty to speak out for him. I'm here for Matt today. I just can't stand by and let messages of prejudice about him go unanswered, because he was an incredible person. So that's my happy thought for the day. My friend Matt."

Then it was time to line up the angels and walk the four or so blocks to the courthouse. I had only one thing in my mind as we formed our single file: It was an image of Judy and Dennis Shepard. This day, the day of the trial in which they would hear graphic testimony from one of the boys who murdered their son, would quite possibly be the hardest day of their lives. I felt such a sense of protectiveness for them, and I knew that if the roles had been reversed, Matthew would have done everything in his power to shield my parents. With all my heart and soul, I *needed* to make sure that when Judy and Dennis Shepard walked into the courthouse they did not have to see Fred Phelps.

As we began to walk, there were some almost comical hitches we hadn't taken into consideration. First, because the wings were so big and, well, effective, it was almost impossible to communicate with the person directly behind you. From the front of the line I'd turn my head as far as I could, hope my halo pins didn't pop off, and scream directions to the angel behind me. If she understood a word of it, she did the same thing—and the message went on back. It was like playing a game of telephone, and I could only imagine what "We're turning left up here!" had turned into by the time the message reached the back of the line.

Another little wrinkle was the fragility of the costume. In order to ensure that the entire thing didn't fall apart, you sort of had to contort your body into it then walk in such a way that no part had to bend or endure any stress. That meant waddling— honchoing forward, sticking your ass out behind you, and walk- ing hip over hip.

We also had to deal with three stoplights. Because we all want- ed to stay together as a group, this meant gathering at an inter- section then—like a gaggle of geese—waddle-running across it. We waved at the confused citizens of Laramie who sat waiting in their cars, then resumed our single file.

Unless you've done it, you can't know what it's like to strut down the street with a seven-foot wingspan. That day I waddle- strutted with the most overwhelming amount of pride I have ever felt. I had a band of angels behind me, and they were the fiercest warriors of all. I beamed as we made our way, shouting "Oh, my God, look out for the mirror on that fucking truck!" and "Ahhh! Watch out for that stop sign!"

As we approached the courthouse we began passing the satel- lite trucks from various news outlets. The trucks completely blocked our view of Phelps and his group. As we turned the cor- ner onto the lawn we saw that almost all of the reporters, camer- apeople, and photographers had their eyes trained on Fred and his signs. There were a dozen or so policemen and a growing number of groups of civilians surrounding him, all with their backs to us. None of them saw us coming. I was able to read some of the group's signs as we approached. They said AIDS CURES FAGS, GOD HATES FAGS, NO SPECIAL LAWS FOR FAGS, and FAGS DOOM NATIONS. I was the first one of us to see them, and I closed my eyes for just a second and hoped my angels would be able to take it. Then I hoped I would be.

We walked slowly to the chain-link bull pen that separated Phelps from everyone else, careful not to trip over the wires from satellite trucks and media tents. All of a sudden, one reporter turned around and saw me. She sort of gasped then said, loud enough for all to hear, "What is this?" She and a few others took a step toward me, and as she moved away from the fence, I saw Phelps's face.

He wore a white cowboy hat. Straggly strands of frizzy gray hair hung down from underneath it, framing jaw muscles clenched into golf ball–size knots. His cheeks were a pale, snowy color and looked as though they had never seen a day's growth of beard, with skin so thin you could almost see his skull. And he looked hideous, like a lifetime of hate had aged him grotesquely.

Phelps was right in the middle of saying something but stopped when he saw me. He looked fearful. Our eyes locked for just a second, and I almost chuckled. In that second I saw him for exactly what he is, a silly and sad old man who has never known love. I wasn't afraid for my angels anymore because it was clear Fred Phelps had no power over us. The man couldn't touch us if he tried.

It took the media a minute to catch up. They'd been prepared to see Phelps—he'd sent press releases to all of them announcing his arrival—but nobody knew we were going to be there. As they moved away from the bullpen to make room for us, we slid into place and, one at a time, turned our backs on Phelps and his group. In a flash, all their ugliness was gone.

"Who are you guys? What are you doing here?" the reporters wanted to know. They were now unable to see Phelps, let alone get to him.

"Give us a minute to get situated," I said. "We're going to hold a press conference in just a minute."

I turned to make sure all my angels were in place. Some were putting in earplugs. Others had tears rolling down their faces. But anyone who was crying was also smiling—and it was clear they were tears of pride.

Dave Cullen, the reporter from Salon.com, ran up and handed me a piece of paper. That past Sunday morning he'd taped me talking about what I thought should go in our press release. "This is it," he said. "This is what you wanted to say." He was beaming and looked like he wanted to say more, to cheer me on in some way, but we both knew there wasn't time.

I pulled the slip of paper out of his hand. "Thanks," I said. I wanted to hug him, but it would have been impossible in the costume, so I smiled and nodded. Then it was off to the media.

I read it over quickly, then took a few steps forward and waited as the hushed media gathered around. There were more cameras than I could count and more expectant reporters than I had ever seen in one place. I took a deep breath.

"Ladies and gentlemen, please allow me to introduce myself. My name is Romaine Patterson. I am from Denver, Colorado. And I am the bearer of a message. We stand before you as a band of angels. We represent hope for our future. Hope that love, respect, and compassion will be the message brought forth this day. So often we find that people are willing to make a lot of noise about what they believe to be true. Aside from this brief explanatory statement, we don't believe we have to say anything at all. Our actions will speak for themselves. Hatred is running rampant through our everyday lives. That is why the angels are here, because as a group we have chosen to lift ourselves above that hate and deliver a message of love.

"It is important to note that the group is widely diversified and does not represent any one religion, sex, age, race, or sexual orientation. They are merely a group of people who, like myself, could no longer sit idly by and watch others bring forth messages that were nothing more than vindictive and hate-filled. As a young person, I feel it is time to show this nation that there doesn't have to be this kind of hatred in our world. And that loving one another does not have to compromise our beliefs; it simply means that we chose to be compassionate and respectful of others.

"With that said, I would like to rejoin my angels silently. If you have any questions, there is contact information on this press statement, and I will be available after we finish up at UW. Thank you for your time."

As I turned to get back in line, I saw all of the police officers. As we'd been told there would be, about a dozen stood in a line between the angels and Phelps. There were also another few dozen cops milling about the crowd and, I noticed as I looked up, another dozen or so on the courthouse roof and the adjacent building. The cops on the roofs wore bulletproof vests and carried sharpshooting rifles. *Oh, my God,* I thought. *They're snipers.*

Amid applause from some of the reporters and almost all of the civilians present, Cathy Renna, the activist from GLAAD whom I had met at the National Gay and Lesbian Task Force conference, walked up. "Good job," she said, smiling and nodding her head excitedly. "Great job, actually. This is amazing. If you give me your copy of the release, I'll run to Kinko's and make copies for the press." I handed it to her and she was off.

I began to move up and down the line, making sure all of my angels were OK, and every now and then sneaking a look at Phelps's group. There weren't a lot of them, 12 at most, but what was so disturbing was that at least half were children, little boys and girls in pink pompom hats who didn't look old enough to be able to read the hateful signs they held, let alone understand them.

I stopped for a minute in the center and turned to look at the press. They hadn't moved. Some scribbled furiously in their pads, while others wove in and out of the crowd to get the best shot with their cameras. A few had tears in their eyes. Others were full-on sobbing.

I'm sure it's not the case, but I remember that moment as being completely silent. It was a serene, profound, life-changing moment, the likes of which I'd only experienced once before—the moment I closed my eyes while my father poured Michael's ashes into the hole he had dug by the creek. I felt life in that moment. I understood who I was as a human being and the kind of person I wanted to be in the world. I believed in what Matthew had so earnestly tried to explain during our last conversation, that one person can make a difference. And in this case, a group of "one persons" could maybe change the world.

We stayed out there as long as Phelps's people did, which ended up being about two-and-a-half hours before they packed up and headed for the University of Wyoming. They had a little group huddle when they realized what was happening and came to the conclusion that because they wouldn't be seen, they were going to have to yell louder and hold their signs higher. That was one of the images I was hoping a still photographer or cameraperson would capture: an angel with huge wings, a halo, and a solemn face beneath a sign, seemingly held by nobody, that said AIDS CURES FAGS or MATT IN HELL. What a beautiful way to juxtapose our messages.

We had left a small space open on one of the sides of the bull pen for reporters to be able to get to Phelps if they wanted to. By that point a frustrated Phelps had only one message: "These aren't angels, these are devils," he repeated over and over in his odd Southern drawl. "They do not represent God. These are not God's angels, these are fallen angels. These angels are sending this nation to hell in a handbasket—in a yella handbasket."

I think I even felt a little sorry for him.

When the reporters lost interest in the group, the group turned to taunting the angels. When they saw that Katie, my favorite one with the shaved head, had forgotten her coat and was shivering, Phelps stood right behind her and started to yell, "Girl, don't you know nothin' 'bout protestin'? You gotta wur a coat, girl, put a hat on your head." Then they moved on and found another angel to pick on. I walked up and down the line during that time. "Folks, don't forget to use your earplugs if you need them," I reminded. "Remember your happy thoughts!"

The people of Laramie were great to us, though before I held my press conference some thought we were actually with Phelps's group. People honked their car horns and cheered as they drove by; others ran home and brought back thermoses of hot chocolate to help us keep warm. One woman brought a thick winter coat for Katie.

We followed Phelps up the eight blocks to the university, but because they drove and we had to waddle, dodging stop signs and side-view mirrors, they were well set up and into their protest by the time we got there. The university had sectioned off an even smaller section of lawn for them. There was also a much smaller police presence and a much larger presence of angry young people, many of whom had actually known Matthew and who didn't necessarily care if they ended up in jail. The situation was clearly escalating toward violence when the angels arrived.

Initially, like the people at the courthouse, the students thought we were a part of Phelps's entourage, so I quickly grabbed my copy of the press release and read it to everyone. Our presence seemed to settle things down considerably, though those students who were intent on yelling at Phelps found ways of doing so. At one point the university president came out to thank us. Several professors brought cookies and sandwiches.

It finally ended around 1, when Phelps and his group, defeated, decided it was time to pack it in. The angels were all so relieved, if for no other reason than it meant we could take off our costumes. The wings were light and easy to maneuver, but after the first couple of hours they began to feel like lead. All of our shoulders were sore.

As we dismantled the costumes, some of the students wanted to try them on. Once dressed in a halo and a pair of wings, they frolicked and danced around, their sheets flapping carelessly in the breeze.

All of the original angels, many university students, and several other supporters lined up on the sidewalk to wave at Phelps and his group as they drove away. We all wore big smiles that said *You just got your asses kicked.* People jumped up and down and cheered. One girl even got down on her hands and knees with a bucket of water and scrubbed the sidewalk where Phelps's people had loaded their truck.

"Good riddance," I heard her say as she scrubbed. "Good fucking riddance."

30 | *The Trial*

After helping pack up Ron's truck with the costumes, I grabbed a quick bite to eat and headed down to the courthouse with Chris and Ladd.

The security required just to get into the building was intense. There was a series of metal detectors and friskings. We all had to empty our pockets more than once. It seemed everyone and his dog wanted a seat in that courtroom. Each would-be attendee had to check in at a security desk where he or she was given an index card with his or her name and a number on it. When the number on the cards reached a certain point, it meant that the room would be at capacity and nobody else would be allowed in.

When I told the man behind the desk that my name was Romaine Patterson, he checked for my name on a list, stamped the word RESERVED on it, then wrote the number 3 in the corner. I found out later that the list had been written by Judy Shepard. She wanted me sitting next to her on the other side of Dennis.

I saw a lot of familiar faces as the courtroom crowd began to congregate in the lobby. Leigh Fondakowski and Greg Pierotti, my long-lost interviewers from the theater group in New York, came over to say hi. They told me that they were going to be back in town in a few weeks with Moisés Kaufman, the artistic director of their group, Tectonic Theater Project, and that they'd like to interview me again. I said that would be fine. I also saw Cathy Renna, who took me around and introduced me to some of the press. And I saw Reggie Fluty, the female officer who'd been first on the scene when Matthew was found. I recognized her from the papers and wanted to introduce myself, but just as I was making my way over, the doors opened and we were instructed to start filing in.

Judy and Dennis Shepard were already seated in the first row on the left side. As we walked in, someone placed a hand on my shoulder and said, "You're going to be sitting over there, next to Judy."

I was nervous. I hadn't seen Judy since March, when we had sat together at a Human Rights Campaign dinner in Denver. But I was honored that she'd thought of me, and I went and took my place. Dennis had his arm around her when I sat down. She looked at me and didn't say anything for a second. Then, almost in a whisper, she said, "Oh, Romaine, it's so nice to see you." She gave me a hug; I noticed she smelled like flowers, and I almost crumbled. I leaned over and shook Dennis's hand. He didn't speak, but he looked me in the eye and we nodded to each other. His forehead was wrinkled as if he'd had his eyebrows raised for the last six months, and there were the beginnings of little dark circles under his eyes. I thought he looked more tired than Judy, then remembered that unlike Judy, he hadn't been able to stay in the United States after Matthew's memorial service. Poor Dennis must have just made the grueling 19-hour flight back from Saudi Arabia for the trial.

It took only a few minutes for the room to fill up. The media was not allowed to bring in any recording devices, so everywhere you looked there was someone with a pad and a pencil. The atmosphere was uncomfortably solemn. There was absolutely no talking and no movement. It was as if any sound at all would have detracted from the seriousness of the event. And there was a feeling of anticipation in the air, as if everyone were thinking, *Let's get this started so we can get this over with.*

The door next to the witness stand in the front left corner of the room opened, and the defense team for Russell Henderson walked in. First was Wyatt Skaggs, Henderson's chief trial counsel, a nondescript man in a cheap-looking suit. Behind him was Jane Eakin from the public defender's office. Eakin, with long platinum-blond hair and wearing a knee-length black leather skirt, looked more like a call girl than a lawyer. Behind her was Henderson himself.

When he entered the room there was a quiet collective gasp from those of us in the benches. It was just loud enough to be heard among those of us who were watching but not loud enough for Henderson to hear. Nobody wanted to give him that satisfaction. He was wearing a navy-blue suit and a tie. He was clean-shaven and had obviously been given a haircut in the last couple of days. That was the first time I had seen him in person, and I was actually surprised at how different he looked up close. He gave the impression of an all-American boy who should have been in his early years of college—well-raised and mild-mannered, not at all like the type who could have done those things to Matthew. Though he walked right in front of us on his way to the defense table, he didn't as much as glance at Judy and Dennis as he passed. But they looked at him. Wrapped in each other's arms, they took a good hard look.

As he sat down, I noticed he wasn't handcuffed, which seemed kind of odd. He slouched in his seat, didn't look at a soul, and held perfectly still—as if willing himself to be invisible. I couldn't take my eyes off him, and I couldn't stop thinking, *You did this, you little fucker.*

Up to that point everybody expected the prosecution to pursue the death penalty for both Henderson and McKinney. Jury selection for Henderson's trial had begun the day before and would have continued that day and the next except that, for reasons unknown, Henderson had requested an audience with the judge that day. It quickly became clear, to the shock of everyone in the room (except Judy and Dennis, who were privy to every detail of the case), that Henderson was there to change his plea from not guilty to guilty. He wanted to avoid a trial he knew he couldn't win.

After explaining to Henderson the ramifications of changing his plea, the judge said, "You entered a not guilty plea earlier, Mr. Henderson. I understand you wish to change your plea today, is that correct?"

"Yes, sir," Henderson, now standing, said meekly.

In the stunned silence that followed, all that could be heard was the scribbling of pens on paper. The reporters, it seemed, couldn't write fast enough. I didn't move. Judy and Dennis had obviously offered some sort of plea bargain, and as the judge continued to speak, it was all I could do to keep up.

"All right. Mr. Rerucha," the judge said to the county prosecutor, a heavier-set man with graying hair who'd been flipping through his legal notepad since before Henderson entered the room. "I understand there is a plea agreement. Would you state that for the record, please."

Mr. Rerucha stood. "Yes, your honor," he said. "Mr. Henderson will plead guilty to felony murder reflecting robbery as the underlying felony. He will also plead guilty to the additional charge of kidnapping. There will be a life sentence for the felony murder and a life sentence for the kidnapping. Whether terms run consecutive or concurrent will be a matter of argument and left to the judge."

A murmur of understanding swept through the crowd. Judy

and Dennis had decided *not* to pursue the death penalty.

A few minutes later Henderson was called to the witness stand, where he was questioned by Mr. Rerucha. Though he recounted what happened the night of October 6 step-by-step, the details of the beating were minimal, and as far as I'm concerned, the same old questions went unanswered. Why did Matthew Shepard leave with you that night? Where did he think you were going? Nonetheless, the Shepards paid very close attention. Over the course of the testimony, I heard Judy weeping softly.

When the questioning was done, and after Henderson's grandmother made a statement for the family, the judge informed Henderson that he had a constitutional right to make a statement if he'd like to do so. Henderson stood behind the defense table and, making a halfhearted attempt to look at the Shepards, said:

"Mr. and Mrs. Shepard, there is not a moment that goes by that I don't see what happened that night. I know what I did was very wrong, and I regret greatly what I did. You have my greatest sympathy for what happened. I hope that you will one day be able to find it in your heart to forgive me.

"To my family, thank you so much for everything. Thank you for being there for me through this. And I hope you can also one day forgive me.

"Your honor, I know what I did was wrong. I'm very sorry for what I did, and I'm ready to pay my debt for what I did. Thank you."

I thought about it for a second then decided it was the most disingenuous load of crap I'd ever heard. There wasn't an ounce of sympathy, compassion, or remorse in his voice. The Shepards were like stone statues by then, completely inert as they listened.

"Mr. Rerucha, I understand that the Shepards would like to make a statement," the judge said.

"Yes, they do, your honor."

"Go ahead, Mrs. Shepard."

I moved over a little to make room for Judy. She stood and spoke about how much Matt had meant to both her and Dennis, about his hopes and dreams, about how he had never judged people before fully knowing them. She spoke poignantly about how much she loved her son and how now that Matt was gone there was a "hole in her existence." She then turned to Henderson directly and told him that he wasn't worthy of any acknowledgment of his existence, that he had murdered her son and had forever changed her family.

I was sobbing by the time she was finished, and I don't imagine there was anyone present who was not.

"Mr. Shepard," Mr. Rerucha said.

Dennis stood to speak. He repeated Judy's statements about how nonjudgmental Matt had been, and he spoke eloquently about how his son had reached out to others who he thought needed a friend. Then Dennis, like Judy, spoke directly to Henderson, telling him he had created a hole in his life that could never be filled.

I had my elbows on my knees and my face in my hands by the time Dennis was finished. Judy, very gently, put a hand on my leg.

I sat up and pulled myself together as the attorneys made their closing statements. It was reiterated that Henderson would spend the rest of his life in prison because of the two life sentences. However, it would be symbolically more severe if the sentences were served consecutively rather than concurrently. That was now what the judge was going to decide. The judge cleared his throat:

"Many people have called this a hate crime. Quite frankly, the court does not find this matter to be so simplistic. For it is quite clear that a number of motives and emotions were involved here: rage, callousness, greed, brutishness, and perhaps others.

"Mr. Henderson, you drove the vehicle that took him to his death. You bound him to that fence in order that he might be more savagely beaten and in order that he might not escape to tell his tale.

"The court finds, Mr. Henderson, that this was a most heinous crime, savage and brutal in its nature, and evidencing a total lack of respect for the dignity of human life, all life, whether different from your own or not, and, quite frankly, deserving the fullest punishment that this court can mete out.

"The pain you have caused here, Mr. Henderson, will never go away. Never. There may be days from time to time when people won't think about this or remember this, but it will always be here.

"Sentencing for count 1 is to run consecutive to sentencing for count 3."

With that the proceedings ended. Henderson was handcuffed and led away. I wanted to clap. Almost immediately Mr. Rerucha grabbed Dennis—who gave Judy a quick kiss—and took him away to prepare for the press conference. A bailiff rushed over to Judy and me. "Please follow me," he said, leading us to a private room where another of the Shepards' attorneys was waiting. Standing quietly by a window that overlooked the lawn where that morning a group of angels had confronted hatred with love, I listened to what Judy had to say. She felt that the trial had gone well and that there was a good chance that Henderson would testify against McKinney at his trial in the fall.

When she and her lawyer were done talking, Judy came and stood with me at the window. Looking out at the lawn, which teemed with reporters gearing up for the press conference, I said, "What did you think of the angels?"

"Oh, Romaine, they were great," she said. "We watched them from right here."

"You did?" I said. "I wasn't sure you'd seen them."

"One of the lawyers came and grabbed us," she said. "He was like, 'Oh, my God, you've got to come see this.'"

I didn't know what else to say, so I smiled at her. And she smiled back. She turned back to the window, perhaps for a quiet moment of reflection. I thought about all the work she'd done and the sacrifices she'd made in Matthew's name since his death. With the money sent by strangers to help cover Matthew's medical costs, she and Dennis started the Matthew Shepard Foundation, a nonprofit organization whose mission is to put an end to hatred and discrimination. (Nearly seven years later, she is still the foundation's executive director.) Judy gave up her comfortable life in Saudi Arabia to carry out that work, and I didn't know how or where she found the strength to be so proactive during a time of such sadness.

The press conference took place almost immediately following the hearing. We were taken downstairs when it was the Shepards' turn to speak, walking out the front doors of the courthouse just as the defense team was finishing in front of the microphones and cameras. I stepped off to the side to be with Chris, Ladd, and Ron as Mr. Rerucha began to speak. Judy and Dennis, back in each other's arms, stood to the left of him.

A group of reporters gathered around me when the official press conference was over. "Do you think justice was served here today?"

"Yes," I said. "Obviously, the punishment best suits the family."

When all was said and done I said a quick goodbye to Judy and Dennis, and our little band from Denver got back in our cars and headed home. The only thing more overwhelming than that day was the idea of going home to an empty apartment that night. I thought about Roni and how great it would be to have her with me that day. She'd have made such a great angel—even though she'd have definitely lost her cool, hopped the barricade, and beaten Phelps's ass. Then I thought about Shannon and how much I missed her. I couldn't wait to get home to call her and tell her all about the experience. But a phone call was not a warm body. Despite my elation at having pulled off the angels, a big part of me felt terrifyingly hollow and sad.

The next morning Chris and Ladd came in to see me at the coffee shop, each carrying a stack of newspapers and Web articles.

"What is all this?" I asked.

"The angels are everywhere," Ladd said as he tossed me a copy of *The Denver Post*. The Henderson trial was the cover story, and there was a picture of the angels in the upper right-hand corner.

"This is all the stuff we found on the Internet," Chris said, handing me what must've been an entire ream of paper.

"And you'll never believe this," Ladd said.

"What?" I asked.

"We were the number 1 story on BBC last night."

"Yeah," Chris said. "We beat out the war in Kosovo."

31 | *The Fence*

Several weeks later, near the end of May, I was back in Laramie with the documentary crew for *Journey to a Hate Free Millennium.* Early on I'd decided never to visit the fence where Matthew was killed, but I agreed to go when producer Brent Scarpo told me Judy and Dennis Shepard wanted the three of us to go together. However, on the appointed day, as the Shepards were being interviewed for another segment of the film, they decided they weren't yet ready to see it after all.

When I was told it was going to be just me, my first instinct was to back out. But Brent insisted that a visual of me at the fence would drive home the importance of my friendship with Matthew. "Romaine," he coaxed, "this image is vital to the central message of the film."

I told him I wanted a few minutes to think about it then stepped outside with Shannon—who, knowing I'd need support that day, had insisted on flying out to be with me.

"I feel like I don't have a choice," I said, as I paced around in a little circle.

She took my hand and made me be still. "Honey," she said, "you *always* have a choice."

"I know," I said, "but he's making me feel like I'm going to ruin his movie if I don't do it."

"Well, hey," she said, "if you're gonna do it, just remember, I'll be there with you the whole time—I'll hold your hand the entire way if you want."

I thought about it for a second. "Yeah?"

"Yeah." Then she flashed the smile that always jump-started my confidence.

The crew was small—two cameramen, a still photographer, executive producer Martin Bedogne, and Brent. As Shannon and I were climbing into one of the two Four Runners they'd loaded to make the trip to the fence that afternoon, Brent stopped us. "Actually," he said, reviewing his notes, not looking at me, "I need Romaine to come alone with the camera crew and me. Shannon can ride in the other car if she wants."

I looked over at Shannon, who scowled and shook her head. "Ah, OK," I said, "but the whole point of her being here was to be able to support me."

"Yeah," he said, looking up at me briefly before returning to his notes, "but you alone are a much better visual, don't you think?" Then before I could answer, "And when we get up there, you should probably walk to the fence yourself. Shannon, you hang back by the cars, OK? Out of the view of the cameras." And with that he turned back around in his seat.

I stood there for a second, stunned by his insensitivity, then turned to look at Shannon, who was still standing outside the car. Her arms were crossed at her chest, and she looked ready to pitch a fit. "I'll be OK," I said.

"You sure?"

"Yeah, I'm sure. I'll see you up there."

Brent fired question after question at me the entire 15-minute drive. I tried to listen, to offer a response he'd be able to use, but was having a hard time focusing. As we drove past the Wal-Mart, one of the last recognizable symbols of ordinary human life that Matthew ever saw, and onto the dirt road that led to the fence, so many things were on my mind. *Here I am*, I thought, *jammed into a car with a microphone stuffed down my shirt, a camera in my face, and a producer firing questions at me from the front seat. What if I have no reaction? What if I get to the fence and feel nothing? What if I can't cry?*

It was slow going once we turned onto the dirt road that led to the fence. Months of pilgrimages to "the place where Matthew Shepard had been left to die" had taken its toll on what had already been a bumpy path. We bounced and shook as we drove, and I thought, *Matthew felt this.* Listening to the sound of my own breathing in the microphone, I wondered, *Was Matthew fighting by now?* Maybe by that point, by the time those two boys drove over that crater-size bump in the road, Matthew was yelling. Or maybe he was already begging by then. Either way, he had been there.

"How are you feeling? What's going through your mind right now?" Brent wanted to know.

I wanted to tell him, "Just shut up and be an observer. Please, just let me experience this moment." Instead, I told him, "I'm fine."

I had positioned myself in the middle of the backseat to see clearly through the windshield as we drove. There were a lot of rocks in the road, I noticed, as we ascended a small hill. Then, as the rise gave way to a sort of plateau, I saw it. The fence. It sat, amid patches of dry green grass and mounds of chocolate-brown dirt, in the middle of the place where the road ends and gives way to the prairie. It looked different in real life, less foreboding, possessing none of the human evil I associated it with. This fence was just a rickety old structure, crudely built, and connected to nothing. It looked like it served no purpose.

But it had served a purpose. That was why I was there.

I got out of the car when they told me to and looked behind me to locate Shannon. She waved when I flashed her a *God help me* smile. "See you in a minute!" she called out.

As I stared at the fence, I saw a house about 200 yards behind it. It was brown and modest-looking, and had what looked like an entire wall made of glass. This wall faced the fence. I turned and looked out from in front of the fence to see what Matthew would have seen. In the distance were rows of backyards, backyards of the houses that made up a little neighborhood. All I had read about that place led me to believe that it was open prairie, miles from civilization, and that no amount of screaming that Matthew could have done would have made a difference. Granted, it was nighttime when he was out there, and it's possible, even probable, that the houses in either direction were so far away that he wouldn't have been able to see them and vice versa. But I had to ponder, at least for a second, the idea that he had seen a porch light or some other indicator that taunted him with the possibility of getting out of that mess alive.

I started to move toward the fence. Two cameramen, one in front of me and one in back, moved with me. I heard a click from the still photographer in the bushes to the left of the fence. I again thought about the microphone and how silly it would sound if I cried too loud. I tried to create a bubble around myself. *I am alone here*, I decided. *I won't see anything but the fence. I won't hear anything but the wind.*

By the time I reached the fence there was no controlling my sorrow, so I let it come. At my feet was a cross made of rocks someone had made. Tied to the fence were pink and yellow ribbons, beaded rosaries, and bouquets of flowers. Beneath it was a basket of dried roses that had been blown over by a breeze, scattering the purplish petals around the base of the fence, a place I knew had once been saturated with Matthew's blood.

Shuddering with tears, I knelt down to lay my head on one of the posts. It felt rough against my cheek, and I couldn't help but think of Matthew tied to it—grabbing at it, trying to twist his body to defend himself. I closed my eyes and tried to imagine what it would be like to be at peace there. In that moment of surrender I felt a breeze on my face. *Was this the same breeze Matthew felt?*

As I gripped the fence and continued to cry, I thought about the circumstance—the road that seemed to lead nowhere that led to the fence with no purpose. And I thought about the events of the previous six months—my last conversation with Matthew, his death and how it was changing the world, and the events that led me to a place where I was able to tell the world about him. It all seemed to fall into place for me then. I can honestly say that as I knelt on the ground where Matthew had lain, as I clutched the fence and cried over the loss of my friend, it became clear to me, beyond a shadow of a doubt, that Matthew had fulfilled his destiny.

I wept until I was exhausted. Then I got up, dusted off the knees of my jeans, and went over to Shannon and let her hold me. Brent tried to ask more questions, but I turned to him and said, "I want to go now." He tried to ignore that. And so I said more forcefully *"Now!"* and climbed with my girlfriend back into the car.

I told Judy and Dennis about my experience at the fence and my feeling of Matthew's destiny later that day. Of course, it may not have been the best or most appropriate time for sharing my revelation, but they were receptive nonetheless. Judy listened intently—nodding with her eyes glazed over in a way that made me think she was trying to picture something. Then she took my hand and held it for a second. I felt relieved then, because more than anything I just wanted to help lessen their fear of going there, to help them understand that, at least for me, the visitation had been healing.

I wondered also if, perhaps, the day would come for them, as it had for me earlier that afternoon, when they would be able to see that while Matthew Shepard had been taken from his family and friends at that fence, it was the same place where he had been given to the world.

32 | Coast to Coast

Once I was back in Denver, it felt like every media contact I ever made wanted to do another story, this one about the angels.

Shannon decided to stay on with me in Denver for the first half of the summer. During that time she became my best friend as well as my closest and most trusted confidant. She always wanted to know how I was emotionally. She wanted to know that I was hugging people and being hugged—that I was not becoming robotic just to cope with all the media attention. She helped me to realize just how sturdy my emotional walls had become—and I began to wonder just how much damage I'd done to myself.

As Shannon's departure date in July approached, I knew I had some tough decisions. She was the first to bring it up one night as we sat on the back porch, drinking tea. "So, what's going to happen to you when I go back to Pennsylvania?"

"I don't really know," I said, though I knew exactly. She had been such a wonderful diversion from the monotony of my routine. Without her there I was sure I'd go back to my miserable existence of working two jobs, answering interview requests for every reporter who asked, and spending whatever free time I had locked in my room talking to the outside world via my computer.

"Do you think…"

"What?" I asked.

"I was just wondering...do you think that maybe you're doing too much for Matthew?"

"What do you mean?"

"I don't know...I was just thinking: The world is never going to forget what happened to him, but eventually we're going to heal and move on. When that happens, what's going to happen to you?"

"I don't really know," I said. "I mean, I know I've sort of lost myself in all of this, but I can't just stop." Or could I? And for the first time in almost a year, I thought maybe I could.

She stopped rubbing my knee, then leaned in close. "Why not?"

"Because," I said, whipping out the stock response she'd heard a hundred times before, "who'd pick up where I left off?"

"I only ask because I wanted to tell you that you're welcome to come with me when I leave. I'd love to have you in Pennsylvania with me."

"You would?"

"Yeah," she told me. "I would."

She left a week or so later, and it took less than a week after that for me to make my decision. I called her and asked if she was serious about her invitation.

"Of course I'm serious!"

"OK," I said, "then I'm gonna do it...I'm coming out to be with you."

And that was that.

After hearing through the family grapevine that I was moving to Pennsylvania, my sister Trish called with some news.

"Remember Leigh and Greg from that little theater project in New York?"

"Of course, why?"

"Well," she said, "they're coming back to Denver to do their final interviews, then they're going to put up a workshop of their play. It's called *The Laramie Project,* and I hear that you're going to be a pretty major character."

"Wow, that's great," I said. "I'll definitely try to get back to Denver before they take it to New York." I got off the phone as quickly as possible.

The truth was that I had no intention of ever seeing that play. I couldn't bear the idea of reliving all those old memories and was secretly relieved to be leaving town.

Shannon flew out in the beginning of August, and in keeping with lesbian tradition, we rented a 5-by-8 U-Haul trailer and towed it behind my car all the way to Pennsylvania. The trip was a disaster from the get-go. Whether it was the trailer's ball bearings cracking, the tires getting all fucked-up, or the car overheating, it seemed we couldn't go 20 miles without some major catastrophe. But I was so happy to be leaving Denver, it didn't matter.

The best thing about Pennsylvania was that I was anonymous there. And for the first time in a long time there was silence in my life—no phones ringing off the hook or answering machines beeping and flashing red lights in my face every time I walked in the door. In a way, I got to be a kid again. I went to parties, stayed out late, and drank too much if I wanted to. It felt like I was having the time of my life.

I still did interviews with reporters who could find me—a number that increased substantially when in August *The Advocate,* the country's leading gay newsmagazine, declared me one of the gay community's "Best and Brightest Activists."

I kept in touch with Jim Osborn in Laramie, who made me promise before I left to come back and do the angels if Phelps returned for Aaron McKinney's trial, which was scheduled for Monday, October 11, a year to the day before Matthew Shepard died. When he called in early October to report the arrival of another "here we come" fax from Phelps, Shannon and I—still broke after the move—took a $60-apiece, 39-hour bus ride to get there.

Our first stop was Fort Collins for the premiere of *Journey to a Hate Free Millennium*, produced by the same Brent Scarpo I'd become so disenchanted with. Mom and Dad met Shannon and me out there to attend it with us. It was nice to be with them, but my father's health was continuing to decline.

The film itself was very well-put-together. It followed the Matthew Shepard case, survivors of the Columbine High School shootings, and relatives of James Byrd Jr., the black man in Jasper, Texas, who died when he was tied to the back of a truck and dragged two miles down a dirt road. Judy's and Dennis's interviews were especially moving, and the footage of the angels brought applause from the audience. During the scene with me at the fence, Mom held my hand and we both cried.

Drained by his radiation treatments, Dad went home the next day—but Mom decided to stay. Having seen how effective the angels were in the documentary, she wanted to come to court on Monday and see them in action. It was quite a shift in attitude from the I'm-afraid-you're-going-to-get-shot speech, and it made me even more proud of our work.

Ask anybody who participated in both angel demonstrations and they'll tell you that the second time had a totally different feel.

For one thing, we knew we weren't surprising anybody that time—and we angels also had a better idea of what to expect. So there was much less tension and apprehension in the air. There were also five more of us, bringing our total to 17, while the number in Phelps's group had dwindled down to six. And though we'd agreed to stand in our own fenced-off area a few yards away from Phelps's group (rather than in front of them), we were no less effective in stealing their thunder. We weren't a counterprotest that time, so we could speak with the townspeople as well as with the press. But it almost wasn't necessary. Nobody was shocked by Phelps that time, and nobody cared what he had to say.

For a number of reasons, I didn't attend McKinney's trial. Sitting through Henderson's had been bad enough, but this was expected to be a lengthy one, not a single-day affair like before—and Shannon and I had to get back to Pennsylvania. I found out later that, like Henderson, McKinney was spared the death penalty in exchange for two life sentences to be served consecutively. In addition, McKinney's plea bargain included a gag order, forbidding him to ever speak publicly about the murder.

Later that evening, back at Trish's house, Leigh and Greg from New York came by for one final interview. They brought Moisés Kaufman, the founder and artistic director of Tectonic Theater Project, and a girl named Kelli Simpkins. Kelli was a tall, square-shouldered woman with gray-blue eyes and a powerful sexual magnetism. The writers hoped she would play me in *The Laramie Project*. She was beautiful, and I was flattered, to say the least.

The five of us and Shannon went out to the backyard and arranged the lawn chairs into a circle while Trish put on a pot of coffee. They told me that they loved the angels—that it had been a beautiful and necessary symbol, and the only effective way Fred Phelps's message could have been stomped out.

"Thanks," I said. "You know, it's interesting; I've done, like, a thousand interviews over the last year, and I really feel like you guys are some of the very few people who really get it."

"Wow," Leigh said. "Thanks, Romaine. Thank you for saying that."

We talked for hours as the sun went down. Moisés asked me the funniest questions in a choppy Slovenian accent so thick that Leigh often had to translate. In addition to asking about my childhood and what age I came out, he wanted to know about high school and my other gay siblings. It seemed that he wanted to know about every aspect of my life. He studied me while I told him stories about my adventures in Principal Edwards's office and my eye-opening summers in Denver. He took note of the way I speak and how I gesture, and seemed especially amused by my laugh.

They let me ramble for at least an hour about how the angels came to be, interjecting questions here and there for the sake of clarity. It was Kelli, who'd been quiet for most of the evening, who asked me about my leather jacket.

"Leigh tells me it's your trademark," she said in her low voice that hinted at a Midwestern accent.

"Yeah," I said. "Ever since my brother Michael died and left it to me, it's just sort of become a part of who I am."

"*Moy*-kal?" Moisés said.

Leigh translated: "He wants you to tell us more about your brother Michael."

And so I told them the whole story.

I gave them each a hug when they left. "Good luck with your play," I told Leigh and Greg. "I'm sure it's going to be big."

33 | *Two Thumbs Up*

Shannon and I had only been back to Pennsylvania for a few weeks when I got a phone call from the Anti-Defamation League, a Washington, D.C.–based organization with a long history of fighting bigotry. Of course, I had no idea who they were. It turned out that every year since 1995 they've held a concert at the Kennedy Center, where a theme is chosen and individual activists selected from a pool of nominees are honored for their work. That year, 1999, the theme was "A Concert for Hope"—recognizing young activists working for a better future. For conceiving the angels and bringing them to life, I was to be one of four young activists honored that year.

They flew Shannon and me from Pennsylvania—as well as Jim from Laramie, because he'd been such an integral part of putting Angel Action together—to D.C. for the event. It was so wonderful to have Jim there to be a part of the celebration. It was hard to know, though, that he was not going to be honored along with me that night—that because I had been the spokesperson for the media, I was getting all the credit. I'd said it to him a hundred times, and I really hoped he'd understood, that I had never wanted it to be that way; that as far as I was concerned we were partners.

My once-wild-but-now-married sister Sabina flew out—as did

my parents, who insisted despite my father's health that they would
be there to see their baby honored in the nation's capital. My father
looked terrible. Stuffed into a suit and tie for the event, he tried to
put on a happy face. His skin was pasty, he walked at a much slow-
er pace, and he complained of a searing pain in his back. Still, he
hadn't lost his proud-papa charm. At the formal dinner that preced-
ed the concert, he asked me to point out one of the other honorees.
I pointed to the table where Chuenée Sampson sat with her family.
Chuenée was being honored for creating an organization called
Students Against Violence Everywhere, or SAVE.

"I'll be right back," Dad said, then he got up and went over to
their table. My family watched in amazement as Dad, gesticulat-
ing almost wildly, had a conversation with, I swear, the first black
family he had ever interacted with. I let it go on for a few minutes,
hoping against hope that he wasn't boring them to death with
embarrassing stories from my childhood, then went over to get
him. "And here she is," he said when I pulled up next to him, putting a protective arm around my shoulder. "This is my daughter.
She's getting an award tonight too."

Cathy Renna from GLAAD joined us for the concert, and we
all took our seats. We listened as the National Symphony
Orchestra played Bernstein's overture to *Candide*—a light, airy
number with overtones of joy and just a hint of darkness, like
something sad is lurking just out of sight.

When it came time for the four of us to be honored, we lined
up on the right-hand side of the stage. The lights were dimmed
and a video screen was lowered to the center of the stage, where a
montage of video clips highlighted what each of us had accom-
plished. There were various news clips of the angels, including one
of me, standing in front of what looked like hundreds of reporters,
reading our first press release.

One by one the honorees were asked to cross to center stage to receive our awards. I was third. When my name was called, I hobbled up awkwardly—as I always did in heels—shook the hostess's hand, and stood staring out at my friends and family while she read a list of my achievements. Cathy and Jim were both beaming at me. Sabina made funny faces, trying to make me laugh while Mom pinched her arm to get her to stop. Dad, when he realized I was looking at him, exploded into a smile and gave me a double thumbs-up. It was the same gesture Michael had made from the back of the room when I won the state speech finals in high school. My father never could have known what that particular gesture meant to me, nor could he have known that for the rest of my life I would remember him flashing it with that proud-papa smile.

After the ceremony was over we all walked out together.

"Now that my daughter's on the East Coast, I hope you'll keep her on the straight and narrow," Dad said to Cathy, who ran GLAAD's D.C. office.

"I can probably do something about the 'narrow' part, but I'm not so sure about the 'straight,' " she quipped.

On the way back to the hotel, Cathy, Shannon and I, and Jim stopped into a café for a cup of coffee. At one point in the conversation, Cathy asked me what I wanted to do next.

"I don't know, go to school maybe." Then, jokingly, I added, "When are you going to give me a job at GLAAD?"

"You want to work at GLAAD?"

"Well, yeah," I said. "Now that I know what you guys do."

Cathy, who'd been stirring her coffee, tapped her spoon against the side of her mug. "OK, well, how about right now?"

"Are you serious?"

"Yes," she said. "I actually have a job opening right now. Why don't you send me your résumé when you get back to Pennsylvania?"

It all happened so fast after that. I drafted up my first professional résumé, wrote a cover letter, drove back to D.C. for my interview, and was offered the job. It was a once-in-a-lifetime opportunity, and both Shannon and I knew it. Even though it meant we would have to do the long-distance thing until she was finished with school, we both agreed that I had to take it.

The GLAAD offices in Washington, D.C., are located in a building just north of Dupont Circle. Scott Widmeyer, a founding partner in the Widmeyer-Baker Group, a large creative PR firm, was on GLAAD's board of directors, and for a minimal amount of rent allowed us to share the office space.

Our office staff consisted of Cathy and me, and that was it. I was working as the regional media manager for the nine East Central states, and there was a lot to learn. It was my job to watch for any form of defamation of gay, lesbian, bisexual, and transgender people in all forms of media in those nine states. That meant monitoring all TV and radio programming as well as newspapers, magazines, and all other forms of print media. If defamation occurred, it was my job to fix it. It was also my job to pitch GLBT-inclusive stories to news outlets, producers, writers, and reporters. Picking up the phone and introducing myself to strangers was the hardest part for me. Cathy encouraged me early on to say when making cold calls, "Hi, my name is Romaine Patterson, I was a good friend of Matthew Shepard's..." Interestingly, with that introduction people seemed more willing to listen.

I talked to my mom just about every day, and she kept me informed about Dad. His back pain had gotten so bad they had to buy him a La-Z-Boy recliner to sleep in. Finally, a few weeks after his six-month checkup, Mom took him to the hospital in Sheridan, where they found a rapidly growing softball-size tumor in the small of his back. This was very bad news.

After intensive radiation treatment, Sheridan Memorial, our hometown hospital, continued to do what it could for my father. But when it became clear after a few weeks that Sheridan didn't have the facilities to treat someone in such an advanced stage, he was moved to Deaconness Billings Hospital in Billings, Mont. Just before he was transferred he was given a morphine drip to ease his pain. I remembered what it meant when they provided this for Michael, and felt a dull pain in the pit of my stomach. *How could this be happening again to me so soon?*

Shannon came to D.C. to be with me for the first week of March, which was more or less when it was expected that my father was going to die. Mom wanted me to come home to be with the family. "But it's not what your father wants," she told me. "He wants you to stay there and keep working on your new job." I told her that I couldn't get away yet, that Dad was right: I had to stay there and keep working. Shannon was supportive of that decision, but every now and then she'd say something like "Honey, are you sure you don't want to go be with your family? GLAAD isn't going to crumble if you take a week off."

On the morning of March 8 I called to check in. Mom said Dad wasn't doing so well. His internal organs were failing and they were going to put him on life support. I stayed close to home for the rest of the day with Shannon. Early in the evening the phone rang. It was my brother Patrick. He was the same one who called when Michael had passed, so I knew before he said anything that this was "the call." Just like before, he gave the phone to my mother.

34 | Disaster in Grant Town

I flew out to Billings the next morning. Mom picked me up at the airport, looking devastated and exhausted. Wearing a sweatshirt and a pair of crumpled jeans, she was the embodiment of a woman who had spent the last couple of months living out of a suitcase. I was more worried about her than anything else that day. I couldn't imagine how it must feel to lose a husband of more than 40 years. I held her hand as we drove, and she told me that I was her rock.

We went to the viewing a few hours later. The entire immediate and extended Patterson family was at the chapel by the time we arrived. Mom took my nephew Raif and me by the hand and walked down the center aisle to the viewing table. Dad was wearing a navy-blue suit and—because he was usually in a flannel shirt and jeans—I thought he looked silly. Mom knelt down in front of him and spent a long time just looking at him. She talked to him a little bit. "Oh, Carl, you look so dead," I heard her say.

Shannon arrived the next day—the day John went to Billings to pick up our father's ashes, just as he had done for our brother—when the rest of the family began to plan Dad's memorial. He had been a very popular man in town, and so at his service I saw a lot of people I hadn't seen in years. At one point Principal Bob Edwards took me aside. "I know your father didn't talk much, but I want you to know how proud of you he was. We all are, as a matter of fact." Coming from the man who once outed me to my father, that statement made up for a lot of old bullshit.

Shannon and I stayed with my family for a couple more days, long enough for my mother to assure all of her children at least a hundred times that she was OK. Then it was back to D.C.

Back to my life.

My father's death turned me into a reclusive workaholic. I was glad to not know a soul other than Shannon (footnote:* She'd come to live with me after graduating in May) in D.C., to not have to talk to anybody else. All I did was work, throwing myself into it as a way of not having to deal with death again. I put in long hours at the office, cold-calling reporters and editors as well as setting up meetings with major advertisers, all in regard to our campaign to stop Paramount from airing antigay radio personality Dr. Laura Schlessinger's TV talk show. I was energetic and eager at work— and Cathy praised me for it. Then I'd go home and eat. For weeks that was what I did: I worked and I ate.

In June I got a call from Leigh in New York City. *The Laramie Project* had opened off-Broadway in the spring, and though they'd been well-reviewed, they weren't sure how much longer the show was going to run. She wanted to make sure that I got to New York to see it before it closed. I tried to tell her that I was busy, that there was no weekend in the foreseeable future that would work for Shannon and me. But this was the third time Leigh had called to extend this invitation, and she wasn't going to accept any more of my lame excuses.

"Romaine," Leigh said, "I know you're nervous, but you'll never forgive yourself if you don't come see this. Besides, I've already booked you and Shannon tickets on Amtrak and they aren't refundable. So we'll see you Saturday."

We got to the Union Square Theater about an hour before the show started, and as Shannon and I hung out in the dressing rooms, it was hard to tell who was more nervous about my being there, the actors—Kelli especially—or me. Before we went up to our seats Leigh showed me a bulletin board overflowing with cards and letters the cast had received from other people portrayed in the show. "This is where we get our energy from," she gushed. "This is where we come before a performance when we need to remember why we're doing this. But we won't need it tonight because you're here."

There was so much about the play that was just so perfectly Wyoming. There's a line somebody has that points out how the Wyoming state sign says "Wyoming, like no place on Earth" instead of "Wyoming, like no place *else* on Earth." It's an especially funny line for me because all throughout my teens, every time I drove past that sign, I'd wisecrack, "Wyoming, like no place on Earth. Thank God." So when that line came up in the play I actually said, out loud, "Thank God," then burst into a fit of laughter. Nobody around me got it.

The first time Kelli appeared—in a replica of my trademark leather jacket—she strutted onto the stage. She had my confidence, my swagger, and my sarcasm. In a later scene, when she explained who the angels were and what we were doing that first day at the courthouse, she had my pride as well as the glow I probably exuded as I stood "toe-to-toe with Fred Phelps." She nailed it. What really bowled me over was the incredible applause from the audience for the angels during the scene on the courthouse lawn.

I did also have my moments of panic watching the play. There's a scene in which the national press descends upon Laramie. This is represented by a number of huge TV monitors being lowered onto the back wall of the stage. The TVs played actual news clips as well as real-time video shot by a number of the actors carrying television cameras. Lost in the world of the play, I grabbed Shannon's hand in fear, imagining that the cameras would soon turn toward the audience and come after me.

The play also depicted the press conferences held by the CEO of the hospital in Fort Collins. It was during the scenes with Jon Peacock (played so brilliantly by Greg Pierotti, who along with Leigh had conducted the preliminary interviews with me) that I cried the hardest. It was just so real. My mind kept jumping back and forth between the present—sitting there in the theater with my girlfriend—and that awful week Matthew was on life support. I relived the confusion and anger of that time as well as my hope— in the face of the impossible—that he would make it, that he would live.

I went back to D.C. feeling incredibly proud of my past. I was so relieved to have faced my demons, and today cannot say how much I appreciate that little extra push from Leigh. I immediately went back to work on the Dr. Laura campaign. It was with what felt like a new zest that I, in conjunction with a handful of people from GLAAD's other offices around the country, coordinated letter-writing campaigns as well as sit-ins and protest rallies against advertisers that pledged support for the show. One by one we were able to convince them that they didn't want to align themselves with someone who so unapologetically spewed hatred—and not just toward gays but also blacks, single mothers, and proponents of a woman's right to an abortion. By the time the show was can-

celed on March 30, 2001, it had received such an abundant amount
of bad press that it had been relegated in most markets to a middle-
of-the-night time slot and was relying on the "psychic" Miss Cleo, a
fraud who ultimately served jail time, as its chief advertiser.

In the first week of July 2000, Cathy, whose cubicle was next
to mine, got a phone call. I started paying attention to her end of
the conversation when I heard her say "Oh, my God, that's terrible." She hung up a few minutes later and, still sitting in her office
chair, wheeled herself over to me.

"Something horrible has just happened in Grant Town, West
Virginia," she said, her voice dry. "A 26-year-old openly gay black
man named J.R. Warren was…was kicked to death by two 17-year-
old white boys in steel-toed boots."

I grabbed my stomach.

"Once he was dead, they stuffed his body into the trunk of a
car and drove it out to a deserted gravel road, where they dumped
it and ran it over a couple of times trying to make the murder look
like a hit-and-run accident."

"Jesus Christ," I said. "What the fuck is wrong with people?"

"It gets worse," she said. "J.R. was born with both mental and
physical birth defects."

She gave me a minute to digest all of that before she continued. I took that time to close my eyes and try not to vomit on the
carpet.

"The story was picked up almost immediately by the local
media," Cathy went on, "and it looks as though the national media
might start paying attention."

"OK…" I said cautiously.

"Look," she said, "that was one of his friends I just got off the
phone with—she really wants us to send someone, and West

Virginia is in your region, so I think it should be you."

There they were, the words I was dreading. Dealing with something like that on the heels of my father's funeral was absolutely the last thing in the world I thought I'd be able to handle. But though my heart screamed *No way in fucking hell! Why don't you go?* my brain told me how incredibly lucky I was to even have that job.

"OK," I said.

Cathy's frown faded into a satisfied smile. "You're the perfect person to handle these things," she said. "You're so qualified to talk about hate crimes. You'll go down there and help them get their story out, it's that simple—and besides...who's better at that than you?"

I first met with a group of J.R. Warren's friends at the boarding house where they all lived. I realized almost immediately that what I had been sent there to do was not at all what those kids had called GLAAD about. They weren't looking for someone to help get their story to the media but to help them *fend off* the media. And they were terrified and frustrated, as well as resentful and distrustful of all of the gay organizations that had been sent there to supposedly help them.

"Of course we wanted the murder to garner a certain amount of publicity," said one of Warren's friends, a chubby blond girl named Faye, "or else those bastards who did it would probably have gotten away with it. But all these various gay groups who've come to *help* us...well, let's just say they've brought their own agendas."

Angela, a thin, stringy brunet, complained of having been outed to relatives and friends by the Human Rights Campaign, who had used her name and image in their petitions to the press to portray the murder as a hate crime.

I felt so bad for those kids, who were clearly at a loss as to how to allow themselves to grieve, continue to ensure that justice was served, and deal with a predatory media—to whom they were being misrepresented by people claiming to be their allies.

I was overwhelmed by how similar my situation had once been to theirs. I was also caught off guard by my own sense of uncertainty. Was it true that Cathy had sent me to Grant Town not to help those kids get their stories to the press, but to convince them that this was what they wanted to do? Even when it probably wasn't? Suddenly, I wasn't sure—then it occurred to me that I was uniquely poised to be there for those kids. Nobody else I knew of, save Jim Osborn, had the experience of living through the onslaught of media attention in the wake of a highly publicized antigay murder. And nobody could more candidly explain to them exactly what they could expect their lives to become if their story was picked up by the national media.

Knowing that what I was about to do went against everything GLAAD had sent me down there to accomplish, I went ahead and gave J.R. Warren's friends the speech I wished somebody had given me. "You need to be sure before you speak," I said, "that this is something you want to do. Because I can tell you from experience that it will change the rest of your life. You won't get the opportunity to go back and be invisible or to hide in the closet if this should explode into a big national story." They seemed not only to have heard me but to have appreciated my honesty—so much so that they enlisted me to help organize the vigil for Warren that was being held the next night.

"And guess who's going to be there," said a girl named Tammy. "That guy, Fred Phelps."

The next morning, as the students set to work on building angel costumes for a counterprotest against Phelps, I went to meet with the local sheriff.

Sheriff Ron Watkins is a tall, skinny drink of water who speaks slowly and gives the impression that he thinks even more slowly. We met in his office in the basement of the county courthouse, where he explained that he'd all but invited Phelps to come protest at that evening's vigil. I was horrified until I realized that the sheriff had no idea who Phelps was or what he stood for.

"He's a Baptist minister who called me up and said he was coming," Watkins said. "He wants to lead a nice Christian demonstration."

"No, sheriff," I told him. "He wants to start a riot." I went on to explain how the police department in Laramie had handled him and that he should follow their lead by building a fenced-off area for Phelps and his group to stand in. But no matter how much I tried to warn him, that good-old-boy sheriff just brushed it all aside. It was all I could do to get him to agree to have some fence-building supplies on hand—just in case I was right.

The sheriff was shocked when Phelps and his group showed up three hours early. I stood next to him, shaking my head, watching the look of shock register on his face as Phelps's group jumped out of their trucks, picked up their GOD HATES FAGS signs and spread out across the courthouse lawn. Almost immediately a general mayhem broke out as the hatemongers got in the faces of towns-people trickling in for the vigil. As police officers dashed onto the grass to break up screaming matches that were escalating toward skirmishes, I drove back to the college to round up the angels.

Back at the courthouse, the sheriff and his deputies had slapped together a corral for Phelps and his group, without any success in getting them to stay inside it. The angels, looking absolutely terrified, tried to surround Phelps's group but ended up scattering to the outskirts of the lawn when they weren't able to get anyone to stand still long enough to effectively block them out.

Knowing that it was my job to stay even-tempered and to handle the press, I turned my back on the chaos and walked over to a small group of reporters. I did my best to put a positive spin on my answers but knew the event had turned into a complete failure.

I turned away from the media and looked at the circus that this vigil had become. Phelps and his group had finally been contained, but they were in the middle of the field. The angels had given up; many of them were in various stages of taking off their costumes, and almost all of them were crying. The townspeople who had gathered to grieve together in peace were literally shoving each other to get into Phelps's face.

The worst part about the whole situation was that I still had to do my job—I couldn't just round the angels up and get the hell out of there. Rather, I had to take these grieving (and now further traumatized) kids and deliver them to the press. I remember turning to look at the members of the media again, hoping to see at least a little compassion coming from them the way it had done during the first angel demonstration at the Henderson hearing. Instead, I saw smiles on a lot of their faces as they rolled their cameras and scribbled onto their notepads. *This story*, I imagined them thinking, *is going to be even better than I thought.*

I began to wonder then: *How did I get here? How have I become so distanced from my own story that I am now able to exploit the pain these kids are experiencing, the same way mine had been after Matthew died?* I knew then from the pit of my soul that what I was doing to those kids was wrong. Even though I had won their trust, I was no better than the vultures I thought I'd been sent there to protect them from. But I did it anyway—I gathered the kids together and told them that it was time to go talk to the press. I watched them stumble over their words as they tried to answer questions and squirmed uncomfortably under the glare of the photographers' lights. They hated it. Intermittently they looked over to me, the person they were counting on to guide them, for help. But I had none to give them. They were in it now. And there was no turning back.

I left Grant Town the next day, feeling as though I'd been lied to and taken advantage of. I had dropped my life to go work for GLAAD because it was an organization I really believed in. But it was clear to me that I had been expected to exploit those kids, to get them to talk to the press, to make them believe that it was their responsibility to their dead friend to do so and that it was the right thing to do. I recognize that it was my job to go there, but I was never going to feel good about lying to a group of people or a community who had just lost somebody they loved by telling them that speaking out will make them feel better—it was a lie that just hit too close to home. I was never going to feel good about telling people that they should sacrifice their anonymity as well as their right to grieve in private for the greater good of the gay community.

On top of that, I really felt like Cathy should've known I wasn't ready to tackle that situation. Not only was I too new in the professional-activist world to have made a real difference there, but with the death of my father having been so recent, how could I have been expected to handle other people's grief on top of my own? The details of this murder were so incredibly horrible, and in many ways so similar to Matthew's murder, that it was like I'd been suckered into reliving my old awful life again—because it was my job to know every graphic bloody detail, then talk to the press about it. Only this time, instead of emerging with a sense of hope and triumph, things had gone wrong. It was like a bad dream.

35 | *Flipped*

I didn't have much time to sort it all out, because shortly after I returned to D.C. from Grant Town, GLAAD flew me to Los Angeles to appear on an MTV reality show called *Flipped*. I liked the people at MTV a lot, and I had grown to trust them over the course of my work as a consultant on *Anatomy of a Hate Crime*, the first of the TV movies to come out about Matthew. When the film aired on January 10, 2001, as part of MTV's "Fight for Your Rights" campaign, I was invited to be a part of a live televised panel discussion hosted by John Norris immediately following the film. It had been a great experience, especially because I had loved MTV since I was a little kid, so I was happy to be working with them again.

The idea of the series was to take a young person who had some kind of bias against a certain group of people and, unbeknownst to them, "flip" their discriminatory attitude by putting them through a series of situations that put the shoe on the other foot. The subject for my episode was a 17-year-old boy (the same age as J.R. Warren's killers) named Sean who was openly homophobic. Sean was told that he had won a contest and the prize was the opportunity to host a one-day program on MTV called *Rookies*, which would be taped that day and aired the next. I was the "producer" of the show and would be fielding cell phone calls throughout the day for our assignments.

The day started at 8 A.M., when I, along with a cameraman and a wardrobe person, met Sean in his hotel room. He was a good-looking young guy, about 5 foot 4, thin, with spiky bleached-blond hair. The wardrobe person dressed Sean in a tight-fitting blue pais-ley shirt, a pair of brown leather pants, and a long brown leather coat. It was quite a change from his baggy jeans and T-shirt—and it was obvious that the intention was to make Sean as stylishly flamboyant as possible. Though he was clearly uncomfortable, he was a good sport about it and smiled through his embarrassment.

On the way to the hair salon Sean told us about the evening before, when he and his friend had gone to West Hollywood and had been approached by a group of "fags" (unaffiliated with the show) who'd wanted to buy them drinks and tried to get their num-bers. He claimed to have felt disgusting afterward. "I don't think I've ever felt more disgusting in my life," he said into the camera. His complaint came across as pure macho bravado, and it fell flat in the absence of his homophobic buddies.

At the salon Sean was introduced to Soell, a straight guy who'd been told to bond with Sean over his frustrations with working in an industry where people constantly called his sexuality into ques-tion. Sean liked Soell; he said he understood how Soell felt, espe-cially since he'd been made to wear "these fruity clothes" for MTV.

One of my favorite parts of the day came after we left the salon. MTV called us and asked us to cover a gay teen support group at the L.A. GLAAD offices. We went into the conference room and sat down with about 12 kids who were asked before we arrived to share their stories if they wanted to once we got there, but to turn the discussion around on Sean and ask him questions when they were finished. The facilitator introduced the topic: hate speech and its impact. Sean was slouched back at the beginning of the discussion, but as the kids went around and one by one gave examples of how their peers' slurs had escalated, he leaned forward in his chair.

"I was terrified to go to school," one girl said. "It started out with just being called 'dyke' then getting slammed into a locker. But then one day I was thrown to the floor and was kicked and punched so many times I had two ribs broken."

"I still get slapped in the face sometimes," another boy said, "by boys *and* girls. The teachers see it and they don't care."

About an hour into the discussion one of the boys asked Sean, "Have you ever called anyone a faggot?"

Sean closed his eyes for a second. He nodded his head. "I admit that I have," he said. "But can I ask you guys a question?"

The kids nodded.

"Do you think kids get this kind of hate speech from their families?"

A lot of the kids nodded. One girl said, "I think it's just a few people whose family values are like this. But it's always them who are the loudest and the meanest."

"Because I was raised by my dad," Sean said, "and he always taught me that gay people are bad. I don't know what to say. I'm so sorry."

Once outside, unaware that he was being filmed, Sean said to me, "Going to the GLAAD office was really good for me. I'm going to remember every story."

A few minutes later my cell phone rang, and—as expected—it was MTV letting us know that the police had been called to a nearby location and that we should get over there and cover whatever was going on. By the time we arrived a crowd had gathered. We jumped out of the van and ran up to where an officer was crouched over a man who lay on the ground, bleeding from the head and face. The officer was trying to get the man's name, but he was slipping in and out of consciousness and unable to speak coherently. Suddenly Sean jumped back, turned, and said, "Oh, my God, that's Soell, the dude who cut my hair this morning!" Though I knew it was Soell, I told Sean I wasn't sure. Sean grabbed the cameraman and pushed his way back to the police officer.

"Can you tell us what happened here?" Sean said to the officer as Soell was loaded into an ambulance.

"It looks as though this was an antigay hate crime. We get a couple of those a year around here. But this one's pretty bad—it doesn't look good for this guy."

Sean dropped the microphone away from his mouth. "That guy wasn't even gay," he told the officer. "We talked about it just this morning."

We followed up with the "sheriff" about an hour later at the police station. The sheriff said that he was positive Soell had been the victim of a hate crime, then gave Sean a list of hate-crime victims across the country who'd died as a result of their attacks. The list had over 100 names on it. "These are all *after* Matthew Shepard," the sheriff said.

Sean didn't know who Matthew was. "He was a young kid," the sheriff explained, "who was picked up at a bar by two other young guys who took him to the middle of nowhere, where they tied him to a fence and beat the living hell out of him. He died about five days later."

Sean shook his head, then sat down with the list of victims. There was a brief description of the crime under each listed name. Sean read some of them out loud:

"Shot 16 times...neck crushed...ribs broken...beaten to death then run over numerous times to make the murder look like an accident..." Sean had tears in his eyes by the time he was finished reading.

"Let's go over some of these pictures," I said, indicating a folder the sheriff had just given me containing graphic pictures of some of the murders Sean had just read about. Sean stopped when he came across a picture of the fence in Laramie.

"Is this where they—"

"Yeah," I said, playing along, "I think that's where they tied Matthew Shepard up."

The next picture in the folder was a black-and-white one of me leaning my head against one of the fence posts. Sean looked at it for a second and was about to move on when I said, "Wait. Do you know who the girl in that picture is?"

"No, who is it?"

"It's me."

He looked at me for a long couple of seconds, then he looked back at the picture. "Are you serious?"

"Yeah, Matthew was a good friend of mine."

"Oh, my God," Sean said, and tears welled up in his eyes.

"Take a look at the next picture," I told him. It was a picture of Matthew in all of his smiling glory. He was wearing a blue sweater, his eyes were twinkling, and his hair was a mass of spiky blond perfection. He had this little smile on his face that projected a feeling of contentedness.

"That was my friend Matthew," I said. Then I moved on to the next picture and said, "This is what those guys did to him." It was a picture of Matthew in his hospital bed. Though it was just a picture of his face, there wasn't much to see other than his swollen black eyes and his bloody lips. The rest of his head was swathed in bandages, and a thick plastic tube had been forced into his mouth.

It was a gruesome picture, one I'd seen only once before. It was hard to look at it again then, especially with MTV cameras in my face, but I forced myself to stay on it as long as Sean did. When he was finally done and closed the folder, he looked at me as if to say *What now?*

I looked Sean square in the eye. "I have it all upstairs," I told him, "in this picture that never goes away. Ever since his death I've been working day and night to make sure that no friend ever has to go through this again. I've dedicated the last three years of my life to this."

Then, with no introduction, Soell the hairstylist, still covered in fake blood, walked into the room. Sean looked at him, said "Oh, my God," put his head down on the table for a second, then jumped up and gave him a hug. "I can't even tell you how glad I am that you're OK."

"If you ever need a haircut," Soell said, "come on down. It's on me."

36 | *Leaving GLAAD*

I was dead tired when I returned to D.C. after that trip to L.A. By then I had been with GLAAD for a year and a half, and it felt like I'd been on the go from day one. They had wanted my face and my name everywhere. Cathy had arranged for me to be the keynote speaker for the Youth Pride March in Washington, D.C., they were constantly pitching interviews with me to the press; and I was scheduled to be photographed in my angel costume by David LaChapelle for a profile piece in *The New York Times Magazine*.

Cathy and GLAAD's communication team—a PR group made up of representatives from GLAAD offices across the nation— pushed me to do it all, with little regard for whether I felt the work was exploitive of my friendship with Matthew, and even less regard for how exhausting the schedule was. Before any interview I would always be coached to open with something about Matthew Shepard and to always mention that I worked for GLAAD. For a while that was fine, but eventually I got tired of it. I had joined GLAAD to take the next step in my career as an activist, not to function as some kind of trophy or prop.

Of course, it's possible I encouraged this treatment by immersing myself in my work to cope with the loss of my father and never setting limits on what I was willing to do professionally. However it came about, as I was traveling almost weekly to New York City for this photo shoot or that interview, it was slowly dawning on me that it had all gone on for too long, and that my job was becoming less about monitoring the media than it was about being personally represented in it, and I began to seriously question my commitment.

My level of exhaustion after the whole fiasco in Grant Town, immediately followed by two days of unreal reality in L.A., was the last straw, and I knew it. Shannon, as usual, was the first one of us to bring it up.

"I've been really worried about you for a while now," she said one night in the kitchen, where I stood at the stove, boiling pasta. "Ever since your father's funeral, I guess. You've just been working so hard at a job you can't seem to stand."

Though I knew she was right, I immediately got defensive. I stopped stirring and leaned against the stove, wielding my wooden spoon like a steaming branding iron. Realizing how much like my mother that was, I turned and put the thing down. "Honey, for the first time in my life," I said, "I have direction...and health insurance, for God's sake. I'm making the best money of my life. This is the best job someone like me, someone without a college degree, is ever going to get, and I can't just friggin' walk away from it."

Please tell me to walk away from it, I thought. *Give me permission.*

"You can if you want to," she said. "That job is killing you. Since you started it, I've watched you go from a spunky 140-pound girl to a miserable and depressed 160-pound girl who never leaves the house for anything but work."

I eyed the pasta maniacally. "Actually, Shannon, it's 180 now, but who's fucking counting!"

Shannon came over to hug me. "Oh, Romaine," she said. "Honey, you always have a choice."

A few months after my father died I had a moment of foresight, in which I thought it might behoove me to keep my options open in case my stint with GLAAD didn't work out. On a whim, and with the hope that I would one day be brave enough to follow my dream and actually study sound engineering, I applied to a nine-month program at the Conservatory of Recording Arts and Sciences near Phoenix. Less than a week after my confrontation with Shannon, I received my acceptance letter from the conservatory. This was a sign. It was time to go.

Before packing up yet another U-Haul and heading for Arizona, Shannon and I spent a beautiful Saturday afternoon on the national Mall where sections of the AIDS Quilt were being displayed. We found Michael's panel in block 02917, and though time and travel had weathered it a bit since John commissioned an artist to paint it in 1998, it was just as beautiful as I remembered. It's a very simple mountain scene set against a white background. There is a brown winding path that leads to a blossoming pine tree in the center of the canvas. At the bottom of the canvas is his name, MICHAEL STEWART PATTERSON, and around the border the words *my joy my love* are repeated over and over again in small print calligraphy. As you step away from the canvas, you notice that the smaller words are connected in such a way that in larger print they form one simple phrase: MY JOURNEY CONTINUES.

37 | *Asking for Help*

The first few weeks in Mesa, Ariz., were nice. The dry summer heat was a pleasant change from D.C.'s often oppressive humidity. Shannon and I found a cute little two-bedroom apartment that we decorated as best we could on our limited budget. We even bought a bed for the spare room and, instead of turning it into an office, set it up for my mom in hopes she'd make good on her promise to come out and spend time with us.

Shannon's coming to Arizona was based on a mutual agreement—she'd find a job and support us for the nine months I was in school, then we'd move to Colorado, where I'd carry her through graduate school. Though money (as always) was tight, we were making it work. Shannon found a job at a car dealership about seven miles outside of Mesa. The commute was significantly farther than she'd hoped for, but the job market wasn't exactly booming there, so it had to do.

For the first three weeks at the conservatory I learned and memorized the scientific principals of sound. Being that I knew nothing of recording and engineering before I got there—other than that I wanted to study it—that time was especially difficult for me. I studied constantly, and Shannon worked constantly, and I missed the little warning signs that our relationship was crumbling.

That is, until strange things started to happen. I'd call Shannon at work just to say hi and she wouldn't be there; she'd leave for work early and come home late; and she never seemed to have a day off. Finally one night, after getting home a little before 2 A.M., she woke me up and broke the news.

"I met someone," she said quickly. She was sitting on top of the covers on the corner of our bed. I thought for just a second that I must have been having a nightmare.

"What?" I said. "Who? What are you talking about?"

"I'm sure you don't understand, Romaine—we love each other, and I'm moving to California."

If I hadn't been in such a state of shock, I would have laughed in her face. My *girlfriend,* whom I just moved halfway across the country with, woke me up in the middle of the night to tell me she was leaving me for a used-car salesman.

But I couldn't laugh, because my panic began the very second she said she was leaving. I knew our relationship wasn't perfect, but the idea of breaking up was unfathomable. We both knew that my staying in school, living in that apartment, and paying the bills would be impossible without her there to support us. I thought about Suzanne from high school and Roni from Casper—then I thought about Michael, Matthew, and my dad. All were people I loved who'd been ripped out of my life. Now Shannon was going to leave, of her own free will, just because she felt like it, at a time when I was beginning to get my life together and needed stability the most?

We talked and fought about it for three days. I suffered horrible panic attacks, one of which landed me in the emergency room, and I hardly slept. Finally, when she realized just how desperate I was, Shannon agreed not to leave until I got help, though I hadn't the faintest idea what sort of help I needed.

In the middle of the night a few days later, I hit rock bottom. I had slowly been gathering pills from around the house and hiding them in the pocket of my leather jacket that was stored in the back closet. I didn't have a plan to take them, necessarily; I just wanted to have a stockpile, just in case. That night I walked into the closet and knelt down beneath my jacket. I was crying harder than I've ever cried. *Everyone leaves the party but me. Everyone I care about leaves. Well, fuck that. I'm going to leave first this time.*

With the pills in my hand, I went back into the bedroom, woke up Shannon, and asked her to get me a glass of water. When she came back with it I stuffed the pills in my mouth and tried to grab the water out of her hand. It took her a second to realize what was going on, but when she did she ran out of the room. "Romaine!" she shouted. "Romaine, spit those pills out. I'm dialing 911 right now!"

I sat on the edge of the bed with the bitter pills turning slimy in my mouth. I spit them out onto the floor and looked at them. I guess I knew that I was never actually going to swallow them. Desperate as it was, I just wanted to see her care about me one last time. The police showed up a few minutes later and stayed for over an hour while Shannon tried to convince them to take me to the hospital. They finally left after I was able to get them into the bedroom, where I showed them the pills I had spit out on the floor.

This was the lowest point of my life, and I knew it. I thought about Matthew then and how desperate he'd seemed almost from the minute we all moved to Denver together. I remembered how much I'd wanted him to call his parents, to engage them in his life and his sadness, how I'd hoped they could make it all better for him. Then, for the first time, I think I understood why he hadn't. Because when you're at the bottom, as I was that night, you don't believe in yourself enough. You don't believe you have the energy or the know-how to scream loud enough or to plead with enough force to make somebody care.

But something nagged at me to try, so I picked up the phone.

"Somebody has to get down here," I said desperately when my mother answered. "Shannon and I are breaking up."

Mom sounded annoyed to have been awakened. "Honey, these things happen."

"No," I said. "Listen to me. Somebody *has* to get down here. I am not in the state of mind where I can do this alone."

"Honey," she said forcefully. "You'll be fine."

"No, no, no, no, no, no! I WILL NOT BE FINE!" I yelled. "Let me spell this out for you because you do not understand how it is. For years I've been pretending—believing, even—that everything is OK, but it isn't. I HAVE ALL OF THIS GRIEF INSIDE OF ME! I thought I could handle it and you thought I could handle it and we were both wrong. I've never asked you or anyone for help, but I'm asking you now and I'm not giving you a choice. I have been in the hospital, I'm having panic attacks, I'm going to have to quit school, and I CAN'T DO THIS!"

"Swee—" she said before I cut her off.

"And I tried to commit suicide today. If you care about me, you'll come. If you don't, you won't."

She took a deep breath then said, "I'll be on a plane tomorrow morning."

My brother John came down with my mother, and immediately I could see how worried they were. Shannon had gone to stay with her grandparents in California. I didn't ask, because I couldn't bear to know, what happened to the boyfriend. With Shannon gone, there was plenty of room for Mom, who decided to stay with me. John got a room at a hotel. At first they tried talking to me, engaging me in quick-fix "What's wrong with you, honey?" conversations over breakfast or lunch. But when they took serious stock of my inability to communicate, coupled with my nightly panic attacks—attacks that left me shaking in a fetal position next to my bed—they accepted that the help I needed was far beyond the realm of their capacities and was going to be considerably more long-term. Within the first week of their arrival they brought me to a psychologist for emergency therapy.

In my family, crazy as we all were from time to time, therapy was never an option. My father had firmly believed—and had instilled the belief, as far as I could tell, in all of his children—that to be emotionally weak to the point of needing a therapist was an embarrassment. So it was a major concession made by my mother and my brother to get me the help I needed.

I knew enough about the level of my family's concern for me to know that, at least for the first couple of sessions, the questions asked by the psychologist were meant to determine whether I should be committed to a hospital where I could be monitored at all times. So I gave the answers that would keep me home. No, I didn't want to kill myself. Yes, my suicide attempt was a ploy for attention. And so on.

Once I felt I was safely out of the woods, I found myself really wanting to open up to my psychologist. I loved being listened to and having a safe place where I could unapologetically talk about how the events of the previous four years had made me feel. Our sessions were scheduled for three times a week, though I knew my doctor was always available if I felt I needed him. He prescribed Klonopin, the antianxiety medication Matthew had been so fond of, which helped control the panic attacks and allowed me some decent sleep. When it also became clear that I was clinically depressed, he added Zoloft.

My healing really began the day Shannon moved out. I finally was able to have some closure with this relationship, and—even more important—on this day was the first time in my adult life I watched my mother come to my rescue. It was a sunny afternoon in November when Shannon came to the apartment to get her stuff. I was in the early stages of my therapy and had been warned that any interaction between us could cause a setback, so I had shut myself in the bedroom.

As she was finishing up, Shannon was walking in and out of the bedroom, making sure she had all her stuff. The first couple of times she came in she didn't say anything, then she'd walk into the room and say "Romaine, I really am sorry" then walk out. She'd come back in a few minutes later and say something like "You know I really do love you," then leave again. In my effort not to beg her to stay, I gripped the comforter so hard my knuckles turned white.

When she heard Shannon's voice, Mom came in and stood next to me by the bed. The next time Shannon entered, much to my surprise, my usually mild-mannered mother spoke up harshly. "Why are you leaving, Shannon?"

Shannon, kneeling in front of one of her suitcases, looked up. There was a puzzled look on her face, almost as if she'd never thought about it. "I just don't love Romaine anymore, not the way that she loves me."

Mom looked her in the eye. "I don't believe that's true."

Shannon jerked her head back as if she'd been slapped. "Look, our relationship just isn't working."

"I don't believe that either," Mom said. "Why are you hurting my daughter in this way, Shannon? Tell me the truth."

Shannon looked away from my mother and thought for a second. "I...ah...have to go put this suitcase in the car," she said as she slammed it shut, then stood to lug it out of the room.

I was trying not to laugh as my mom paced the room. She had cupped her chin in her hand and was shaking her head the way Michael used to when he was contemplating something serious. I wanted to thank her for saying things to Shannon I'd been too weak to say myself, to tell her how much her validation of what I was going through meant to me, but speaking at that moment seemed somehow inappropriate.

Shannon was back a few minutes later, standing in the doorway. My back was to her, and I didn't turn around because I was afraid that if I saw her face I'd burst into a fit of laughter or tears. "Romaine, I'm really sorry to be doing this to you," she said, "but I have to go now. I just want to say—"

"Shannon!" my mother snapped. She'd stopped pacing and was facing the door where Shannon stood. All her features were scrunched into the center. Her eyes were squinted and her teeth were clenched. My family called that her bulldog face. It was a face she rarely made, but when we saw it we knew that someone's ass was about to get kicked.

I turned to look at Shannon; I had to see her expression. Her eyes were wide, and she had lost all of her color. I had told her once about this side of my mother, and now she was rightfully terrified.

"If you are going to leave, you need to leave now! Stop coming in here and making this worse for Romaine. If you're going to go, then get out!"

With that, Shannon turned on her heel and was gone.

As my therapy continued and I learned how to talk about what I was going through and had gone through, my mom and I had conversations that I never would have thought were possible. She talked about my dad and how badly she missed him, and, of course, we talked about Michael. I told her stories about my summers in Denver and about Matthew and Roni. For the first time I talked about the press with my mother and how at first I'd been grateful for the opportunity, but that I eventually came to understand my involvement in telling Matthew's story as one of many catalysts for my downward spiral.

Probably inaccurately, I remember those conversations as always basked in the glow of early-morning sunshine; with Mom and me, still in our pajamas, giggling over coffee and toast. There is a certain something to that image, though, however inexact the actual picture may be, that does do justice to the transformation, rebirth even, of our relationship.

After my mother left I had to relearn who I was. I stayed in therapy, where I came to understand that my overriding stumbling block was a fear of loss—a fear that had been instilled in me due to the extraordinary circumstances under which so many of the people I loved had been taken out of my life. Shannon's leaving had triggered that fear in me and had pushed me as close to the proverbial edge as I could have come without falling off. Without the help I received in therapy, God only knows what would have happened to me. Sometimes I wonder how that fear of loss affected my earlier decisions. Did it make me a person who was easily taken advantage of? A people pleaser? Had it all started when I was 11, when my mom began imparting to me her fear that she and my father would die before they got to see me grow up?

Thanks to my brother John, I didn't have to quit school.

"School is important," he said one sunny afternoon over lunch, "and you need to be here. So don't worry about money—I'm going to take care of you as long as you're here."

As I slowly acclimated myself back into society, I began to seize the opportunities that are presented to a person who knows nobody in the city where she lives. Figuring that I could go back to the normal Romaine I had always been once I finished my program and left Mesa, I tried on as many new faces as I could while I lived there. I went to bars alone, flirted with strange girls, and experimented with my feminine side—I even went out and bought some makeup.

In February, as Laramie began to gear up for the premiere of the HBO version of *The Laramie Project* as well as the NBC made-for-TV movie *The Matthew Shepard Story*, I started getting calls from my friends there who wanted me to come up. I thought about it for a few days before deciding that I wasn't going to go. I told Jim and everyone else that I couldn't miss school: that you were only allowed to be absent five days and that I'd already used up three for various therapy appointments. The truth, however, was that, though I wanted to be there, I saw it as a potential setback. My time in Arizona had become about me fixing what was wrong with my life, and frankly, my life's having become so intertwined with Matthew Shepard's death was a major part of what was dragging me down. Perhaps it's selfish to think of it that way, but even if it is, I know in my heart that Matthew would understand.

In March I was sent advance copies of both movies, so I got a group of friends together to watch *The Laramie Project* with me. HBO Films had called me while making the movie and asked if I could come to the set and spend a few days with Christina Ricci, who was to play me, but I was working for GLAAD at the time and couldn't get the time off. We then tried to coordinate a phone call, but that didn't work out either. Finally, I was assured that Kelli Simpkins, the woman who'd portrayed me in the play, would work with Christina to get down the necessary Romaine-isms. Needless to say, I was very interested to see what the outcome would be.

All in all, Christina did a fine job—especially in the scene when she talks about how Matthew's smile can light up a room. She does a quick impression of him in the film, and I've got to say, for someone that never met the kid it was pretty dead-on. She played me a little more girlie than I would have liked—and Greg Pierotti, who had a small part in the film and worked with her a bit on my mannerisms, would tell me years later that she had actually tried to play me tougher but that the producers had encouraged her to "take the edge off." She was very charming, and I was flattered that she cared enough to play me in a movie.

The Matthew Shepard Story was a lot harder to watch. Chris and Ladd, my two friends from Denver, were at the premiere in Laramie and had warned me not to watch it alone. Unlike in *The Laramie Project*, Matthew is actually a character in that movie, and scenes from his murder as well as the rape in Morocco are depicted. Stockard Channing, who won an Emmy for her portrayal of Judy Shepard, brought such a human element to the film it was almost unbearable. As I sat and watched it with my friend Theresa, I had to pause the tape at certain points so I could cry. I don't know why I made myself watch the whole thing; maybe I thought it would help me move on—like a final purge, or something like that.

I spent the two months leading up to my June graduation trying to decide what my next move was going to be. As I saw it, I had two options: L.A. or New York. L.A. seemed like the obvious choice because it was close and would have made for an easy move. But there was something about the allure of New York City. I had wanted to live there ever since I was a little girl, reading of the legend of Madonna, who moved from Michigan to the lower east side with $36 and a can of peanuts. At the time my brother Sabin, who was illegally subletting an apartment in that neighborhood, said I could crash on his couch until I found a job and a place to live. If I was ever going to make that move, it was going to be then.

And so I made up my mind. I put just about everything I owned in storage in Arizona (where it still sits three years later) and got on a plane.

38 | *Return*

New York City is a hard place to live in. It was especially hard in June 2002, nine short months after 9/11. In addition to recovering and rebuilding, the city was downsizing and laying off. The economy was bad; the job market was even worse. So, like many qualified and forward-thinking people who can't find anything better and are desperate for health insurance, I got a job at Starbucks.

It was a humbling summer, to say the least. When I got fed up with Starbucks, I got a job at the café on the fourth floor of the Barnes & Noble in Union Square, which, interestingly, is about 100 feet from the Union Square Theater. Which—by pure coincidence—was where *The Laramie Project* made its New York debut.

I was recognized often by customers who'd seen me on MTV or remembered me from the article in *The New York Times Magazine*. Then, one at a time, books that featured pieces of my story started to come out. The one I was most proud to be a part of is a coffee-table book put together by Judy and Dennis Shepard and the Matthew Shepard Foundation called *A Face in the Crowd: Representations of Gay Life in America*. On the cover is a picture of me in my angel costume, taken from the series shot by David LaChapelle. My coworkers started referring to me as the resident celebrity. I smiled when they said things like that, but I was living on $2 pizza and free coffee at work.

Jim called at the end of September to tell me that he'd just received another fax from Fred Phelps. Phelps said that he and his group were coming to Fort Collins that October, the town where Matthew was hospitalized and ultimately died, to protest at Colorado State University's homecoming football game (against the University of Wyoming) on the four-year anniversary of Matthew's death. Jim wanted me to come out and speak at UW, where he still worked, and help him lead a counterprotest at the game. Naturally, I still felt the need to break away from all that angel stuff—but this was *Jim*. So, of course, I agreed.

The atmosphere at the game in Fort Collins was almost playful. A lot of the original angels showed up to be part of the counterprotest, as well as a lot of new people, young people—a lot of whom had seen *The Laramie Project* and had heard that we would be in town. As it was at the second trial, the angels were kept separate from Phelps. We were stationed in the front of the parking lot while Phelps and his group were in the back, so as people drove into the stadium we were the first thing they saw. We held up signs that said MATTHEW'S ANGELS and RESPECT, LOVE, FAMILY. People honked and cheered as they drove by, then silently rolled past Phelps.

I was nervous about going into Laramie after the game. I hadn't been there in two years. Four years had gone by since Matthew had been attacked and murdered, and I was sure most of the kids who'd been at the University of Wyoming when it happened were gone. As far as I could tell, it had always been the university students who'd tried to keep Matthew's memory alive in that town, a town where people seemed otherwise just as happy to put the incident behind them. With the kids who were so personally affected by Matthew's death now gone, I wondered if there would be any sort of tribute at all to Matthew's memory on that day.

The first thing Jim and I did in Laramie was participate in a panel discussion for a social work class at the university. Basically, we sat on desks and answered questions about Matthew and what it was like to be gay. After that we were taken to an auditorium to participate in a community discussion about Matthew and the changes we had seen in the community and the world since his death. Along with Jim and me, the panelists included Rob DeBree, who had been the chief investigator for Matthew's murder, and Dave O'Malley, the detective division head at the time of the murder who later became Laramie police chief.

Aside from the panelists, four people showed up. Four. It was sort of devastating. We pushed the start of the discussion back 15 minutes, hoping more would arrive, but nobody else did. The whole time I kept thinking, *There's nobody here. Nobody wants to talk about this anymore. How can Laramie be forgetting Matthew?* Then my own internal conflict came to the forefront of my mind. I knew I deserved the time I was taking for myself, out of the spotlight of being Matthew's friend, and I knew I needed that time to heal. But how could I in good conscience take that time if nobody was going to pick up where I left off?

I think it was that moment when I knew I had to pull myself together and find a way to make activism in Matthew's name a priority again. I didn't know yet exactly how I was going to make that happen, other than that I knew it would entail finding a way to make public activism a *part* of my life, one component among many, rather than the entirety of what my life was about.

The only good thing about the panel discussion being so small was that it ended up being more of a group conversation than a Q&A. I was glad for that, because there were a few things

I had always wanted to ask the police department but had never had the opportunity to. I specifically wanted to know what jacket Matthew was wearing on the night that he was attacked. Over the years I had put together in my head what he would have looked like out there on the fence, but the jacket had always been the missing piece.

"It was a brown corduroy jacket with a shiny silver zipper," Rob said.

I knew exactly which one he meant. He had bought it in Denver, and it had quickly become his favorite article of clothing. He wore it the night Roni and I went to dinner with him and his deaf boyfriend. It wasn't a heavy coat, but at least it was something.

The other thing I wanted was to be able to put to rest the rumor that Matthew had left the bar with Henderson and McKinney because of crystal meth—either to buy from or sell to them. It was a nasty rumor that had been circulated in the wake of his death within, as far as I'm concerned, a certain segment of the population's need to blame the victim in order to justify the horror of the crime. My own sister Trish had even tried to sell me on various meth-related stories—living in Laramie, she sometimes talked as though she had insider information, claiming it to be common knowledge among those in her inner circle that Matthew was somewhat of a local drug dealer. I never bought any of that talk. The entire time I had known him, Matthew used pot and prescription drugs to deal with his depression and social anxiety. I knew him better than just about anyone, and I would have known if he'd been lying to me in our last conversation, when he talked about how happy he was, the new friends he had made, and how well he was doing in school. He had no need for any of his vices when he was feeling that good about himself.

To this day, almost seven years later, rumors that Matthew left the Fireside Lounge to buy drugs with Henderson and McKinney have not dissipated. On November 26, 2004, the ABC newsmagazine show *20/20* ran an hour-long piece for sweeps month to boost ratings. Host Elizabeth Vargas theorized that Matthew's murder was not at all a hate crime but rather a robbery attempt gone terribly wrong—so Henderson and McKinney would have money to buy drugs.

I knew from sources at GLAAD and the Matthew Shepard Foundation about six months ahead of time that *20/20* was working on the piece and that, based on the list of people the show had lined up to interview, it was going to be unfavorable. As part of the plea agreement that spared him the death penalty, McKinney had agreed to never publicly discuss the case. That part of the agreement, however, could not legally be enforced, so once we heard that he as well as Henderson had agreed to be interviewed, we knew *20/20* had a scoop—the first public interviews with Matthew's killers since the murder—and would go full speed ahead with the story.

The tone of the piece was even worse than I expected. Vargas was sympathetic to the killers' plights as she described both Henderson's and McKinney's fatherless childhoods before showing Henderson a picture of himself as a teenager receiving his Eagle Scout badge from the mayor. "What happened to that young man?" she asked him, sounding oh, so concerned.

Vargas later gives the killers a chance to put to rest once and for all the idea that they beat Matthew to death because he was gay. Henderson says, "The reason he was targeted was not because he was gay. It's not because me and Aaron had anything against gays or any of that." McKinney adds, "No, I have gay friends, I know other gay people. You know, that kind of thing don't bother me so much."

Vargas seemed satisfied with that. So satisfied, in fact, that she didn't deem it necessary to bring up that fact that Henderson and McKinney approached Matthew at the Fireside only because he, in McKinney's own words, looked "like a fag." Nor did Vargas mention that the boys later admitted to winning Matthew's trust and getting him to leave the bar with them by pretending to be gay. Nor did Vargas mention that McKinney, in his taped confession just a few hours after the murder, admitted that he started the beating that resulted in Matthew's death when—he claimed—Matthew made a pass at him in the truck by putting his hand on his leg.

The show did mention that Kristen Price, the mother of McKinney's child, appeared on 20/20 just days after the crime saying that McKinney confided in her after killing Matthew that "a guy walked up to him and said that he was gay and wanted to get with Aaron and Russ. They just wanted to beat him up bad enough to teach him a lesson: not to come on to straight people." After showing the old clip, Vargas says, "But now, six years later…Kristen says her initial statements were not true." What Vargas failed to ask was: *If you lied then, how do we know you aren't lying now? And does that mean you perjured yourself when you testified at the hearing?*

What I found so infuriating was that the show offered no evidence of drugs being the motive. It included a strange interview with an expert who talked about the behavioral effects crystal meth has on the body—as a response to the claim that McKinney was coming down off a meth binge—but makes no claim to it being McKinney's motivation for killing Matthew. They also interviewed a "former Laramie police detective" named Ben Fritzen—whom I had never heard of—who claims that "what it came down to really is drugs and money and two punks that were out looking for it." That is a direct contradiction to what Dave

O'Malley had to say. He stated in the 20/20 special that the arresting officer—who was, the show failed to mention, a narcotics specialist—reported that neither Henderson nor McKinney exhibited any signs of having been on or coming down from crystal meth. Dave's statement was supported by Rob DeBree, the lead investigator on the case, when I finally got to ask the question that day at the panel discussion.

"It is absolutely untrue," Rob said definitively, "that drugs had anything to do with this. There was no scrap of evidence found to support that theory."

The show also failed to mention that Judy Shepard agreed to be interviewed for the show to be given the opportunity to maintain that Matthew's murder was an antigay hate crime. Her condition was that her lawyer, Sean Maloney, sit next to her during the interview and that he be in every frame that she was in. Not only did 20/20 not hold up its end of the deal—Maloney was only in one brief shot, while Judy was in quite a few—but it took a few of her quotes out of context and made it seem as though she agreed with Vargas's assertion that Matthew's was not killed due to his being gay.

It was obvious to me by the end of the piece that Judy had been duped—that 20/20 had a specific role in mind for her when it decided to include her in the piece. She was to be the grieving mother who had never fully gotten over the loss of her son. Of course Judy is a grieving mother, but her intention for the interview was to set the record straight—that homophobia is at the root of this issue; that her son was killed because he was gay.

Judy was furious about how she'd come off. I, of course, completely understood—I can't even count the number of times my quotes were taken out of context to fit a reporter's agenda in the years after Matthew's death. So often the media just sucks.

39 | *New Perspectives, New Beginnings*

On the evening of October 6, 2002, four years to the day after our friend Matthew was tied, beaten unconscious, and left to die, Jim and I decided to take a walk out to the fence where it happened. Though Jim—having guided many people, friends as well as strangers, on their pilgrimages to the fence—had been out there numerous times, that was only my second trip. I wanted to wait until dark, to see what my friend saw the night he was dragged there against his will.

Sometime after 8 P.M. Jim and I began the hike down the battered dirt road that led to the prairie. The fresh tire tracks and footprints in the dirt indicated that we weren't the only people who wanted to see that place on that day. As we walked we shared stories, Jim-and-Romaine stories about the crazy experiences we'd had over the last four years, and it was amazing how much comfort I took, and still take, in being Jim's friend. Nobody understood the things I had seen and experienced the way Jim did, because he'd seen and experienced them too.

We walked very slowly, I think because we were afraid to get there. It was cold enough to see our breath when we spoke. With every step, bundled up in a sweatshirt and my leather jacket yet still shivering, I thought about Matthew in his thin corduroy jacket, and I no longer took comfort in knowing he was wearing it. He still would have been freezing.

As we walked up the last little hill in the dirt road, the fence came into view. It was different from when I had seen it the first time: It was a little bigger and had been moved a few feet from its original location. Jim had tried to prepare me for that; he told me that some work had been done on it—to, he thought, discourage people from coming out to the private property on which the fence stood. Instantly I was angry. "This is wrong," I said over and over again. "This fence never should have been messed with."

I feel that way even to this day. Tampering with that fence, in my opinion, is desecration of a piece of gay and lesbian history. That fence in the years since Matthew's death has become a symbol of the gay and lesbian fight for equality. It should have been put in the Smithsonian.

After a little while Jim and I turned and sat where Matthew would have been that night. For a few minutes we didn't say anything; we just looked at what he would have seen—the twinkle of the lights of Laramie that reflected a white glow in the sky. As we sat there, I thought about how all over the world Laramie was being remembered, honored even, as productions of *The Laramie Project*, the second most produced play internationally that year, told a piece of the town's story. And I thought about the irony of Laramie's desire to move on, to disassociate itself from Matthew Shepard altogether.

"Laramie is a town that is forgetting," I said. And was I forgetting too?

"Yeah," Jim said. "And it's too bad, because most of the people here did damn good."

Judy Wieder, corporate editorial director for LPI Media, the largest publisher of gay and lesbian magazines and books, took me out to lunch a few weeks after I got back to New York City from Laramie. She had been a mentor and friend for some time by that point, and we both looked forward to the opportunity to catch up. Over lunch I expressed to her my discouragement and confusion about how quickly Laramie seemed to be willing to forget about Matthew Shepard.

"On my very best day," I said to her, "I think about Matthew once or twice, but there is not a day that goes by that I don't think about him." The same was true about my brother Michael and my father. "It just seems to me that there are certain things in life that should stay with a person—or a town, in this case—forever. Evidently, Laramie feels differently."

I was hoping for words of wisdom, some sort of insight that would help me to understand. Instead, what I got was really good advice. Judy said, "I think you should write about this." She began to nod with conviction when she saw the incredulous look on my face. "I'm serious," she continued. "Writing your story down is part of the road you're on. The answers for you are already in you, so just write!"

For weeks I tried and I failed. I filled page after page of my journal with memories of times and places, smells, recipes, pictures, newspaper clippings, and everything else I could think of to jog an idea or a moment from my past. But something was missing, an element that was necessary to bind all of those things together.

In the early part of March, amid the frustration of trying to conceive a book about my life, I got a call from John McMullen. For years John had been the mastermind behind an Internet radio station geared toward the gay community called GayBC. He had interviewed me countless times while I worked for GLAAD, and we had remained e-mail buddies after I left the organization. As John explained it, Sirius Satellite Radio had hired him to produce on one of its 100 channels the first-ever radio channel to broadcast gay content 24 hours a day, seven days a week. He had a talk show in mind for which he was looking for a lesbian cohost and producer. He wanted me to come in and talk to him about it.

I was immediately overwhelmed when I stepped out of the elevator on the 36th floor of the McGraw-Hill building on the corner of 49th Street and 6th Avenue—the site of Sirius. Never had I seen an office space so beautiful—everything, it seemed, was made out of glass; even the freestanding staircase in the middle of the lobby was transparent. And the floor-to-ceiling windows that lined the walls provided the most amazing view of Manhattan I'd ever seen.

The secretary called John, then pointed in the direction of his office. As I walked down the hall, past the glass-enclosed studios, I began to salivate. The whole place was like a dream come true for a kid like me fresh out of recording and engineering school, jonesing to get her hands wet in a studio like one of those.

I listened patiently as he told me about the show he was considering me for. "While the channel will focus primarily on political shows, the one I want you for is the sex–relationship–pop culture show."

I thought for a second about how slutty I'd been since I moved to New York, and I stifled a chuckle when I said, "You have no idea how right I am for this job."

"Good," John said with a smile, like he was reading my mind. "The show will basically air five nights a week from 7 to 10 P.M., then on weekends we'll replay the highlights."

"Wow, it sounds awesome," I said.

"Romaine, I just know you'd be perfect for the job," he told me. "It's yours if you want it."

It seemed almost too good to be true. Not only was I *not* going to be asked to talk politics on the job, but I was going to be encouraged to talk about sex, and my own personal sex life. And it also meant that I could quit my stupid job at Barnes & Noble. I couldn't say yes fast enough.

I met my soon-to-be co-host, Derek Hartley, for the first time a few nights later for drinks at a restaurant called The Park. We had spoken briefly on the phone to set up the meeting. He said he'd be the boy at the bar with the bouffant hair; I chuckled and said I'd be the dyke in the leather jacket.

Other than that he was a columnist for PlanetOut.com, I knew nothing about Derek, so I was nervous when I walked into the place. It wasn't that I thought Derek wouldn't like me or that I wasn't sure I'd be good at my job—I was nervous because I was wondering, *What if this guy is some political queen? What if he's not fun in any way, we have no chemistry, and I lose my chance to host a talk show about sex?* But then I saw him. He was sitting alone at the bar, teasing the female bartender, who was smiling at him and laughing loudly with a look of mock shock on her face, like he had just made a joke about her tits. When I went over and introduced myself, he stood up and gave me a hug.

"Let's get this girl a drink," he said to the bartender. "What are you having?"

"Vodka tonic," I told him.

"And I'll have another sex on the beach."

We sat on a comfortable black leather couch next to a roaring fire. With its brown throw rug, low lighting, and soft music, the room was cozy, and it felt—as Derek and I talked and drank (and drank) for hours—like we were sitting in one of our living rooms getting reacquainted with an old friend. He told me about his family, how he had grown up in Salt Lake City part-time with his Mormon father and had spent the rest of his time with his sister and mother in California. I told him about being the youngest of eight and my adventures with my three gay older brothers, and, of course, all about Michael. By 4 A.M., as the place was closing down, we were shit-faced and we loved each other. We both knew our show was going to be amazing.

The show, which came to be called *Derek & Romaine*, made its debut on Sirius OutQ 149 on April 14, 2003, and was a runaway hit. We had no real guidelines when we started, an because it was on satellite radio, we had very few restrictions as far as what we could say, so with every show we tested the limits. We interviewed a porn star who got naked and introduced our listening audience to his friend and appendage, "Monster," by having him tap it against the microphone. When there was nothing else to talk about, we brought our own hilarious sexual misadventures to the table. Frequently, as the show developed, I couldn't believe we were getting away with it. But our switchboards lit up almost every night, and we consistently got more listeners' calls than any other show on the channel.

I think what amazed me most about the show was how healing it was for me personally. I recognize now how broken I was when I hit New York City and that I'd spent my first year here trying to find myself in a crazy new way. My attitude was: Fuck love,right now I'm all about me. And so, in my attempt to flee from everything that looked like responsibility, I partied like a rock star—and had a blast doing it. I discovered I could have sex with more than one woman in a night, that karaoke is more fun when you're doing it naked, and that I liked tattoos (so I got a couple, including a pair of angel wings on my back). I learned that getting—and staying—

drunk on $10 a night is an art form, and that I could crawl back
to my brother; s apartment in the East Village sometime after 6
A.M., pass out for a couple of hours on the tiny bed he made for
me in the corner of his living room, and be ready to do it all over
again by the time the sun was going down. But when the Sirius gig
presented itself, it seemed like the appropriate time to take a step
back from the craziness my life had become.

I love my job. I can't imagine my life without it, though professionally it's the hardest thing I've ever done; the responsibilities
that come along with producing the show as well as hosting it are
tremendous. What I get in return, however, is the opportunity to
be myself—no holds barred—and to have fun doing it. That, to
me, is invaluable. Sometimes our show is naughty to the point of
being downright raunchy, and I understand that turns some people off, but to me it's incredible. I think of Derek and myself as
trailblazers—no one cusses on the radio like we do, and no one
tells dirtier and more truthful stories about their sex lives than we
do. What's most amazing about our format is the way our listeners
respond; the best callers are those who ask us questions they
wouldn't dare ask their friends. When that happens, a dialogue is
born—a dialogue in which we can speak freely, using actual ter-
minology. These types of calls almost always end up feeling like an
intimate conversation between old friends.

I'm also proud of the fact that while my job may not always be
activism in a "traditional" sense, the show, because it's funny and
doesn't beat anyone over the head with a political agenda, is acces-
sible to people who might not otherwise listen. It's interesting, for
example, that a large contingent of our regular listening audience
consists of straight truckers. This fact was shocking to me; I'd
never imagined truckers to be an especially gay-friendly group of
people. But they love us. In fact, it's not unusual for us for to get

a call a couple of times a week that are very similar to the one we got early on from a trucker named Bob who called in and said, "You know, I never thought I liked gay people. I used to think they were sinners who are going to hell. But I've been listening to you guys for a while now and I think you're great. I'd give anything to hang out with the two of you."

And then there are the times that I sometimes imagine a gay 17-year-old boy in Utah or a young lesbian in Alabama who, unable to come out of the closet, feels all alone in the world. In my fantasy the boy or girl borrows his or her parents' car, turns the channel to 149 and, listening to Derek and me being silly, know that they aren't alone and that being gay will eventually be less scary for them, that someday it will be fun.

Though it's difficult to estimate the number of our listeners, it's clear that our demographic crosses all lines of age, race, sex, and sexual orientation. It's an interesting thing to see what kind of people out there want to listen to a gay guy and a lesbian talk about their sex lives for three hours a night. It's an even more interesting thing to discover how easy it is to do that—to bare my soul on the radio, even if the Romaine people are listening to is sometimes an exaggeration of the real thing.

As the radio show came together, I continued to work on putting together my book. The harder I worked on the radio show, the more obvious became the missing piece that would complete a book about my life's work. I recognized it nightly as I shared pieces of my story and as I took questions from and gave advice to listeners. It is the same element that makes my radio personality work, the element that inspires the sort of trust that makes people want to listen. That element is honesty.

Certainly, the thought never occurred to me to lie. But when compiling the stories of my life that make up my experience, putting my name on them, and handing them to the world in the hopes that someone will glean an understanding from them or that they will affect somebody in a helpful way, there is an almost instinctual urge to pretty up the parts that aren't pretty and to ignore the irrational emotions, misunderstandings, and mistakes. When I realized that I could let myself be a human being, complete with all the inherent flaws and imperfections, telling my life story suddenly seemed worth it.

Before I began, I thought about my brother Michael and how we came to know each other; I thought about my friend Matthew Shepard and how my need to tell the world the truth about his life changed mine forever; and I thought about my father. At first it seemed that my life was marked most noticeably by the loss of those three people, and so I told myself my favorite stories about them then dug deeper and rediscovered some of the others I had locked away. But having looked closer, I see now that loss is not the glue holding my story together, but the ability I have gained to survive that loss, to learn from it, and to grow in the face of it. This, not loss, is the essence of my story.

And so I began to tell this story, holding close to my heart the most important lesson I picked up along the way. It was taught me by a friend, a close friend who fate decided would pay a horrible price so the whole world would know how true the lesson is: One person can make a difference.

Do your part. Use your voice.

Make the world a better place.

Acknowledgments

This book was started late one night in a dark bar in the lower East Village of Manhattan. Upon introduction, Patrick Hinds swore he would get me to write a book about my life. I, on the other hand, wasn't so sure. In an attempt to appease him I gave him my card and told him to call me—which he did every day for nearly a month. I don't think I had much choice after that. Patrick has spent countless hours with me working on this book, and I could not—and probably would not—have done it without him. So thank you, Patrick, for being so passionate and dedicated to this story.

My mom was a librarian and certainly has love for books. I hope that this one makes her as proud as I am to call her my mother. I am truly blessed to have such a strong and supportive family. Each of them in their own way has helped me grow and develop into the person I am today. Thanks, guys, for never letting me get away with anything!

I want to thank Judy and Dennis Shepard for their love and understanding. They, along with the entire staff of the Matthew Shepard Foundation, have given us all an amazing example to follow.

To Jim, Chris, Ladd, Ron, and Roland, thank you for being such inspirational friends and angels in my life. It has been an honor to be in your company.

I want to thank Judy Wieder for her friendship, support, and guidance. Your faith helped me put pen to paper. My thanks to everyone at Advocate Books, including Dan Cullinane, Angela Brown, Tiffany Watson, Greg Constante, and my incredibly hard-working editor, Terri Fabris.

Thank you, David LaChapelle, for so generously allowing us to use your photo for the cover of the book. The day we took that photo is one I will never forget.

Lisa Hagan, you had to bust your ass to find the perfect publisher for my book, then tolerate the many questions of new writers. I don't know how you did it, but thank you!

Eric McCool, you always take such good care of me. You are the best Webmaster a girl could ask for. Erin Byrne, thank you for reading rough drafts and sharing your one-of-a-kind insight. Amber, you have put up with the mood swings and crazy moments of this process. Even after it all, you still managed to love me. You have helped me in so many ways that words can not express my gratitude. Becca Jones, your faith in me is something unmatched by any other person. Thank you for never allowing me to give up and always inspiring me to do better.

What would my days be like without the banter I share with Derek Hartley? Derek, you have tolerated a lot while I was writing this book. Often you had to pick up the load of the radio show while I stressed over edits and Web sites. So thank you. I look forward to many more years of "on air" laughter with you. Thanks to all the "bitches" out there who picked up a copy of this book to show your support. You are the kind of friends I always dreamed I would have one day.

Saving the best for last, I'd like to thank the men who've had the most influence and impact in my life. While neither of them has been here to appreciate all the events of the last few years, I know that each would have been proud of the choices I have made. Thank you, Michael, for teaching me the power of my voice. You taught me to be proud of who I am and to stand up when needed. Matt, you taught me about the power of one person and our ability to change the world. Knowing you was an adventure. Remembering you has been one of my greatest honors. —Romaine Patterson

I would like to express my sincere thanks to the following people:

The four incredible women who made this book happen: Romaine Patterson, for trusting me to help her tell her story; Lisa Hagan, agent extraordinaire, who believed in and nurtured this story from the moment she heard of it; Terri Fabris, our editor, whose insight and creative genius breathed new life into this story at a crucial time; and my mother, Pam Parker, whose patience in reading draft after endless draft and whose support and encouragement in this and everything I've done has been one of the greatest gifts of my life.

Also, my wonderful siblings: Sarah Picard, PFC Rebecca Hinds, and Nick Hinds, as well as my mother's incredible wife, Carol Jenney—the best family one could hope for. Mike Jensen, for a million things, but most importantly for being the best friend I've ever had and always believing that I could do it.

And all of the great people who've supported me over the years: Ellyn, Anna, AJ, Ashley, Camille, Christian and Mike, Seraphin, Jordan, Kathleen, Levon, Marianne, Max, and Tyler. And a special thanks to Allison Rice, Ann Rebello, Jessica Edwards, and Marie Johnson at Housing Assistance Corporation on Cape Cod.

To all of the great people at Alyson Books, especially Judy Wieder, Angela Brown, and Tiffany Watson. Everyone at the Matthew Shepard foundation, especially Chris and Tina. And to Jim Osborn in Laramie for his patience and answers. And finally, to Mrs. Shepard for her kindness and support. —Patrick Hinds